Mosquito Coast Murders
By
Bob P-S

ISBN 978-1-84799-971-9

Bob P-S. Orkney Isles, Scotland. UK.   bob.p-s@virgin.net

To my wife Janet for her patience, help and understanding.

Author's Notes

The people and locations in this story are fictitious as are many of the places; however some of the places do exist and have been given their correct names. This has been done deliberately for reader recognition purposes. The situations and actions are derived from many places and most of it is from my imagination. As with many novels the writing can be a lonely journey and that was the case with this novel but I was joined at the end by Suzie Woodward and I would like to thank her for her help and assistance with proofreading and some editing.

Chapter 1 Arrival

Adam Zander shuffled through the photographs depicting the battered body of Elly van Dam. The body was sprawled on what looked to be a kitchen floor. The vivid colour of the blood splattered across the worktop surface and up the wall and over the water container above the sink showed the ferociousness of the attack. There was something about that water container but he could not put his finger on it. The blows to the back of the head were so hard it seemed as if the head had virtually exploded like a watermelon when hit by a baseball bat.

Zander wondered what to expect from a Third World country like Vanmalla. He knew it was in Central America and having read Jenny's fax, he also knew that there was considerable poverty and corruption. He also wondered if he had bitten off more than he could chew when agreeing to investigate Elly's murder.

He took the information pamphlet from the pocket in the back of the seat in front of him. He flipped through the pages until he came to a map of Vanmalla. It is a country one hundred miles north to south and sixty-five miles east to west. The west of the country is secondary jungle and the east coast is low level and mainly mangrove swamp. The population consisted of many races, Hispanic, Carib, and Creole and there were also many European and North American expatriates.

The main industry of Vanmalla is farming with sugar cane, oranges and bananas being the main crops with tomatoes, cucumbers, mangos and melons following close behind. There were still some teak exports under licence and some smuggled but very lucrative. In recent years it was becoming very popular as a diving and deep sea game fishing resort.

The stewardess placed another whisky and water on the armrest of his club class seat. Zander was a heavy whisky drinker and the flight from Heathrow gave him the opportunity to indulge his passion.

'Thank you, how much longer before we land in Vanmalla?'
'About an hour, Sir.'
'Thanks.'

Zander scanned the fax that his sister Jenny and her husband, Stan Jones, had sent to him.

"To: Adam Zander, Private Investigation Agency.
Dear Adam,
*   A very dear friend of ours has been killed and the less than competent local police force has arrested her fiancé, Marty Martens, and accused him of the murder.   We know he didn't do it.   He loved her and would never do such a thing. We know that all those close to a murderer say he or she couldn't do it.   But Adam in this case we can assure you it is true.   The ex-pat community is up in arms about it and we know someone from the American Embassy who hinted that you would get their cooperation if you took up the case.   We've told them you are a retired detective chief inspector and that you now run your own investigation agency.   What we are worried about is, if he is found guilty, he will hang.   The thing is there is no telling what might be concocted if they can't find enough evidence to get the result they want, the local police that is.*
*   We have sent photographs of the murder scene and the initial police report by special delivery.   The American Embassy obtained them for us; Elly and Marty are both American citizens.*
*   We know there is a lot of drugs and corruption out here and we think Elly's murder could be part of that. Will you please HELP?"*

Zander sent a positive reply; his agency was now well established in London, and his partner and the investigators could handle the present workload.

He finished off his complimentary whisky and water and asked for another as the captain warned them of the possibility of turbulence on the approach to Vanmalla International Airport. The Boeing 737 Vanmalla Airways daily flight from Miami swept in over the steaming tropical jungle of Vanmalla. The turbulence was most violent as they crossed the coastline minutes before landing.

'Welcome to Central America, Adam,' announced Stan Jones as his brother in-law stepped off the afternoon flight and was enveloped in the tropical jungle heat.

'Thanks, Stan, is it always this hot?'

'No, Vanmalla's normally hotter; it's only twenty-eight centigrade today and we are not that far from the equator.'

Stan weighed 100 lbs and was five foot six tall. His long white socks, white shorts and short-sleeved white shirt with a Panama Jack hat hinted at his previous colonial service. His clothes were in distinct contrast to his red hair. They walked from the steps of the aircraft across the apron to the arrival area.

'I will contact the Americans first thing in the morning, Adam.'

'I would prefer you to do that today, Stan; I want to get started as soon as possible'

'All right, I'll do it when we get home.'

'Good. Where's Jenny?'

'She's at home preparing for the dinner party tonight.'

'What's the party in aid of?'

'It's to welcome you - Adam Zander, the celebrated private detective!' 'That's good of you, Stan, but there's not much that's celebrated about me. I only celebrate now and again when I find a missing person or get a good roll of film on a husband or wife who's been playing away from home and the spouse pays well.'

'What about all the murder cases you've solved?'

'Well, I only "help the police with their enquiries" as they say, when paid by interested parties, of course.'

'But didn't you solve murder cases when you were at Scotland Yard?'

'Yes, I did, and many of them over the years.'

'Well, I'm glad about that. I hope you aren't going to be this reluctant in front of my friends because I've told them you are a tough, notorious and ruthless detective with the suave good looks of Clark Gable. You're my brother-in-law, Adam, and I'm proud of you.'

'Okay Stan, I'm here to try and solve this murder, but you know I love my work and I'll be only too happy to talk to your friends about being a private detective. But then I want to get on and solve the murder of this young American girl. I was just being a bit mercenary.'

'Thank goodness for that; you had me worried for a minute. Let's collect the bags and go to Riverside - that's the name of our house and you will see it's appropriate.'

'I read on the plane that Vanmalla is about a hundred miles north to south and about sixty five miles east to west.'

'That's about right, not so small!'

The arrival area at the airport was primitive by most standards; it consisted of just a few corrugated tin sheds with zigzag lanes made from two-inch scaffold poles. At the end of this were a few upturned packing cases to put the baggage on for inspection by the customs officers. The customs officers seemed totally disinterested in Zander and his luggage. They were more interested in little old ladies carrying shopping bags full of goodies from America. Jones picked up Zander's suitcases and put them in the back of his Bronco. It was a five-minute journey to the house, which was located in secondary jungle on the edge of a river. They pulled out of the airport car park onto a tarmac road and were nearly hit by a huge late sixties Pontiac, which was driving straight at them

'Look out, Stan!'

Stan swerved and went on to the verge.

'What happened there?'
'Looked like a taxi; the driver was most probably high on wacky baccy - it's a tolerated pastime here.'

A little further down the road Stan turned off the tarmac road and on to a track, which was a mass of potholes. Mary, the maid, and Winston, the gardener, met them at the front of the house. The utility room, Mary's room, two guest rooms, a double garage, carport and the twenty-thousand gallon water tank were all at ground level, and the Jones' lived on the first floor. Zander and his brother-in-law walked up the concrete steps at the front of the house. Mary and Winston took the luggage around to the back, and Jenny met her husband and brother at the front door.

'I see you are well-protected against insects,' said Zander.
'Vanmalla is often referred to as the Mosquito Coast, Adam, and with good cause,' said Jenny.
'Are the fly-screens effective?' Zander asked.
'Yes, we've had the whole house done. You will notice there are thousands of biting insects that seem more active after the sun has gone down,' Jenny said.

The fly-screen door banged shut as they went into the house. Zander embraced his sister and Spark, the Jones' Doberman, greeted Zander; he sniffed his leg and shoes and then started to growl. Zander put his hand down to stroke Spark, but he backed off.

'He seems a bit shy."

'No, he's just wary. A dog is essential here in Vanmalla; we don't encourage friendliness until we have made the introductions.'

Stan called Spark over and got him to sit.

'Okay, Adam, pat and stroke his head; good, now you're friends. Spark knows the rules. He will let some people in, but they can't get out and he will contain them, aggressively if necessary.'

Spark wagged his three-inch stump of a tail.

'Thanks for the introduction, Stan. I see what you mean.'
'I think you've put on a bit of weight, Adam?'
'I'm only eighteen stone, Jenny, and at six-foot four that's my best fighting weight.'
'Well I hope you're not going to do any fighting while you're here.'
'Metaphorically speaking, of course.'
'I hope so. Would you like a cold beer?'

Zander nodded. He could not speak at that moment, as his tongue and mouth were busy getting rid of what must have been the only flying insect inside the screens.

'Mary, two beers please.'

Mary fetched the two cans of Slitz and poured them into pewter tankards and they sat out on the large veranda overlooking the river. The veranda was twenty-feet square, totally enclosed by insect screens with a manhole cover in the middle.

'What's the manhole cover, Stan?'
'That's the access to the water storage tank. When it rains it runs off the roof and into the tank. Every couple of months we

mix in some water-sterilising powder and some taste-removing crystals and this cleans up any contamination from birds and the like and makes it just about palatable. We usually do it every three months or when Jenny gets a rumbling tummy - she's sensitive to that sort of thing,' said Jones as his wife joined them.

'We're sorry we couldn't get away to come to Tracy's funeral. I know we didn't make your wedding either so, we never got to meet her. I expect it has been difficult for you' Jenny said.

'It was very traumatic. The Metropolitan Police were very sympathetic after the event. However, I just wish they had been more sensible when they sent that vehicle on what I think was an unnecessary blue-light journey across London. As you might remember I had become disgruntled with the increased paperwork and bureaucracy that was creeping in. It seemed to be more important than catching criminals. Tracy was a police constable passenger in the car that night when it crashed into a double-decker bus. As you know we had only been married for two years.   I resigned from the force the following day and have no regrets.'

'How's your agency getting on?' Stan asked.

'Very well. My partner is looking after things while I'm away. He's an ex-Met' copper as well. Who's coming to this party tonight?'

'A few businessmen and some of the military from the nearby army camp,' said Stan.

'Well, this beer is certainly welcome. I think the next thing I need is a shower.'

'Your room is at the end of the corridor and the bathroom is en-suite,' declared Jenny indicating the corridor off the veranda.

Zander moved off down the corridor followed by Spark who stopped at the entrance to the bedroom and lay down on the cool hardwood floor. There was a power shower within the sunken bath unit and there were sliding glass doors along the edge the bath. After some minor adjustments he had a water

massage across his shoulders and neck. As he dried himself he
heard something scuffling about in the roof space above the
bathroom.   He made a mental note to ask Stan about it.
Zander walked out of the bathroom and into the bedroom, still
drying his brown wavy hair. He took his head out of the towel
to see Mary standing in front of him; she was admiring his
naked body while holding his bathrobe. He moved towards her
as she lifted the robe for him to put on. He was so surprised
that he didn't have time to be embarrassed. He slipped his arms
into the robe and turned his back on her. She handed both ends
of the belt to him by putting her hands around his waist.

'I hang your cloths up, Mister Adam, okay?'
'Okay,' said Zander as she turned to leave the room.

With a nervous action she stepped over the dog and looked
back over her shoulder at Zander and winked. He felt a tingling
sensation run through his body. He knew that he had achieved
a sub-conscious aim, without having consciously set a target.
Mary was about five foot two with long black straight hair
down to her waist. She was twenty-three years of age and
single but living with the gardener. She was of Hispanic/Carib
descent with brown eyes and skin. Zander's mind wandered as
he got himself dressed into planters, Mary being uppermost in
his mind. Consequently he had tied his tie and realised it was
too long and hanging below his belt so he pulled it apart and
tied it again. On completion he went back to the living room.

'What's all that scrabbling up in the roof, Stan?'
'Bats; vampire bats, in fact. We got rid of them once but
they've recently returned.'
'That's all I need, a blood-sucking bat to come through the
ceiling.'
'They won't do that.'
'How'd you get rid of them?'
'They get in under the eves, so we put twenty pounds of
naphthalene balls into the roof space. They hate the smell of

the mothballs so they leave and then we block the eves up with newspaper.'

'Obviously it didn't work.'

'It did, but some of the paper has been pecked out by the birds for nesting materials - nature's cunning ways.'

'Perhaps you could get some more mothballs to scare them off whilst I'm here?'

'I'll do it tomorrow.'

'Good, thanks. Oh, what time are people due to arrive?' Zander asked.

'In about an hour at seven thirty. Would you like a beer or something?'

'Large whisky and water please.'

'And I'll have a beer,' said Stan.

He did not make a move to fetch the drinks and a few minutes later Mary entered with the drinks on a tray.

'You must show me how you do that one of these days.'

Stan Jones smiled as he sipped the foam off the top of his beer. As he took a gulp of his drink, Adam wondered if he should ask if it was rainwater in his whisky.

'This doesn't taste like rainwater, Stan?'

'No, it's not, it's bottled. We make ice and all cold drinks from bottled water.'

The first guest to arrive was Jon Morris.

'Nice to meet you, Jon, what do you do here?'

'I own and run a cattle farm about fifty miles inland and a pig farm on an island about a half mile off the eastern shoreline. That's where Elly and Marty lived. I also own an ice cream factory in downtown Malla. And you?'

'I'm a private investigator in England.'

'Interesting work?'

'Sometimes, but there is a lot of leg work and repetitive questioning.'

'I don't s'pose you'd be interested in tracing a missing person for me would you? I'll give you ten percent plus expenses.'

'Ten percent of what?'

'A certain person owes me fifty thousand dollars U.S. and he's gone missing.'

'I might be interested, but I think I'm going to have my hands full investigating the murder of Elly van Dam. If I do get time I'll be in contact, but of course I'll need all you have on this missing person.'

'I'll let you have the full dossier next week.'

'Is that your wife talking to Stan?'

'No, it's my girlfriend. My wife's back in the States with the kids. She hates the jungle.'

Zander thought he must be in his fifties because his hair was greying at the sides but his physique was that of a much younger man. He got the feeling that Morris was a bit of a ladies' man. He excused himself and moved off to meet another group and introduce himself. He met an elderly schoolmaster and his wife and daughter, and a rather obnoxious Frenchman and his wife. The Frenchman challenged Zander about taking water in his whisky.

'Why do you ruin a perfectly good whisky by adding water to it?' said the Frenchman.

'I rather enjoy the flavour, and I get a little bit touchy when people I don't know comment on me putting water in my whisky. I didn't comment on the fact that you hold your drink in your left hand,' said Zander trying to be casual.

'I am left-handed.'

'Exactly, it comes naturally; well it's natural for me to have water in my whisky as it has been for many thousands of people around the world since whisky was first distilled over five hundred years ago. A comment like yours makes me think you couldn't tell a malt from a good blend - am I right?'

'Yes, I don't drink, and that's the third drink you've had in less than half an hour,' said the Frenchman.'

'I didn't realise there was a limit here in Vanmalla.'

'There's not.'

'Well, why mention it? Are you some sort of temperance preacher?' Zander could feel his anger rising.

'No, I'm a psychiatrist.'

'Enough said. I've never had much time for trick cyclists and you seem determined to be confrontational, but I'm not going to play your stupid game. I'm not a closet alcoholic or a dipso; I just drink a lot now and again but I often go for many days without a drink. Now, are you satisfied that you've antagonised me enough?' Without letting him answer Zander continued.

'As a result of your success could I suggest that you go ride your trick-cycle somewhere else, unless in the future you want to clean your teeth with toilet paper? If you have difficulty understanding what I say, perhaps you would like to step outside and I will demonstrate what I mean.'

The Frenchman went grey and shook his head. Zander turned his back on him and asked Mary for another whisky.

'And make it a large one, please, Mary.'

There were fourteen for dinner and he had just enough time to introduce himself to them all. The last person he met was an officer from the nearby British Army Training and Defence Unit Vanmalla (BAT & DUV). Major George Galpen commanded one of the companies. Zander explained what he did for a living and Galpen was impressed.

'Perhaps you would like to come across and meet the boys from the Royal Military Police, in particular the SIB. That's the Special Investigation Branch chaps.'

'Yes, I'd like that. I've an associate who's an ex member of the SIB.'

Zander looked around the room and wondered if any of the assembled company was involved in the murder. Stan called them to order and allocated them their seats. The oblong table was of panelled rosewood with matching chairs. There were six on each side and Jenny and Stan had an end each. Zander was sitting with Sal, Jon Morris' girlfriend, on one side and Mrs Day on the other.

'Where do you live, Mrs Day?'
'Just aways down the track,' she replied with a prominent Jamaican accent.

Zander immediately sensed hostility.

'Do you enjoy living here?'
'I can tell you're police. All you do is ask questions, and the answer is yes, I do like it here; I was born here.'
'I thought I detected a Jamaican accent.'
'You did indeed - that's observant of you. My parents were Jamaican.'

Mrs Day did not disclose her first name and Zander had difficulty in breaking through her frosty exterior. She was in her mid thirties with long fair hair and blue green eyes. Zander looked straight into her eyes and as she looked back she seemed to look straight through him, although he thought he detected a flash of a sparkle as she looked away. He felt he ought to say something but as he was about to speak, her husband looked up. Zander looked around quickly to see what the rest were doing. They were all busy talking or their heads were down eating crayfish curry. Arnold Day was in his fifties and it showed, as many years in the sun had parched his skin.

'Do you get out to the islands much?'

'They are called keys, spelt c-a-y-e-s, and yes I do; we have a holiday house on one. We have a cabin cruiser and go out most weekends.'

'How do I break through this hostility, Mrs Day?'

'After dinner,' she replied in a lowered voice.

Zander turned to Sal.

'How do you enjoy Vanmalla?'

'I don't, but as long as I get laid regularly, I don't give a shit.'

'I suppose that's one way of putting it'

'And the answer's no. I'm off limits till Jon's out of town.'

'I wasn't asking.'

'Well, just in case you were.'

'Is everyone in this place so aggressive?'

'What's aggressive? You're single and you're trying to find out what's available.'

'Not really; I'm just trying to make polite conversation,' said Zander with a slightly raised voice.

'She givin' you a hard time?' asked Morris from across the table.

'No, I just seem to be in enemy country.'

'I spec it's 'cause you're a detective and they all think you're investigatin' 'em all. Must have summit to hide.'

'I can assure you, Jon, that I'm here to solve Elly van Dam's murder and when I start grilling people they will know about it.'

Either Zander's statement eased the tension or the Californian wine was having an effect. They had brandy snaps and cream followed by port and coffee. Arnold excused himself and went to the lavatory, and Mrs Day turned towards Zander and looked him straight in the eyes - he was hooked.

'He gets jealous if I show the slightest interest in anyone, he go crazy'. He's going deep-sea fishing on Tuesday so call me,' she said handing him her card, which she had taken from her small purse.

They moved away from the dining table to the living room and the veranda.

'Why don't you come across to the camp for Beating Retreat next week, Adam?' Galpen asked.
'I would like that. What's the form of dress?'
'Planters or a Marcos shirt.'

'What's that?'
'Some government officials have taken to wearing Filipino or Mexican-type embroidered long-sleeved shirts without tie. The British and most others wear ties. Rather stuffy, but you have to have standards or everything goes to pot. Don't you agree?'
'Yes, as a matter of fact I do. However, if everybody kept to the standard law, I would be out of a job.'

George laughed and slapped Zander on the back.

'Yes, good one, Adam. Mind you, the law of averages says you've got a job for life.'

There was a sudden crash and a thump and Arnold Day was lying on the living room floor. His wife and Jenny went to help him. He was out cold. One of George's young subalterns looked rather shocked.

'What happened?' Galpen demanded.
'I was chatting to the young lady and that brute threw a punch at me. I stepped back and he fell over, Sir.'
'All right, Nigel. Make your apologies and leave before he comes round.'
'Yes, Sir. Mrs Jones I'm...'
'Oh, don't be silly, Arnold often has these little turns, doesn't he, Heather?'
'Yes. If a couple of you could lift him into the chair he'll be fine' said Mrs Day as she unfastened his top button and tie.

Arnold came round rubbing his elbow.

'I must have slipped; I didn't do any damage, did I?' Day queried watching Heather sweep the broken glass away to the edge of the room with the sole of her shoe.

Mary entered more or less unnoticed and swept up the glass with a pan and brush.

'Nothing to worry about, Arnie,' said Jenny. 'Would you like a cup of coffee?'
'Please.'

The incident was soon over and the hubbub of conversation resumed. The subaltern was still hovering so Galpen gave him the eye.

'Good-night, I must go, really,' declared Nigel, as he waved away Jenny's protestations.

Heather looked at nobody but Arnold for fear of more trouble. The party was thinning when a whimper came from Zander's room.

'Help!'
Spark was sitting at the bathroom door with his teeth bared and making a deep-throated growl.

'It's only me,' whined Sal.

Jenny called Spark away from the door.

'How long have you been in there?' asked Zander.

'About thirty minutes. I tried calling but there was so much noise out there you obviously didn't hear me. Every time I opened the door he snarled,' she complained, pointing at Spark.

'I'm sorry, Sal; he doesn't mean you any harm. He is just being protective. Spark, say hello to Sal.'

Sal started to move back into the bathroom.

'Stay where you are,' whispered Jenny.

Jenny took Spark by the collar and walked him to Sal. She froze to the spot. Spark sniffed her feet and legs and then his tail stump started to wag and his tongue came out and he started to pant.

'Okay, you're friends now.'

Sal was obviously not as confident as Jenny; however she managed to pat his head. The excitement over, the party broke up and Zander, Jenny and Stan sat on the veranda while Mary and Winston came in and started to get the place cleaned up.

'There are some interesting people in this country, particularly that Frenchman'
'I'm not so sure interesting is the appropriate word, Adam, but you have noticed that they are not all normal,' declared Stan hesitantly as he seemed to be searching for the right phrase. "The Frenchman, Henry, is a bit of a prat. He can't go back to France because of a malpractice case against him, something about a patient committing suicide.'
'Why did you invite such a rude person to the dinner?'
'Oh, he's all right. His abrupt manner just takes a bit of getting used to.'
'I don't wish to get used to him, thank you very much.'
'You might have to; he's a consultant forensic psychologist with the Vanmalla government.'
'I thought he said he was a psychiatrist not a psychologist.'
'You're correct of course, but he is also a psychologist. He treats the mentally ill but he also studies behaviour and does psychological profiling.'

'Whose palm did he grease to get a job like that?'

'I don't know, but he's been here a couple of years.'

'What's his second name?'

'Henry; he has a German first name - Deitmar.'

'Ah yes, I remember now; it was mentioned during the introductions. Thing is he made me angry; he was so rude that I must have had a memory lapse while trying to control my temper.'

'Let's hope you don't have to deal with him then. He was here with his wife; she's Vanmallen and they were here because she is a secretary with our company.'

'What does Arnold do for a living?'

'He exports furniture made by local craftsmen and made in his factory; he also does a bit of this and that, and imports a bit of this and that,' said Stan with a smirk.

'What's the police force like?'

'As I've mentioned they're not the best but they're trying - some would say very trying. Some are good and some are.... otherwise. There is corruption and it is fairly widespread.'

'Thanks for warning me.'

They had a few more drinks and talked about old times. Mary and Winston said goodnight and they all went to bed. Mary had switched on the air conditioner in Zander's room and as he entered his room, the cool air enveloped him. He took a shower, got into the king-size bed and was asleep in minutes. His sleep pattern was upset as a result of crossing the time zones during his journey so he woke early, but he read for an hour and then went back to sleep.

Chapter 2 Meeting the Accused

Zander eventually got up at nine o'clock. After his shower he lay naked on the bed under the fan, which was blowing down cold air from the air-conditioner.

'You wan' to eat, Mister Adam?" Mary asked while walking down towards Zander's room.

He heard the bare feet padding down the passageway so he quickly covered his middle with the corner of the sheet before she arrived.

'Yes, full English please.'
'Anyt'ing you wan' in bed?'
'Tea, please.'

Zander knew by the look in her eye what she meant and while she fetched the tea he made up his mind he was not going to oblige. Mary set the cup and saucer down on the bedside table and sat on the edge of the bed.

'Is Jenny or Stan out there?
'Mr Stan he gone out, Missy Jenny having coffee.'
'Would you like to go and get my breakfast ready because I have to go out this morning.'

Mary made such a face that he thought she was going to explode. She didn't of course, but let out a long stream of air that exceeded any sigh Zander had ever experienced.

'Sorry, Mary,' he called after her as she stomped off down the corridor.

He finished his tea and went through for breakfast.

'Ah! You're up. I thought I'd let you sleep, jet lag and all that. Mary looking after you?' Jenny asked from the kitchen.

'Yes, fine thanks,' said Zander as he sat down at the table.

'I've been shopping this morning. I had to take Winston with me this morning as I had a lot of heavy stuff to get. What are your plans for today?'

'I thought I'd go across to the BAT& DUV and meet the RMP.'

'Okay, use the Bronco. You might as well use it for the length of your stay. As you go towards the airfield take what they call Army Road - it's on the right and passes the end of the runway. Oh by the way, they call it Batdove.'

'Will I have trouble getting into the camp?'

'No, I'll phone George Galpen and tell him you are on the way. As you go out you'll find a map in the top drawer of the bureau. It's quite simple really; there are only two roads out of town - one running south and one west. The Capitol Highway - and I use the word highway with my tongue firmly in my cheek – has a turning that goes north. There's a hand-drawn street map of Malla, "downtown" as they call it; it's in the glove compartment.'

'Thanks. Is there anything from the Americans?'

'Yes, they will get back to you later today.'

'If they do, tell them where I am.'

Mary served his breakfast and when he'd finished, Zander picked up the keys and drove the automatic, air-conditioned Bronco into camp. The camp was situated to the side of the runway. It had a main entrance and a side entrance that went directly to the RAF and Army Air Corps hangars. The main en trance had a manually-operated barrier with a sentry box to protect the soldiers from the elements. The guardroom was a single-storey building painted olive green. There was a hatchway where enquiries were made and soldiers booked visitors in and out of camp and there were six cells for miscreants. George Galpen was standing at the barrier.

'Morning, Adam, how are you?' Galpen asked as Zander pulled up alongside.

'Fine, George, how's things with you?'

'Couldn't be better,' declared George as he got in beside Zander.

Zander pulled away from the guardroom and the sentry saluted Galpen. They drove the four hundred yards to the police post where the Royal Military Police Company Sergeant Major met them at the entrance and saluted.

'Good morning, Sirs,' snapped the CSM.
'Morning, I'm Adam Zander,' he said offering his hand. The CSM shook his hand and introduced himself.
'Sarn't Major Murphy, Sir.'
'Please call me Adam, and what do they call you?'
'Spud, Sir.'
'Okay, Spud, and what have you got to show me?'
'We'll start in the evidence room.'
'I'll pick you up for lunch, Adam; at about twelve thirty if that's all right?
'Suits me; you Spud?'
'For sure.'

Murphy gave him a conducted tour of the department and ended up with the Warrant Officer Class 2 SIB.

'This is WO2 Fred Oxbee. He looks after all the special jobs - theft, rape and robbery et cetera.'
'Rape? You have rape here in the camp?'
'No, but it has occurred in the quarters area in town,' affirmed Oxbee.
'I'm intrigued - tell me more.'
Oxbee was only able to tell a couple of stories before the major arrived to collect Zander for lunch.
'Fred, I don't suppose we could meet for a beer somewhere later? I'd love to hear more.'
'What about the Majestic at ten tonight?'
'I'll be there.'

The officers' mess rear entrance had a white picket gate and, leading in to the mess was a four-foot wide concrete path which was thirty yards long and overhung by mango trees. An iguana lived under the concrete, which had been eroded by numerous tropical downpours.

   The officers' mess dining room was an atap-covered (palm leaf thatching) structure at the rear of the main mess complex and a fine mist formed and descended over any occupants who were there during heavy storms.

   'Adam, this is Sandy Medows, the Station Medical Officer. He's been here five months and is giving a lecture on snakes one evening later in the week in the education centre.   Would you like to attend?' George asked.
   'I would indeed. If there is one thing that fascinates me a great deal, and frightens me a little, it's snakes.'
   'Sandy is carrying out a study for the School of Tropical Medicine and is somewhat of an expert.'
   'I wouldn't say that, George, but thanks anyway. I look forward to seeing you there.'

   Galpen, Medows and Zander collected their meals from the hot plate and joined Sarah, the QARANC Matron, at the back of the dining area. They sat down at the six-foot trestle table in fold-flat wooden chairs.

   'Sarah has just a few days to do and is meeting her replacement off the plane tomorrow afternoon,' said Galpen.

   Zander looked at the extremely attractive major and noticed that she was not wearing a wedding ring.

   'Not married then, Sarah?' Zander queried.
   'I was, but my ex preferred men to me.'
   'The man's a fool!' exclaimed Zander.
   'Fool he might be, but queer he certainly is,' proclaimed Sarah with a tad of venom in her voice.
   'Well, it takes all sorts,' said Zander shrugging his shoulders.

'I'm having drinks in the bar at 1830 hours just after the flight arrives. Why not come and meet my replacement? There will be a few eats, some drink and a lot of people.'

'I'd like that. Do you know your replacement, Sarah?'

'Yes, we joined the army together some ten years ago. Her name is Perky Perkins, Iris actually, and she holds her drink better that a lot of men.'

'Sounds interesting; I instinctively like someone who can hold their liquor,' pronounced Zander with a smirk.

'She is not lesbian if that's what that smirk infers?'

'No, it doesn't infer anything, other than I'm looking forward to meeting what sounds to be a lady of repute.'

'Are you married?' asked Sarah.

'No, I was but my wife was killed in a car accident a couple of years ago.'

'Oh' I'm sorry I didn't mean...'

'Don't be, I'm over it now. We had no children but we had a short but marvellous marriage.'

The mess staff sergeant entered the dining area and went up to Galpen and whispered in his ear. Galpen left the table and was gone for a few minutes and when he returned he approached Zander.

'Adam, would you come with me please?'

Zander got up from the table and with a bemused expression on his face he excused himself and followed Galpen to the mess office.

'What's up, George?'

'It's the American Ambassadors office. They're pleased you've arrived and want you to get started on investigating the murder; you will be given a fee plus expenses. You know Jon Morris, the pig man? Well they want you to go and see him this afternoon. They're having difficulty getting clearance.'

'What's the problem?'

'They didn't say but I'm sure you'll find out eventually. Things like this don't move very quickly here. I've some info about Elly and Marty; I don't know how relevant it might be, however, I've mentioned it to the police.'

'What's that then?

'I went to a party the other night at a house in the town. Marty was there but Elly wasn't - apparently she will have nothing to do with one of the guests. She came to pick him up and there was a bit of shouting match outside; then the truck started and they left. The following morning she was found dead.'

'Sounds interesting, but if I understand it correctly the local ex-pat community believe him innocent, which means it will most probably have little bearing, but thanks. I need an introduction to the policeman in charge of the case and I would also like to meet whoever is employing me.'

'You won't need that here - there are no formalities.'

'Perhaps not, but I think it's good to see who's going to pay me. If I'm to get cooperation during my investigation, firstly, I must have the authority to carry out the inquiry and secondly I must have the local constabulary on my side.'

'You have to go and see Jon Morris. He has an office in town and when you go and see him he will most probably be able to arrange something without upsetting anyone.'

'Okay, point me in the right direction.'

'Jon's office is next to the Majestic Hotel, but do come and finish your lunch.'

They went back to the table and Zander finished his meal after which he stood up and said his goodbyes. Zander looked for the Majestic Hotel on the hand drawn map. It wasn't difficult to find but that first journey into town, trying to avoid the potholes, was an adventure in itself. Morris was on the phone to the American Embassy as Zander entered the office.

Looking around, Zander thought it was quite obvious that Morris liked wood. The office was pine-panelled and air-conditioned. The majority of the furniture was rosewood and there was a network telephone system on his desk as well as a CB radio. The one thing that struck him as perhaps a bit odd was that there were no windows in the room, yet the buildings overlooked the sea and the cayes, in particular No Trees Caye, where the pigs were kept. 'Git back to me will yah, thanks,' said Morris putting his hand over the mouthpiece. 'Only the Prime Minister can give you clearance to conduct an investigation, and he's out of town at present and due back in a couple of days so, there's not going to be a decision until he's contacted. They've asked me to give you all I can 'til they get you the okay.'

'Let me have a word with them, please," said Zander holding out his hand for the phone.

Morris passed over the handset to Zander.

'Zander speaking. Any chance of a meeting. I have some things I would like to discuss' The response was negative, 'Not at this stage...... okay, well what about giving me some information now? Like what do you expect of me?'

The conversation continued for several minutes and eventually Zander put the phone down with a sigh of relief.

'Everything okay, Adam?'
'Yes fine. The Americans don't want to be formally involved. They should use their own people but the PM is against that. But at least I know what they want and what they are prepared to pay. Now what do you know, Jon?'
'The farmhand went back to No Trees Caye with the ice and water after taking Marty Martens to the office. When he got there he found Elly's body lying on the kitchen floor with her skull smashed in.'
'Anything else?'
'Yeah, they have arrested Marty for the murder.'
'Will they let me see him?'
'They are holding him at Police HQ; let's go and find out,' said Morris picking up his car keys.
'Jon, if I'm going to investigate this case I must be able to do it my way.'

'That's okay with me, but I thought you might need my influence to get to see him.'

'Yes, you're right, I most probably will, but I'm not sure I want pointing in any particular direction just yet.'

'Okay, buddy, but I don't think Marty did it. They might have had fights but I think they were only verbal. He has never laid a finger on her, that I do know.'

'Good, fill me in on their background.'

Morris gave Zander a short life-story on Elly and Marty.

'When were they due to get married?'

'In three months. They've been saving for over a year now and Marty was due to bring the money in that morning so that Sal could buy the flight tickets. They were planning on a two-week break - one week to organise everything and get married at the weekend in between. We were all going back for the wedding and then they were going to have a honeymoon in Florida for a week and then back here for another two year contract.'

'Thanks for that. Let's go and see the police.'

They cooperated when it came to visiting Martens, but they would not answer questions on the case or let Zander visit the scene of the murder. They walked down a six-foot wide passageway with cells on either side; they varied from the single cell to the multipurpose holding-cell, which was twenty feet square. Morris and Zander were escorted to the cell where Martens sat hunched on his bed.

'Hi, Marty, this is Adam Zander, an English private detective. The embassy has asked him to help with the investigation,' said Morris.

'What happened, Marty?' asked Zander as he sat down on the crumpled and very hard bed.

'I'll leave you with this one, Adam; if you want me I'm in the office 'til six. Hang in there, Marty.'

'Okay,' said Zander without looking up.

Marty's face was tear-stained and he looked pale and was still hunched.

'I didn't do it, Adam. She was okay when I left, I swear.'

'Tell me exactly what happened'

'Pancho came and picked me up from No Trees that morning by boat as usual at seven o'clock on Monday morning. It's a few minutes by speedboat and then a few more by truck to the office. Pancho went to the ice-cream factory to pick up ice and freshly-treated water and take it back to the house.'

'Don't you have water on No Trees?'

'Oh yes, but it's rain water and we only use that for showering and feeding the pigs, and we'd completely run out of fresh.'

'Are you sure there was no water?'

'Absolutely. I helped Pancho load the empty cans into the boat.'

'What about the money you were due to take in that morning?'

'Elly told me she had to come over shopping that morning and she would go and see Sal, so she could get our air tickets.'

'Obviously Sal didn't get the money, so where is it, and who knew you had a lot of money at the house?'

'I don't know. Lots of people knew we were saving to get married. Where the money is, I don't know. Elly had a secret place but even I didn't know where that was.'

'Did they know you were keeping it in the house?'

'Possibly, but I don't trust these local banks and the exchange rate changes can be so volatile

'Could anybody land on the island and go and help themselves?'

'No, we've ten vicious dogs that're zealously provocative, and strangers would have to kill the dogs or put them to sleep.'

'How do visitors get to the house?'

'There is an intercom system between the dock and the house. Elly would have to put away the dogs that are in the compound around the house and then they would be able to go ashore.'

'How many people could get on to the island when the dogs are out?'

'Fifty or so.'

'As many as that?'

'Yes, just about everybody from the mainland farm, Two Snakes, and the office. The dogs are security dogs and change between properties.'

'Okay, why did they arrest you?'

'Pancho went to the police station after he found Elly.'

'He didn't go to the office first?'

'No, the station is on the way. When he told them what he'd found, they took him straight back to the island and searched the place, which had been trashed. They found my stash of hash, so they arrested me.'

'So you haven't been charged with murder?'

'No, but if I ask for bail, they say I will be.'

'Okay, we must force their hand. Jon told me he was getting you a lawyer. Any idea when he's due?'

'Soon I hope'

'If it's any consolation I usually get a gut feeling about these things and I don't usually get it wrong. I don't think you did it, Marty, and I'm going to get you out of this mess. How big is No Trees Caye?'

'Half-a-mile long and 'bout a quarter-mile wide.'

'Who do you think did it, Adam?'

'At this stage I have my suspicions, but really it's an open field. Anyone who could get past the dogs could have done it and that includes fifty or so of the company's employees, most of them from the farm. I'm going to start with a simple system of alibi elimination, which could be as easy as checking a list of names in the office to find out who was not at work at the time of the murder. "Do you know if that's been done?"

'No, I've no idea.'

'All right, Marty, I'm going to have to leave you now but keep your chin up and think positive. If I can't nail this bastard, even I'll admit I did it - that's how confident I am. I know Pancho is lying'

'How?'

'He said Elly was dead on the floor when he arrived back with the water and ice but that's obviously not true if what you say is true.'

'I don't get it.'

'Well, I've seen the photographs of the kitchen and Elly was in the process of making a cold drink because I could see the jug with liquid in it on the worktop at the side of the sink, and the blue plastic water container above the sink had water in it.'

'That is amazing! You haven't been here twenty-four hours yet and you've got me off the hook.'

'Not so fast. I've a lot more work to do, but if you are confident that there was no water or ice on the island, then there are grounds to point the finger at someone else.'

The jailer let Zander out, when he got outside he realised the Bronco was at Morris' place. He was about to go back inside and phone when he saw a military Land Rover coming up the street. He recognised the driver as Nigel, the young subaltern, so waved to him to stop and asked for a lift back to Morris' office. When he arrived there, he found Morris was at his desk.

'Jon, I need a list of all the people in your company, including executives, who were not in their normal place of employment on the morning of the murder.'

'You've got it. What about illegal access?'

'I think it's a non-starter, don't you? What I must do is get a look at the scene of the murder, and the sooner the better.'

'I've had word from the embassy and the Deputy Prime Minister will not permit outside interference. He stated, "You have murders in your country and you wouldn't permit us to get involved so you must let the law here take its course." So we will have to wait, Adam.'

'All right; there is nothing more I can do, so I'm going out for the evening. Please let me know when I have clearance'

Zander went to the Majestic Hotel that evening and met Fred Oxbee as planned. The music was exclusively Caribbean and loud, and the lights were dim except in front of the band. Oxbee was at the bar waiting for him.

'What are you having, Adam?'
'Whisky and water please.'
'I would advise against the water - it's awful.'
'I'm a whisky man but I like it with water.'
'They use rain water here and in most bars in town.'
'Haven't they heard of bottled water?'
'Yes, you can have soda, mineral or spring water but they are all carbonated; no still water other than out of the tap. Not many people drink scotch here unless it's with Coke,'
'Any particular reason.'
'The ice is made from rain water as well.'
'I'll try a local rum and Coke then.'
'Two doubles please, Roland.'
'This rum's not bad. It's a bit harsh on the back of the throat but it seems to have a bit of a kick.'
'It'll be better when you've had a few. Oops, I think someone's giving you the eye, Adam.'

Zander looked in the direction of the dance floor.

'I see what you mean. Who's she with?'
'She's not; she's freelance.'
'You'll have to brief me. Is that good or bad?'
'Difficult question and intelligently put without considering the work that might have to go into formulating an answer. To be blunt, unless she offers to pay you, don't bother.'
'You're a bundle of fun; here's me looking for a bit of skirt and you go all academic on me.'
'No, actually she's not that bad. If you give her a few drinks you might get a freebie.'

Zander returned the stare and she responded with a smile. She was only five-feet tall and so unable to look over her dance partner's shoulder; however, she did look around him.

33

As she walked off the dance floor she made a point of going the long way around and walking past Zander, and as she did so she brushed her breasts against his back as he was seated at the bar. He realised immediately that he was not going to pay for it.

The music started and Zander looked in her direction. She pursed her lips and lifted her head slightly indicating the dance floor. He was tempted to go over and ask her for a dance but having a little bit of a chauvinistic streak he decided to let her make the first move.

'I think she's hooked, Fred. I'm going to give her a little longer,' he explained as he looked straight at her across the dimly-lit room.
'You obviously don't know where she lives, so I had better explain where it is. She lives in a village on the way back to camp; it's the turning on the left just before the bridge. The thing to remember is that you will have difficulty in turning your truck around in front of the house. Your best bet is to go straight up to the house and reverse back around the side of the house. The temptation is to do it the other way. Don't! – or you will end up in the river.'
'Thanks for that. Where's the gents?'
'Over there in the corner.'
'I'll speak to her on the way back if she doesn't speak first.'

The lavatory was rather primitive and the galvanised metal urinals were half full of naphthalene balls, which still did not mask the terrible stench of the uncleaned toilets. He walked back to the bar and made a point of going past her table.

'Hello, big man,' she purred.
'Would you like to dance?' asked Zander.
'Yeah, okay.'

The music was unfamiliar to Zander so he used an old tactic lift a foot every time the music beats and within seconds she was rubbing her outer hip and thigh against his crotch. It had

an instant effect and the front of his trousers started to fill out.
They danced to several tunes and Zander was already thinking
of how he was going to get back to the bar without everyone
noticing his reaction as he walked off the dance floor.

'I'm Adam Zander. What do they call you?'
'Elloween or Weenie.'
'What a lovely name.'
'Yes, and before you ask, I *was* born in October.'

When the music stopped, Weenie let go with both her hands
and turned her back on him, and as she did so she grasped his
left and right hand in her hands and pulled Zander in against
her back and wrapped his hands around her waist. Once they
were amongst the tables she released her grasp.

'You've done this before, Weenie.'
'Uh, huh.'
'Come and join us at the bar.'
'Okay.'

Weenie went back to her table, picked up her purse, made her
excuses to her companions and joined Zander and Oxbee.

'What would you like to drink?'
'White rum and Coke, please.'
'Any preference?'
'Bacardi, if you can afford it?'
'Well, perhaps just the one,' announced Zander with a wry
grin.
'Only one, eh?'
'I didn't think we would have time for anymore. I thought we
were going to bed,' declared Zander.
'You pay me?'
'No.'
'Why not?'
'I might not like it, so that would be a waste of money but if
you are pleasurable we might come to some agreement.'
'What sort of agreement?'

'It depends on how good you are.'

'I'm the best in town - ain't that right, Mister Fred?'

'By reputation you are certainly in the top ten.'

'You try the other nine and then me. Then you know I'm best.'

'I don't go with other women, Weenie,' stated Oxbee.

'You queer?'

'No, I'm happily married, but Adam's single.'

'Oh, okay Mister Adam; I give you freebie tonight but tomorrow you pay double.'

Zander drained his glass and said, 'I'm going to check out Weenie's attributes. I'll give you a call at work.'

Zander reached out and gripped Weenie's hand and she resisted a little. He looked back at her and she screwed up her face in a playful and tempting fashion but he gave her a quick jerk and she came up off the barstool still resisting slightly. She stepped down off the stool and shook her hips as she made the first reluctant steps and then she was alongside him. Zander looked over his shoulder at the group she had been sitting with and noticed they were all in a huddle.

'What's that hip wiggling all about?'

She played dumb for a while then admitted it was their way of communicating a freebie. Elloween wore a long white clinging rayon dress and no underwear. In the light of the Majestic Hotel lobby, Zander's attention was drawn to her breasts where her nipples could now be seen, erect and tantalising.

Chapter 3 Superintendent Confrontation

Weenie asked Zander to turn the air conditioner off in the Bronco and then explained where she lived. As they pulled away from the kerb she put her head in his lap.

'If you start that, we're not going to make it back to your place.'
'I keep warm till we get there.'

Zander parked as Oxbee had advised and they went into the house, which was on stilts. As they went past a room on the right of the passage she pointed to it and wagged a finger indicating out of bounds and mouthing the word "parents." They continued down the central passageway, which was about forty-foot long, with doors on each side that were all closed.

Her room was at the end of the passage; it had an en-suite shower and lavatory. The room was sparsely furnished; the dressing table was covered in trinkets and small ornaments of animals, and the luxurious king-size bed was covered in cuddly toys, which she immediately moved to the settee.

Zander sat on the edge of the bed and removed his shoes and socks; then Weenie insisted on removing his other clothes.

She seemed to be able to find every sensitive spot on his body, which she gently touched with her fingertips, and when he was naked she pushed him back onto the bed. Her right hand went between the upper part of his thighs she bunched her fingers and then gently and slowly splayed the fingers, lightly touching the flesh on the inside of his thigh. Weenie continued this jellyfish action with her hand until Zander was sexually aroused and breathing hard and fast.

Weenie stood up and Zander made a grab for her but she pushed him back. She seductively slipped the straps of her dress off her shoulders and it slithered down her body revealing a light brown skin with small firm breasts and large dark erect nipples; her hips were thrust forward with a triangular patch of hair below her inverted navel. She turned and walked away from him holding out her hand and Zander realised they were heading for a shower.   It was only the atmospheric temperature that heated the water so it was cool and invigorating and the sticky sweat of the day was removed straight away. Weenie soaped him all over and stroked and squeezed his manhood to see if there was any contagious discharge.

'I haven't got a dose if that's what you're checking for'
'I don't want a dripping dick in me - bad for business.   I don't like rubbers either; also bad for business.'

Weenie handed him the soap and turned her back on him. He moved his right hand around the front and down to the inviting bulge of hair between her legs. He rubbed the soap on his hands and then onto her body, paying particular attention to her breasts, which were firm and smooth. Zander snapped his hand away and picked up the soap and returned it to the vital spot. As the soap foamed she backed into him and his erection pressed into the middle of her back.

'A knee-trembler is out of the question with our height difference,' gasped Zander excitedly.

Weenie took up the showerhead, and with a few quick flicks of the wrist, washed off the soap-covered areas of their bodies. She pulled him out of the shower and scooped up two towels, threw one on the bed and shook the other open and vigorously rubbed him down. Zander picked up the other towel and repeated the process on her. Weenie switched off the oscillating fan as it brought a waft of cool air to her body.

Zander sat on the bed where her waist was level with his eyes. He bent his head slightly and blew a stream of warm air into the fluffy hair; it was not harsh pubic hair but soft and downy.   She clasped her hands behind his head and thrust her lower body into his face. He rubbed his bristly chin into the extremely sensitive area and she threw her head back and gasped. Zander leaned back and Weenie fell forward and his face went up the front of her body, coming to rest between her breasts. He kissed her left breast and enveloped the nipple in his mouth; breaking away he kissed her neck, chin and lips. Weenie put her hand between their bodies and guided them together. Zander rolled her over and they thrashed, thrust and heaved until climax. Afterwards they lay in each others arms, drained and exhausted.

   Their love-making continued throughout the night. At seven o'clock Zander got up and dressed, and as Weenie slept he tucked a hundred-dollar note into her hand and left. As he moved off in the Bronco he noticed where numerous vehicles had gone into the river and momentarily remembered Oxbee's advice.   Zander went back to his sister's house where he carried out his ablutions and then went to the office of Jon Morris.

   'Any developments, Jon?'
   'The lawyer has seen Marty and he is hopeful of release today.'
   'Anything from the embassy?'
   'No, but they will be acting with telling effect by now.'
   'I desperately need to get to the scene, Jon. Who's looking after the pigs and dogs et cetera?'
   'Two of the boys from Two Snakes - that's the inland farm.'
   'Have they got access to the house?'
   'No, they are staying in the bunkhouse.'
   'So, I could visit the island then?'
   'I should think so.'
   'Can you fix it for me please?'
   'Okay, have some coffee and I'll see what I can do.'

   Morris made the arrangements and Zander went off in a company truck to the jetty where he was collected by speedboat and taken to the island. The house was taped off and guarded by several uniformed policemen but the dogs in the area of the house were locked up, and this gave Zander the opportunity to poke around the out-buildings. He was tempted to try and bluff his way into the house, but realising he had been there over an hour he thought a phone call to Morris was perhaps the better thing to do.

The approaching police launch had a large uniformed policeman standing at the stern; his legs were spread apart against the wallow of the launch. He had a silver-headed swagger cane grasped firmly in both hands horizontally behind his back and his chin jutted forward in an arrogantly aggressive manner.

'Good morning, Sir. I hope my request to visit the scene of the crime has not made things too difficult for you.'
'T'ings? What t'ings?' Superintendent Kaba blurted as he got out of the launch.

Zander realised he was wasting his time. He ignored the superintendent's reply and followed him into the house and as they entered the large front porch, he noticed slatted racking, similar to that found in a greenhouse. There were five five-gallon clear blue plastic containers each full of water and they all had a tap at the bottom edge. Zander scanned the kitchen cabinets as he went in and observed that above the sink was an aluminium shelf bracketed to the wall with steel struts.

'Has anything been removed?'
'Not by us,' snapped the superintendent, 'except the body of course.'
'Has someone else moved things then?'
'The murder weapon has gone; it was some kind of blunt t'ing hit on de body.'

Zander surveyed the blood-spattered worktop and noticed the jug of homemade lemonade. He had another look at the sixth water container above the sink and noticed that it was nearly full.

'That, superintendent, is a break,' announced Zander pointing to the jug.

The policeman looked at it and shrugged.

'It shows that Pancho was lying.'
'How?'
'There was no fresh water in the house when Mr Martens left for the office. If Pancho brought the fresh water in, then Elly wasn't dead when he arrived, unless of course he stepped over her dead body, installed a container of water above the sink and made a jug of lemonade.'
'Unless Martens was lying about the water,' snapped the superintendent.
'We only have to check with the ice cream factory to find out how many containers of water Pancho collected. Despite your doubts, I think it's time to have a word with Pancho. Do you know where he lives, Sir?'
'No, but I can find out from HQ.'
'Okay. Was the rain water storage tank inspected during your search?'
'Dun know.'
'I would like to check it now if that is possible?'
'Why you wan check?'
'I've seen my sister's tank and it's a good place to hide things."

'Like what?'
'A body!'

The superintendent looked shocked.

'I t'ink it's outside.'

They walked outside and found the tank at the side of the house. Zander clambered up the steel structure supporting the two thousand-gallon tank and lifted the inspection hatch and saw a small plastic ball floating on the surface. He picked up the ball and found nylon fishing line attached, and when he pulled in the line he discovered a heavy-duty plastic bag attached to it and there was a metal cash box inside.

'I think this is the flight money, superintendent,' he said handing the box over. Shall we go and find Pancho and tell him what he missed?'

The superintendent set his jaw and was determined to be unsociable. He hardly spoke during the return journey to HQ and then on to Pancho's. On arrival at Pancho's tin shack they could see that someone had left in a hurry.

'Am I allowed to look around?'
'I don't see why not. He's not here to stop you,' stated the superintendent.

This was becoming very difficult, thought Zander, and if this arrogant buffoon of a superintendent doesn't stop getting under my skin I'm going to crack him one. The shack which was made from corrugated iron had a bed in one corner and a wardrobe in another. Zander searched the shack and found a blood-stained blue and white checked shirt under the bed.

'I think we have our man, superintendent. We had better speak to Martens and then get this analysed.'

Zander looked at the policeman and waited for some reaction. He seemed to be going over things in his mind but then there was a reluctant show of acceptance spreading across his face.

'Okay, you win,' declared the superintendent with a sigh.

They went back to the police headquarters where they left the shirt for analysis in the coroner's department, which also housed the pathology laboratory, mortuary and forensic department, all under the control of Doctor Sir George Roberts. On arrival at the headquarters Zander opened the main entrance door for the superintendent.

'May I telephone Jon Morris?'
'Yes, if you wish; there's a phone over there at reception.'

The sergeant on duty handed Zander the phone.

'Ah, Jon, just the man. I'm at the police headquarters and I'm just about to see Marty; he's going to be released. Would you send the Bronco? Thanks. See you later.'

Zander was then taken to Martens' cell, where the superintendent joined him.

'Marty, how many containers of water did Pancho collect?'
'Six. We only have six and they were all empty.'
'What shirt was Pancho wearing when he told you about the murder?'
'A white T-shirt, and he told me about the murder just before the police arrived.'
'What was he wearing when he picked you up that morning for the office?'

Martens had to think for a minute or two.

'A blue and white checked short-sleeved shirt.'
'Satisfied, superintendent?'
'Okay, let him go.'

Martens could hardly believe his ears. He let out a little yelp and started to straighten himself up.

'Thanks for your cooperation, superintendent. I will leave it to you to find and arrest Pancho.'
'Okay.'
'He's full of enthusiasm that one.' remarked Zander as he and Martens got into the Bronco.

'Back to the office please,' said Martens to the driver. 'I hope you don't mind, Adam, but I don't want to go back to No Trees.' They pulled up at the office building. 'I won't come in, Marty, as I have a few things I would like to do.'

The driver got out and Zander slipped in behind the wheel and started to pull away.

'Adam!' yelled Jon Morris from behind the Bronco.

Morris broke into a little jog to arrive at the Bronco as Zander got out.

'I'm glad I've caught up with you, Adam. I have that dossier on that missing money. Would you like to come up to the office and have a look?'
'Yes, my few odd jobs can wait; it's going to be a little quiet now we know who was responsible for Elly's murder - let me re-phrase that - we know who killed her, of that I have no doubt.'

'You've found out who did it? Really!'

'Yes, it was Pancho. Now, whether he was self-motivated or just persuaded to do it is the one doubt in my mind at present.'

'What doubt is there?'
'Well, firstly, he worked for Elly and Marty for some time so he was obviously aware of the proposed wedding and the arrangements, and most probably the money in the house. But the money was not in the house; it was in the rain water storage tank outside the house. And why did he choose the day that the tickets were being purchased because there would have been many other opportunities when the house was unoccupied?'
'It's obvious he's the killer so what else is there to look for?' Morris demanded.
'Yes, you are most probably right, but if I get these ideas they usually turn out to be true.'

'Yes, okay. Let's go and see the dossier on the man who owes me money,' suggested Morris as they headed for the office. 'I'm afraid there isn't much to go on but I have his name and last address, and also a copy of the agreement he signed when he got the loan.'

'But surely you didn't loan fifty thousand dollars without checking his details?'

'No, of course not; it wasn't fifty, it was one hundred and fifty, and he has paid back a hundred and the rest is now three months overdue.'

'Do you want me to take him to the local police and get the money off him or bring him back to you?'

'I think the best idea would be to get the money and dispose of him, but that. . .'

'Stop!' interrupted Zander. 'Before you say any more, that is not what I do. I do not kill people for money. I might in self-defence but never for money; so, I think the best thing I can do is forget we ever had this conversation. I will leave you to make other arrangements for the collection of the fifty thousand. It's five thirty already so I must dash,' declared Zander as he turned on his heel and walked out of the office.

Morris was left standing with his mouth agape; he had never been dismissed like that before. He called after Zander, but was ignored. Zander went out into the evening sunlight, and drove the Bronco back to his sister's house and during the journey he thought hard about the significance of what Morris had tried to do. He came to the conclusion that there was more to Morris than he had first thought, and that was still on Zander's mind while he was having a shower.

'Oops! I'm sorry, Mary, I have to go out,' said Zander as he was surprised yet again by Mary holding the robe for him.

He shrugged into the robe and felt invigorated as he rubbed the towel robe all over. He was hardly able to resist her and he could tell by the look in her eyes exactly what she wanted, but he knew his sister was in the dining room. Mary pouted and hung her head in a mock sulk as she laid his things out on the bed and then left. Zander arrived in the dining room just as Stan returned from the office.

'How's the case going, Adam?'

'Fine, it wasn't the butler, it was the farmhand,' declared Zander with a smirk.

'Well I never! Would you credit it? I wouldn't have thought Pancho capable.'

'Yes, I've a problem with that too, but I think he might have done it under duress or perhaps he did it for the flight money; that's how it looks.'

'I'm sure you'll solve it.'

'I'll need to find someone else with a motive if it wasn't just the money. I'm going to the officers' mess to say hello to the new matron so I'll see you later.'

'I'll phone the mess and tell them you are on your way,' said Jenny.

Galpen met Zander at the barrier.

'Good evening, Adam, I hear you've solved the Elly murder.'

'Well, it looks that way, but Pancho hasn't been arrested yet, George.'

'Matter of time, old boy, and they will have him tucked up in jail waiting for the hangman's noose.'

'Do they still hang them here then?'

'Yes, indeed; they only recently stopped doing it in public but by that I mean a few of the public were permitted to go into the jail and observe.'

There were about fifty people in the mess bar. The bar was L-shaped and the serving area was set in the corner backing onto the dining area and adjacent to the atap ante-room where the weekly film shows were shown. The ceiling fans were having little effect in reducing the effect of the tropical heat which was made worse by the number of bodies packed in shoulder to shoulder. The bar was only ever this crowded on flight days when there were departures, arrivals and visitors out from the UK usually on a jolly and everybody met at happy hour. Sarah waved at them from the far end of the bar and then jiggled her hand in front of her mouth asking what drink they wanted. In return, Zander mouthed beer and Galpen mouthed G and T and they stepped back under the fan and waited for their drinks.

'Hi there,' chirped Sal, 'My hero! You've solved the murder and now I hear you are going to get Jon's money back.'

'Well, I would say there is a distinct possibility that the murder has been solved, but getting the money back, no. I remember a couple of days ago when Elly was murdered you didn't seem too worried about it, but now you seem interested.'

'Nah, she used to be my competition and I didn't like her too much, that's all.'

'Competition - for what?'

'Jon Morris, that's what.'

'Really! Well that puts a different light on the matter.'

'What did I say?' Sal asked.

'Jon and Elly!' queried Zander.

'Yes, Jon and I were fooling around back in the States; then he moved down here about three years ago and now spends one week a month in the States on business and pleasure. Up until a year ago, I was his pleasure back in the States, shared with his wife. Now I'm his assistant, and sometime pleasure, down here. Whereas Elly was his pleasure down here until Marty turned up about a year and a half ago and they hit it off and then Jon asked me to move down here which I did and all's been well since.'

Sarah arrived with the drinks followed by Perky. Sarah made the introductions and Zander noticed that Perky had a vice-like handshake to go with her shapely body. Her pint mug was in her left hand which was curled up against her left breast, and as she took it away to take a drink, it left a wet patch on her white cotton blouse.

'Not quite like UK pints; the outside of the glass here is covered in condensation,' explained Zander nodding his head towards the wet patch.

Perky pulled the blouse away from the skin and the damp patch then settled over her nipple, which could be clearly seen through the material. She then brushed it with the ends of her fingers as if to flick something off but this made the nipple stand out like an organ stop. Galpen and Zander averted their eyes and Perky smiled.

'Sorry about that. I'm so used to cuddling my pint that I forgot about the condensation. I'll have to go and change.'
'Sal, where's Jon?'
'Gone out to Two Snakes; they've got trouble with one of the cows in calf.'
'Does he always get involved in that sort of thing?'
'Yeah, he loves it.'
'So you're in limits now that Jon's out of town.'
'Yeah, sure. Yah wanna get laid.'
'The thought had crossed my mind, I must admit.'
'Okay, keep an eye on me and keep me sober, and later on we'll go to it.' Sal raised her hand and made a finger wave and moved off into the crowd.
'That's the fastest chat-up success I've ever heard,' declared Sarah.
'I'm next,' snapped Perky, 'and that's faster.'

Zander smirked at the comment.

'What's up? Have I got my fly open, George?'
'No, but your tongue is hanging out.'
'Ah, that's what it is; I didn't realise it was that attractive.'
'I'd better introduce you to Doc Medows, Perky. As I mentioned earlier he's your boss until his replacement arrives in a fortnight's time,' proclaimed Sarah.

The two matrons moved off just as Nigel, the young subaltern, started to play the piano.

'He's good on that piano, George. What's he doing in the army?'

'The army sponsored him through university and now he is doing his time. Actually he will make an extremely good regular officer, in the fullness of time and I just hope he decides to stay in.   He's enjoying himself at present as the Regimental Signals Officer.'

'That's Shearing's *"Buccaneers Bounce"*, isn't?' asked Zander.

'Possibly, but I'm not a musical person; however, when the regiment is back in the UK Nigel plays at a jazz club in London.'

It was nearly ten o'clock and Nigel was still at the piano.

'Can you play *"Stormy weather"* Nigel?' asked Sal.
'If you can sing it, I'll play it.'

Everybody was impressed with Sal's rendition but none more so than Nigel and when she had finished he gave enthusiastic and loud applause bouncing on the piano stool excitedly.

'Is there anything else you would like me to play, Sal?'
'What about *I Left My Heart In San Francisco*?'
'Okay, come and join me,' said Nigel patting the stool.
'From the way Nigel is looking at Sal, Adam, I think you might have missed your opportunity to "get laid."
'Yes, I think you're right.'
'No he's not, I'm still here.'
'Hello, Perky, I thought you'd gone.'
'No, I'm still waiting to be next.'
'I'm sure that can be arranged,' said Zander holding out his hand to her.
'Where are we going?'
'Around the corner for a knee-trembler.'
'Oh, I thought you were heading for the female accommodation area but we're obviously not, which is good because it's out of bounds to visitors.'

'See yah, George,' said Zander over his shoulder as he walked out of the bar with Perky.

When they were outside on the veranda Perky took the lead. The verandas, made of slatted-wood staging about four-foot wide, surrounded each single storey building and were all interconnected.

'Where are we heading?'
'Matron's night room,' whispered Perky as they entered the hospital by the back door. 'Wait here.'

Perky went down the corridor about twenty yards, made sure all was clear and then waved Zander in. The room was like a single bedded side ward, except that there was a desk, chairs, a couple of armchairs and a coffee table and there was also a drugs cabinet on the wall.

'Drink?'
'Scotch, please.'
'Sex?'
'Please, but hang on, what's happening here? We don't even know each other and we're about to have sex.'
'I fancied you from the minute I set eyes on you, Adam. Your Clark Gable looks make me want to ravish you.'
'The loving and tender person that I am, drives me to let you have your wicked way, if that's what you want'

Zander smirked at her posturing, and his own for that matter, and felt slightly embarrassed, however, that did not last long because she started to undress and his attention was drawn to the comeliness of her body. Their lovemaking lasted several hours and Zander eventually woke at two in the morning with Perky purring gently with her arms wrapped around him and her head on his chest. He eased himself out of bed as she adjusted her position and curled up into the foetal position.

He left via the back door and headed towards the mess car park and as he approached the mess he heard the piano. Nigel was still playing with Sal still sharing the piano stool with him. There was only the two of them so he left them to it and got into the Bronco.   The sentry gave Zander a strange look as he lifted the barrier to let him out of the camp.

Chapter 4 Another Death

On Sunday Zander settled down for a day of fishing on the river at the back of his sister's house. The riverbank was shored up with logs driven in to make a landing place. Zander gulped a mouthful of cold beer, which seemed to hit the right spot as it generated a smack of the lips and an ahh of satisfaction but as he relaxed back into his chair the phone rang in the house behind him.

'Adam!' called out his sister; 'It's the superintendent for you.'

Zander acknowledged the call with his hand and reeled in his line. He put the rod down by his chair, picked up his beer and went back up to the house.

'Hello, Superintendent, Adam Zander here.'

'Mista Zander, Pancho is dead; you wanna come to the station? We have his body in the morgue here.'

'I'm on my way,' stated Zander putting the phone down.

He turned to his sister, 'Is it all right if I use the Bronco again?'

'Yes, by all means; it's yours while you're here. What's the problem?'

'Pancho has been found dead so I'm off to the police morgue.'

Zander approached the police desk.

'May I speak to the superintendent? I'm afraid I don't know his name but he's the man in charge of the Elly van Dam murder.'

'You wan Super Kaba. He with the death doctor through that door,' announced the Desk Corporal pointing at a door that had morgue written on it in white letters.

The door to the morgue was brown and the paint was peeling, as was the paint on the walls, but this was in contrast to the door leading into a brightly-lit air-conditioned waiting room, which was sparsely furnished with just six chairs and a low coffee table. There was a sign on the door leading to the morgue which said, *"No persons beyond this point without authorisation and police escort."* Kaba opened the door and waved Zander into the morgue.

'This is the coroner, Sir George Roberts,'
'Hello, Mr Zander, nice to meet you.' Zander did not offer his hand as the doctor was wearing rubber gloves, which were covered in blood.
'Any idea of the cause?'
'Yes, here; a bullet through the heart from close range.'

Zander looked where the doctor was pointing and could see a black smudge around the small hole. Sir George eased the side of the body up to show Zander the exit hole, which was large and ragged.

'A lot can be deduced from the entry and exit wounds. The shot was made at close range so he most probably knew his killer et cetera, but I'll leave that to you. My initial report will be ready in a couple of hours but my first impression is that he has been dead about twelve hours, shot at close range with a .22 calibre bullet, which went right through him. He was not killed where he was found.'
'So, we're looking at a time of death about ten o'clock last night?" Zander quizzed.
'Yes, he was found at the side of an old logging track by some back-packers at seven thirty this morning,' stated Kaba.
'My theory is that either he wouldn't be found or he would appear to have had an accident and that would be the end of it, but somewhere along the line it has gone wrong and so my theory is out of the window. The person who wanted Elly out of the way had to kill Pancho. This means we still have a trail to follow and   I think I know who is responsible for Pancho's' death but now I have to establish the motive.'
'What do you mean by that, Mista Zander?' asked Kaba.

'Elly was Jon Morris' girlfriend some time ago and I think there might have been some sort of blackmail going on. You might like to question him about that, Superintendent. Meanwhile I'm going out to Two Snakes to check on his alibi for last night.'

Kaba looked quizzically at Zander. 'You serious about Morris?'

'Yes, extremely serious.'

'But he was instrumental in getting you to investigate the case.'

'That's not true. I was briefed by the Americans and asked to investigate this case, and that's what I'll do, even if he's involved. Anyway I'll let you know as soon as I get anything concrete.'

Zander went out via the reception desk and phoned Oxbee.

'Fred, I'm going out to Jon Morris' farm. Do you want to come?'

'Yes. When?'

'Now, and could you bring your evidence-collecting bag of tricks.'

'Okay, but won't that upset the locals?'

'No, I'm on a roll now; if I leave it to Kaba and his boys it'll never get done.'

Zander and Oxbee arrived at Two Snakes late in the afternoon. The entrance to the farm was manned by one of Morris' employees and he questioned them before he would let them in. There was an inner fence some ten yards inside the outer fence and this enclosed area had security dogs loose within it. At the rear of the employees' accommodation, which backed onto the jungle, dogs were tethered to static lines and they patrolled menacingly for four hours at a stretch. Zander introduced himself to the farm manager, Red Hodson.

'I see why they call you Red. With a mop of red hair like
that, anybody would be hard pushed to call you anything else,'
stated Zander as he shook hands with the six-foot, two-
hundred–and-fifty-pound farm manager.

'Well, my Mom named me Cedric, so Red suits me fine. Mr
Morris has mentioned you to me, Mr Zander, so you can have
access to everything,' said Hodson in a slow Texan drawl.

'Where're you from Red?'

'San Antonio, Texas.'

'Was Jon Morris here last night?'

'Yes, he went over to the bunkhouses. I had a few beers and
then watched the football game on TV so I didn't see him when
he left.'

'Didn't you have trouble with a cow calving?'

'Yes, that was yesterday afternoon. She had twins and it was
a bit of a struggle but they're okay now.'

'Didn't he come to help with that?'

'No, he went to the bunkhouses.'

'Which one?'

'I'm not sure, I think you'd better ask them,' said Hodson
pointing to a group of workers near the bunkhouses.

Zander and Oxbee headed for the little group of huts on the
edge of the compound. The huts were twenty feet long with an
atap roof and there were six beds in each. They questioned
several of the cowhands who all played dumb, and one of the
hands was a bit agitated when questioned but he eventually
admitted he let Morris have a box of tools.

'Why tools?' asked Zander.

The Hispanic cowhand was reluctant to offer more
information and it took Zander several minutes prising out of
him that Morris had taken one of the farm trucks.

'What time was that and where did he go?'

'About seven, and he went out to the old logging area; we are
clearing another fifty acres for more cattle grazing.'

'Would you like to show me on the map where that is?'

'I don't want to lose my job.'

'Mr Morris is not back yet, so maybe he has had an accident, and we should go and look for him.'

'Okay, I'd better take you there.'

Zander could not believe his luck. He looked at Oxbee who raised his eyebrows and then winked. They travelled along a metalled road for about six miles and then turned off onto the logging track and eventually came across a police Land Rover at the side of the logging track.

'What's going on, Officer?' asked Zander as he pulled up alongside.

'Ah, Mr Zander, this is where they found Pancho.'

'Have you found any evidence?'

'No, Sir. I think the body was just dumped here. We are searching the area but I doubt that we'll turn anything up.' There were several police officers thrashing about in the jungle at the side of the road.

Zander spoke over his shoulder to the cowhand in the back of the Bronco. 'You know Pancho?'

'Yes, he works on the island.'

'Not any more - he was killed last night.'

A quick glance in the mirror told Zander that the cowhand did not know Pancho was dead.

'Can we go back now?' pleaded the cowhand.

'No, we're going to where you were going to take us.'

'I'm frightened, Mr Zander; maybe I die like Pancho.'

'No, I don't think so,' declared Zander as he pulled away from the scene.

They travelled along the track for another mile and the cowhand directed them off the logging track and into the secondary jungle. The track, which showed signs of recent use, was painfully uneven and they bounced about unceremoniously in the Bronco.   They entered a clearing of some fifty acres where the new grass was well-established, and on the edge of the clearing was a tin shack.

'Did Pancho stay here?'
'Maybe, I don't know,' spluttered the nervous cowhand.

The door was not locked so Zander opened it cautiously and lit a hurricane lamp that was hanging from a crossbeam.

'It looks as though someone has been here recently. See if you can get any prints, Fred.'
'I can see plenty of prints on that melamine table top without dusting.'
'Good; start collecting.'

Zander went outside to where the cowhand stood.

'Are there any other buildings around here?'
'Yes, there is the Master's cabin; it's back there in the jungle; just follow the track.'
'I'll leave you to it, Fred. I'm going over to the cabin.'

Zander opened the door and went into the entrance hall and then into a pine-panelled room where the ceiling fan was whirring.

'Jeez, I thought I was never going to be found.'
'Jon! What the hell are you doing here?'
'Slowly bleeding to death, I think. I've stopped the bleeding using pressure, but I've lost a lot of blood so much so that every time I lift my head I get dizzy and sometimes pass out.'

Zander looked at the wound in Morris' left shoulder.

'By the look of this wound you were shot from behind.'
'I was, and no, I don't know who did it.'
'What were you doing out here anyway?'

57

'I've been fooling around with someone else's wife. Her car broke down so she used my Bronco to go back to town and dropped me off at Two Snakes on the way. I picked up some tools and a truck and came back out here to fix it.'

'Where is it now?'

'I'd moved it down the track and was coming back up here for the truck, so that I could tow it back to Two Snakes and as I was walking towards the door I felt this searing pain in my shoulder. I heard nothing; I just felt the impact and fell forward onto my face.'

'Do you think you could sit up? I need to look at the entry point.'

With Zander's help Morris sat up on the bed and leaned forward; there was a considerable amount of blood on the sheet, some of which was partially congealed.

'The point of entry is small so it looks like a .22. There is a slightly larger exit hole and the bullet has gone straight through and it doesn't look as if it's been deflected by bone.'

'Hold on to me, Adam, I'm going to pass out again.'

'Okay, I've got you, but I've got to take your shirt off to try and dress the wound, and it's still oozing a little blood.'

Morris did not hear what Zander was saying as he had already passed out, and it was at that point that Oxbee walked into the cabin with his bag of tricks. Zander held Morris in the sitting position to make it easier for Oxbee to access the wound.

'I've got a small first aid kit in my bag,' uttered Oxbee.

'The flies have not been active, but the wound needs to be sterilised as soon as possible.'

Oxbee removed a plastic sachet of sterilising fluid from his bag. He snipped the top off the sachet and poured some onto the wound, and it took him several minutes to clean and dress the wound.

'It doesn't look as if it has touched the bone, Adam, but we will have to compensate for the blood loss.'
'Yes, that's what I thought,'

Oxbee laid Morris back down and moved his hand beckoning Zander away from Morris and over to the doorway.

'Look to the right of the entry point, Adam. Would you say that puncture was the site of an injection?' Oxbee whispered.

Zander went back to Morris.

'Could be; we'll have that looked at.'

Morris started to come round as they went to the bed.

I won't be the Boy Scout and offer you a cup of hot sweet tea, but how long have you been like this?' asked Zander.
'Looking at the light outside it looks like dusk so I should think about twenty-four hours.'
'Let's get some liquid into him, Fred, and then we can move him back to Two Snakes. Where's that cowhand?'
'I left him back at the shack.'
'Okay. Would you mind getting him and the Bronco over here?'
Oxbee scooped up his bag and left the cabin.
'Jon, were you involved in Pancho's killing?'
'No! I didn't know he was dead. What on earth made you suggest that?'
'The obvious, I'm afraid. You had a motive for getting rid of Elly with her being your ex-girlfriend and possibly blackmailing you with the threat of telling your wife.'

'It's not possible to blackmail me when it comes to other women and my wife because she knows all about my philandering, so that's not a problem.'

'Well, there have been two murders and Pancho was found not far from here only a few hours ago. Now there has been an attempt on your life and it would be a bit naive to think they were not related.'

'You're most probably right, but I would like to think I was the unintentional target of a local hunter taking a pot shot at something that moved.'

'There's little chance of that; I would suggest you are on someone's hit list. Have you got the keys to her car and the truck? I'll get Fred and the cowhand to take them back.'

'Yeah, sure, in my right pocket.'

Oxbee arrived back with the cowhand and under the direction of Zander, and with the help of Oxbee and the cowhand, Morris was lifted into the Bronco and driven back to the farm whereupon Oxbee summoned a doctor via the farm manager. Zander and the cowhand carried Morris into the house. The house had a white-washed wooden lapboard exterior and was air-conditioned throughout. The housekeeper met them in the entrance hall and directed them to an L-shaped room on the ground floor where there was a large king-sized bed in an alcove to the right. Zander helped Morris undress.

'I have to go to the bathroom, Adam, would you mind?'

Zander assisted him to the en-suite; although weak Morris was capable of walking slowly on his own. Once Morris was in bed Zander went to see the farm manager and left Oxbee at the house.

'Red, how does that fan in the cabin operate?'
'There is a generator in a building about fifty yards back in the jungle and there is also solar power.'
'How do you start the generator?'
'With a pull cord.'

'Thanks for that.'

'Adam, the doctor's arrived,' called Oxbee from the entrance to the farm manager's office.

'Okay, I'm on my way.'

The doctor was preparing an injection when Zander went into the bedroom.

'What are you giving him, Doctor?'

'And you are?' demanded the doctor indignantly.

'It's all right, Doc," said Morris. "He's an investigator friend of mine, Adam Zander, helping the police with the Elly van Dam murder.'

'All right. I'm giving him antibiotics and a pain killer. He'll be fine. The bullet went clean through his shoulder and the wound area shows no signs of gangrene yet and that's a good thing. I should think, as long as the velocity didn't kill the flesh as the bullet went through his shoulder. But I'm going to give him a local anaesthetic and clean it up properly. I'll also set up a plasma drip and arrange for a nurse to come and keep an eye on him.'

'Are you from America, Doctor?' asked Zander.

'No, I'm English actually, originally from Camberley in Surrey. Mark Smith; I've been here over twenty years and spent some time in the States, which most probably accounts for my mid-Atlantic accent.'

'Did you come out from town?'

'No, I was out this way on a call and the office got me on the radio, and as soon as I found out it was Jon, I came straight across.'

'Well, thanks for all you've done, doctor. I must be off because I need to have a few more words with the farm manager. Would you mind if I had a few words with you before you leave?'

'Not at all.'

Zander met Oxbee who was coming out of the office and they went together to see Hodson.

'Red, have you got any hunters amongst your farmhands?'
Zander asked.

'Yes, several; the two in today are Manuel and Otis but most
of the hunting they do is illegal. They hunt big cats - puma,
mountain lion and stuff. They are protected species but there is
a market for them and they usually kill to order and make big
bucks.   If a tourist wants a skin or carcass of a particular type,
they go out and get it.'

'Have they been out recently?'

'I don't know. I usually hear about it after it's over, and as
long as they do it on their own time ...what the hell.'

'Don't you try and stop them?'

'I'm not a cop; and anyway, I've a farm to run.'

'But it's illegal.'

'So is speeding but what do you do about that when you see
someone exceeding the limit?'

'Point taken. Would it be all right if I had a word with them?'

'Yeah, sure.'

Zander and Oxbee headed off to the bunkhouse in search of
the two hunters and on the way they met Doctor Smith heading
for his truck.

'Did you see that puncture wound just to the right of the
bullet entry point?'

'Yes, why?'

'I thought it might have been where someone injected
painkiller before or just after the shot. What do you think?'

'Yes, it could be, but why would anyone do that before the
shot?'

'That's something I have to work out. Thank you, Doctor.
I'm not so sure, Fred, that the bullet that hit Jon is the same sort
of round they would use for big cats. What do you think?'

'Yes, I tend to agree with you, but, there has to be some sort
of connection. I'm sure a .22 high velocity bullet in the head

would knock down a puma. Let's hope these two hunters can shed some light on the matter.'

The first cowhand they met was the one that had taken them to Morris in the first instance.

'Do you know where Manuel and Otis are?' inquired Zander.
'Yes, in the other bunkhouse, but only Otis is there.'
'Thanks, pal.'

They walked the length of the first building and onto the veranda of the second.

'How are we going for time Fred?'
'It's ten thirty.'
'Bit late; let's hope they are not all in bed. Where's Otis?'
'Over there,' said the hand.

They approached the cowhand who was sitting on a bed reading a magazine and it was obvious that his demeanour was somewhat hostile.

'You police?'
'No, not really, we are making inquires about hunting activities in recent days.'
'Don't know not'in'.'
'I know you are a big cat hunter but I'm not interested in that as such. I just want to know if you were out last night, and if not, do you know who was?'
'No and no.'
'I can see I'm going to have difficulty with you. Now you can either cooperate with me or I shall turn you over to the authorities with a story that will take you weeks to talk your way out of jail,' pronounced Zander.
'Like what?'
'Like you shot your boss because he was onto you as a hunter?'
'I shot no man; I only shoot animals.'

'Where is your rifle?'

'In there,' drawled Otis pointing to the cupboard in the corner of the bunkhouse.

'May I see it?'

Otis got up and ambled over to the cupboard. He opened it and took out a rifle.

'Here,' he snapped thrusting the rifle towards Zander.

'That's a FN 7.62 Fabrique Nationale. Belgian I think, semi-automatic. We used to have them in the British Army before the SLR.'

'Where did you get it?'

'Bought it.'

'You got a licence?'

'Yes.'

Otis went to the table by the side of his bed and took a folder out of the draw.

'Here's my hunting licence and firearms certificate.'

'Your licence says crocodiles, wild pig and iguana but nothing about big cats.'

'I don't shoot protected animals.'

'Oh, I see. Do you use a .22 calibre rifle?'

'No, poachers use them.'

'What for? Big cats?'

'Yes.'

'But a .22 wouldn't bring a cat down, would it?'

'Yes, it would if you hit it in the right place or used poison.'

'Poison?'

'Yes. The poachers seal flying-death poison in the hollow point of the round, which leaks out on impact, and it only takes a few seconds before it takes effect. It is used on the tips of arrows.'

'Why do they use poison?'

'Because then they can use a silencer and a low-velocity round with a telescopic sight and it can be effective up to about four hundred yards - so you can poach undetected.'

'Who do you know who has one of these rifles?'

'Manuel has one, and yes he was out hunting last night.'

'Where is he now?'

'Still out hunting, I think.'

'Have you any idea where?'

'No, but I could most probably find him if you paid enough.'

'Two hundred bucks?' offered Zander.

'Okay, when do we start?' spluttered Otis.

'First light tomorrow. See you in the morning.'

'But surely, Adam, Manuel might be back by then,' said Oxbee.

'He's not due back to work for another couple of days, and if he shot his boss he's not likely to come back anyway. Besides, Jon Morris says he doesn't know who shot him; it's all assumption on our part,' declared Zander with a smile.

'Do you think this poison will kill a human?' Oxbee asked.

'Yes, I suspect he's referring to curare. It needs to get into the bloodstream, but is harmless when swallowed. Whoever it was that shot at Morris obviously didn't want to kill him by using flying death - an indication perhaps that it wasn't a local hunter.'

'It could have been just to scare him off,' inferred Oxbee.

'You could be right, but scare him off his own cattle-grazing land? No, I don't think so; maybe muddy the waters a bit to try and deflect the investigation, but it's a point to ponder on during our journey back to town. What we're going to do now is quickly go back up to the cabin and check that generator,' declared Zander.

'It's a bit late, Adam.'

'Yes, I know but I'm curious as to what was running that fan. If it was the solar-charged batteries, okay, he would just have to have flicked the switch after being shot. But if it was running on the generator, either he started it or someone else did. If he started it, he did it before he was shot, in anticipation of having to stay there until discovered. But he was just getting the truck to go and pick up the car on the "A" frame and go back to Two Snakes, so the generator would have been switched off.'

'You're obviously switched on, Adam, let's look.'

Chapter 5 Yet Another Killing

They arrived back at the cabin and Zander collected the torch from the glove compartment and headed for the generator building. The generator was not running but it had been recently because it was still warm. Zander checked the fuel tank and found it to be empty.

'It's out of petrol. Looking at that tank how long do you think it would run?'

'About twenty-four hours. It's similar to the one on our standby generator.'

'Do you want to come and look for Manuel tomorrow?'

'As much as I would like to, I can't. I have to work, investigating drug-taking soldiers, et cetera.'

'Okay, will I see you at Beating Retreat tomorrow night?'

'Yes, why don't you come to the Sergeants' Mess afterwards for a few drinks?'

'Thanks, but there's a curry supper in the Officers' Mess with the Prime Minister and I think I'm down for that.'

Zander dropped Oxbee at the camp gates and went back to his sister's place and it was past 1 o'clock in the morning by the time he got into bed. His alarm went off at five thirty, and after a quick shower, Zander dressed, had a cup of coffee and drove to Two Snakes.

'Morning, Otis. Do you think we will need that rifle?'

'I hope not, Mr Zander.'

They drove back to the cattle clearing and then headed off into the jungle.

'What are we looking for, and where are we going?'

'You say Mr Morris was walking back to the cabin so, looking from the cabin to the only place that the shot could have come from, I think it must be that ridge.'

'How far would you say that is?'   Zander asked.

67

'Two hundred yards or so.'

'It was dusk when he was shot so how could he see the target?'

'Lights from the truck or the cabin? He would only need an outline.'

'Is Manuel that good a shot?'

'Yes, he's better than that. I'd put a month's money that he could hit a person at five hundred yards.'

'Do you think he would do it?'

'It's possible.'

'You mean if the money is right?'

'Yeah.'

'Murder here is a hanging offence.'

'If it was Manuel, he didn't want to kill him, because he could have. If he gets caught he will say it was an over-shot and an accident, and that's only if Mr Morris presses charges.'

They moved on up the track for another half-mile and came to a clearing where logs had been stored and loaded.

'Teak logs?'

'Yes, if you follow the track around to the right there's an old disused bunkhouse.'

'What about this tin shack?'

'It was a tool store, but I don't advise you to go in there; it's now used by the hunters for keeping their skins. They salt them down for a couple of days until they have all they need, and then they bag them and take them for preservation. Some go to the animal trophy processor for mounting while others are just treated and tanned.'

'You know a lot about this trade.'

'I used to do it about ten years ago but they tightened up on it and a few went to jail so I gave it up.'

'I think we'd better have a look and see if there is anything there.'

'Okay, I'll have a look for you.'

Otis opened the door and there was Manuel's dead body lying on top of a couple of racoon skins.

'He's been shot in the back of the head, Mr Zander. I think he was shot while standing in the doorway. You see that spatter of blood over there on the opposite wall - I expect we will find a bullet there somewhere in the stud or there will be a hole in the tin.'

Zander gingerly stepped around the body and skins and went to the far wall. The stench was overbearing but he persevered. He couldn't find a hole in the tin so he made a close inspection of the studs. Two of the studs had blood on and the dim light made it difficult to see but he found it masked with blood. The bullet hole was filled with blood which had run down the stud.

'I'll leave the bullet for the forensic boys to dig out. Can you see a weapon anywhere?'
'No.'
'Let's have a quick look at the bunkhouse and then we'll go back to Two Snakes to get the police. I need to get out of here before I'm overcome by the stench. How do hunters like Manuel get the skins of the endangered animals out of the country?'
'The person who wants the skin usually arranges it. There used to be a local contact when I was doing it but he died and I don't know who does it now but there are shipping companies that will transport them.'
'What good is a skin?'
'There's a trophy processor in Texas.'
'You mean a taxidermist?'
'Yeah.'
'Texas. Does that involve Red Hodson?'
'No, I don't think he would get involved in that sort of thing.'

They moved over to the old bunkhouse; it had been used but there was nothing of significance that caught their attention.

'If we wanted to go to where that shot came from, we would have to more or less double back on ourselves along that spur.'
'Yes, we can go there now.'
'No, let's get the police here first.'

Zander walked back towards the Bronco; he was about ten yards behind Otis when suddenly there was a whistle and a thwack, and Zander threw himself to the ground.

'That was a shot' cried Otis.
'Yes, someone is shooting at us,' gabbled Zander as he crawled towards the corrugated tin shack.

Otis realised there was only one direction the shot could have come from so, he moved to get the shack between him and the rifle.

'Over here, Mr Zander. The shot came from behind you.'

Zander crawled to the side of the hut and stood up.

'That was dammed close; I felt it whistle past the side of my head.'
'I don't think it was actually meant to kill you. If it was the same person that shot Manuel, and I suspect it was, he is good enough to have hit you.'
'I'm glad I parked the Bronco at this side of the shack.'
'Whoever it was is long gone.'
'Okay, let's go,' snapped Zander as he dashed to the Bronco.

Zander pulled the Bronco up at the farm manager's office.

'Morning, Red. I'm afraid Manuel has been killed. Do you mind if I call the police?'

'Go ahead,' suggested Hodson with a worried look.

Zander contacted Superintendent Kaba and explained about the attempt on Morris and Manuel's death. The response was not favourable and Kaba was most put out because he had not been told about Morris the previous evening.

'Kaba can be extraordinarily ungrateful. I tell him about a murder and he threatens to throw me in jail for withholding evidence. Strange man.'

'No disrespect, Mr Zander, but I find all cops strange.'

'That's all right, Red, I'm a retired policeman.'

'You know what I mean?'

'Yes, of course, I take it as a compliment, because if I was normal I don't suppose I would do what I do. Anyway, how is Jon this morning?'

'The nurse says he's fine but reluctant to stay in bed as the doctor ordered.'

'I think I'd better go across and see him.'

As he went out onto the veranda of the farm manager's house he met Otis.

'Here you are, Otis,' said Zander as he handed him $200.

'I haven't really earned this much Mr Zander.'

'Keep it on account.'

'On account?'

'Yes, on account of the fact that I might need you again.'

'Thanks,' chirped Otis with a beaming smile.

Zander proceeded to see Morris and the housekeeper let Zander in and he followed her to Morris' room.

'Morning, Jon, how are we this morning?'

'Good,' he replied registering a certain amount of surprise in his facial expression. 'I'm sore, and I have a head like a bulkhead. I want to get up but Attila the Hun there won't permit it.'

'Morning, nurse. Patient being difficult, eh?'

'Just a little, but I shall put that right in a minute. He's due an antibiotic injection at ten,' she stated as she left the room.

Morris winced and looked at Zander pleadingly.

'Don't look at me, Jon; you've brought it on yourself.'

'I was hoping for some support.'

'You have it. I support you in whatever the doctor recommends.'

'That's all I need - everybody ganging up on me.'

'Not everyone, but there is a distinct possibility that the husband of the woman you have been having a bit on the side with might have a grudge.'

'Not to try and kill me though - he's a preacher? Jeez, perhaps I shouldn't have said that.'

'You've been fooling about with a vicar's wife?'

'Well, yes. She is a lovely, warm, caring and mature woman, who likes the idea of a flirtatious individual like me making advances towards her.'

'How long has this been going on?'

'Couple of months or so.'

'Does Sal know?'

'I haven't told her but I'm sure she has her suspicions, but that's not a problem as we have an arrangement. When I'm in town, I'm in town; when I'm not, I'm elsewhere.'

'You don't think she would arrange to have someone put the frighteners on you, do you?'

'No, as I said, we have an arrangement.'

'I found Manuel this morning; he had been shot through the head, and as I was about to leave someone fired a shot at me.'

'This must be someone who has flipped and is shooting at anything that moves.'

'That is a possibility, but Otis thinks that if the person doing the shooting wanted to kill me, he would have done so.'

'But surely he must realise that people like us don't scare easily.'

'I've been thinking… perhaps Manuel killed Pancho and someone has been hired to kill Manuel, and whoever did that is likely to be killed also. Which means I have to find the common denominator but the only consistent thing seems to be the .22 calibre of the weapon used. With a bit of luck the police should be able to dig out some bullets from the tin shack besides the one that killed Manuel, and there might even be a bullet in the cabin that you were walking towards. I didn't look when we found you because it was too dark.'

'If Kaba reacts true to form, he will flood the area with policemen.'

'If he does that I will go back up. The chances of someone taking pot shots with the place crawling with armed policemen will be reduced considerably and I think some direction might be in order. I'm going to call Kaba and see what his plans are.'

'Use the phone in the study; it's the door opposite. Oh no! Here comes Attila again.'

'Excuse me gentlemen. Mr Morris, it's time for your injection. Over onto your tummy please and trousers down.'

Morris complied with a groan.

'I'll leave you to it, Jon. Get well soon.'
'Thanks a bunch,' whined Morris sarcastically.

The study had a highly-polished rosewood floor and was air-conditioned, and there were a couple of over-stuffed leather chairs and a large teak desk across one corner. Zander sat in the large high-backed leather swivel chair and reached for the phone.

'Hello, Superintendent, have you cooled down now... Good - I thought I'd call and find out who is directing operations at the scene... Oh you are, I see... what time are you arriving? You're not; you are with the Chief of Police today, all day. I see.'

Zander's conversation was a bit one-sided as Kaba seemed reluctant to get involved but Zander eventually persuaded him to let him show the chief inspector in charge around the murder scene.

'Thank you, Superintendent. Who will be in charge?'
'Chief Inspector Kaba. He's my brother and he's on the way now.'
'Thank you,' declared Zander putting the phone down.

Zander went back to Morris' bedroom, knocked and walked in, and as he did so, he heard a quick flurry of activity in the direction of the alcove. As he peered around the corner the nurse was straightening the bed and she looked a little flushed. Zander smiled but made no comment and the nurse discreetly left the room.

'Ah, Adam, how's it going?'
'Fine, Jon, just fine. I see you two are now on better terms.'
'Yes, we seem to have a mutual understanding.'
'Enough of that. I'm going back up to the scene. Would you mind if I used Otis for the day?'
'No, buddy, he's yours as long as you want him.'
'I also need some information on the vicar's wife. Firstly, she needs to know that her car is ready, and secondly I would like to find out about the vicar's whereabouts over the last couple of days.'
'She knows the car is ready and the vicar Rev. Reg Bray is on his way to pick it up. We have to keep her out of this. She told her husband she was out for a drive and the car broke down and that our mechanic would fix it today.'
'That can't be done unless you want me to question him about his whereabouts?'
'Okay, her number is on my phone pad under Reverend Bray. She's called Jessica.'

Zander thanked Morris as he left. Otis as expected was in the bunkhouse.

'Otis, I've spoken to Mr Morris and he's agreed you can tag along with me for the day, so would you keep an eye out for the police and let me know when you see them head out towards the cattle clearing. I'm going to make some phone calls from Mr Morris' study.' Zander sat down in the swivel chair again and phoned the vicar's wife.
'May I speak to Mrs Jessica Bray please?'
'Speaking!'
'Hello, Mrs Bray, I'm Adam Zander, a private investigator working on the Elly van Dam murder. Would it be possible for me to have a chat with you at some time?'

She was deliberately evasive and unwilling to cooperate until Zander explained that Morris had been shot at.

'Tuesday afternoon is the only time I have free this week,' she replied.
'I'll see you then. Will three o'clock be all right? Good, see you on Tuesday.'

Zander walked out of the office and bumped into Otis.

'Ah, Mr Zander, two police vehicles have gone past.'
'Thanks. Let's go and join them.'

As Zander went out of the farm gate the vicar was driving in, in Morris' truck. Zander contemplated going back to have a word with him, but decided against it. Zander knew who the chief inspector was without asking as he was clearly a younger version of the superintendent.

'Hello, Chief Inspector. I'm Adam Zander, private investigator. I've been...'
'Hello, Adam. Yes I know, you have permission to investigate this case. Sydney Kaba,' he announced stretching out his hand to Zander.

Zander was slightly taken aback, and it showed.

'You've obviously met my brother; he's one of the old school. I completed my training in England, and as you most probably know our law is based on English law but it has a long way to go to be as effective, but we are making progress.'

'It's good to meet you, Sydney. The only reason I asked your brother if I could come up here was because I was not impressed with the work done at the scene of Elly's murder. But if you've done your crime scene training in the UK you won't want my help.'

'Thank you, I appreciate that. I only got back from America yesterday; I read all the reports last night and my brother has briefed me this morning and brought me up to date with your background. Never look a gift horse... as you might say. Anything you have... I would be grateful for the input.   I'm blowing my own trumpet a bit but I'm the best the country has. The Prime Minister personally had my attachment to the Miami Police cut short.   Now, what about you?'

Zander briefed the chief inspector on his past experience and training. The chief inspector was impressed with Zander's potted history.

'What's your theory on this latest batch of shootings?'

Zander gave him his thoughts on the matter and concluded that if bullets could be found here and at the shack, and that they had come from the same weapon, it would narrow the options.

'The one thing that strikes me as strange is that this person has killed at least once, so what difference would Morris and I make if we were added to his list as targets instead of misses. I have a theory that he is a hired gun that hasn't been paid to kill us yet. He doesn't seem to have much nous, because he is only bringing more trouble on himself, unless he is going back to his paymaster with "I missed them this time but I can finish it if you pay me." He has most probably come in from outside and is confident that he can get away scot-free.'

'Do you think he is hiding out in these hills?'

'Yes, that's possible but it is more likely that he's fled. A good idea might be to search that ridge over there; it can be seen from here and from the shack where Manuel was found.'

'I have no trackers with me but I do have some good shots.'

'If you let me have a couple of good chaps who can shoot, I'll go. Otis here is a registered hunter, and I'm sure we can find the place where the shots came from,' stated Zander glancing at Otis expectantly.

'I know where that is; we can get there by logging track,' stated Otis.

'Okay, Adam, take the two with rifles. They can use the other Land Rover because it has a radio so you can contact me if necessary.'

It took them nearly an hour to get to the ridge because some of the track had not been used for many months and was overgrown. The only way they knew there was a track there was because there were wheel ruts, which they followed. The Bronco was badly scratched and had picked up a few dents, which were cause by branches springing back from the proceeding Land Rover. The track ran just below the ridge for most of the way and soon the vehicles broke out of the thick vegetation into a small clearing where fresh vehicle tracks were in abundance. The Land Rover stopped and the Bronco pulled up behind it and they all got out. Zander had a quick scout around the area, which was all he needed to determine the vantage point that had been used by the killer.

'This chap is either unprofessional or he is trying to show he is just a local hunter using a .22 and then leaving the empty cases at the scene. What do you make of it, Otis?'

'I agree with you, Mr Zander. A professional hit man wouldn't leave evidence unless he was in a hurry, and this guy had all the time in the world. He could even see us leave the cattle clearing and head in this direction.'

'Where does this track lead?'

'It goes along this ridge then down the end of the spur and on to the Capitol Highway; it's about three miles.'

'Corporal, would you like to get the chief inspector on the radio?'

'Chief Inspector Kaba for you, Sir,' said the corporal.

'Sydney, we've found the site from where the shot was fired and there are all sorts of bits and pieces of evidence here. I get the feeling some of it might have been deliberately planted to confuse matters. I will leave your chaps here with the Land Rover. I think it's best if I follow the vehicle tracks as they will most probably lead to the Capitol Highway. You never know though, he might have had an accident or something. If there is no contact I will go back to Two Snakes, okay?'

'Yeah, okay, Adam, see you later.'

Zander's journey to the Capitol Highway was uneventful; they turned onto the highway and headed back to Two Snakes and on the way Zander noticed the vicar drive by in his wife's car.

'That's the vicar, Otis; he has obviously stopped and had a word with Jon Morris. Ah, sorry, you don't know about that.'

'You mean about Mr Morris screwing the preacher's wife? We all know about that - the bunkhouse has ears.'

'Do you know about any other assignations?' Zander realised he had put Otis out of his depth. 'Does he have many other female friends?'

'Yes, many, but I don't think he screws them all'

'Tell me more.'

'Nothing to tell.'

'Did you say you wanted to get out and walk?' Zander snapped pulling over to the side of the highway. There was a sandy verge along the edge of the highway; it was about a

yard wide and where the poles to prevent aircraft landing had
been located.

'No, I just want to stay alive.'

'I understand that, but if the whole bunkhouse knows what's
going on, how is anybody going to know it came from you?'

Zander was amazed by some names mentioned by Otis, some
of them prominent members of the community. Most of their
husbands would be angry or embarrassed if they knew about
the unescorted visits. Otis finished listing the visitors, some of
which he was only able to describe and Zander took notes in
shorthand which amused Otis.

'What's all those squiggles?'

'Shorthand, it's a method of writing quickly. Thank you for
that; you've given me plenty to think about. It's nearly
lunchtime; would you like something to eat?'

'Wouldn't mind.'

'Okay, we'll stop off at that place by the orange plantation. I
hear old Joe has been there for years and produces freshly-
pressed orange juice, the best there is apparently.'

'You may have heard about the old Canadian's orange juice,
but have you heard about his wife, Mr Zander?'

'No, I've not met her, but I think she might be out of my age
bracket.'

'You mean too young?'

They pulled into the car park in front of "Joe's Joint" where
the sand and gravel surface had numerous potholes, which,
Zander initially attempted to avoid, but he eventually gave up.
As he parked the Bronco one of the wheels dropped into a large
pothole, which was full of water.

'I knew there was a reason for me being cautious. Now
what's this about his wife?'

'That's her at the bar now. She's a cracker, and a relative of
mine and she's only twenty five.'

The bar area was furnished with crudely-made wooden tables and metal-folding flat chairs. The building itself was made of corrugated tin sheets with an atap roof and the walls were about three feet high, and above that there were five-foot hinged shutters, which were propped open.

'Hello, a jug of orange juice and a couple of beers, please, and what have you got to eat?'
'Rice and beans, chicken, steak, hamburger and most of what's on the chalk board,' explained Joe's wife.
'Steak for me; you Otis?'
'Rice, beans and chicken.'

Zander got his wallet out and was in the process of offering money when Joe entered.

'Hi guys, how's yah luck?'
'Not so bad, I don't suppose you have seen any strangers about have you?'
'Yeah, you and some black guy, an American I think; he didn't talk much, had a beer and a hamburger to go. Drove a green Dodge truck.'
'Did you see which way he went?'
'Yeah, he went back the way he came, towards town.'
'Thanks for your help,' declared Zander.
'No problem. Hey, let me buy you guys a beer and I'll have one with you,'

Joe's wife carried their food to the table and set it down. She was wearing a short skirt, reminiscent of the sixties and she didn't need to bend but as she stood at the table her knickers could be seen quite clearly beneath the hem of the skirt. Joe put his hand on her bottom and squeezed, and she just smiled.

'Nice woman, don't yah think?'
'Yes, you're an extremely lucky man.'
'You bet; got four kids as well'...

Joe stopped in mid-sentence as two of the kids burst into the bar area screaming. They were fair-skinned with dark hair.

'Go pick and juice me some oranges, kids,' snapped Joe.

The children aged about seven and four ran off towards the plantation.

'It keeps you young, fathering children, particularly when you are in your sixties like me. The woman keeps me young as well, tired, but young.'

They spent an hour over their meal and finished it off with the freshly-pressed orange juice. Joe tried to persuade Zander to stay but without success. Zander and Otis returned to Two Snakes where Otis went to the bunkhouse and Zander went to see Morris.

'How are you feeling, Jon?'
'A lot better now that I've received comfort from the vicar. I almost feel guilty about sleeping with his wife.'
'You mean to say that he knows you're fooling around with his and other men's wives?'
'His, I don't think so; if he does then he keeps a poker face when talking about my indiscretion, but he knows about many of the others. Yeah, the husband is always the last to know. Most of the husbands know about my encounters but do not know about my relationships with their partners.'
'Would you like to name a few of these people; there must be a link between your philandering and your injuries.'
'I've thought about that but I don't think any of the men - if I could call some of them that - would have the guts to talk to anybody about it let alone hire? A hit man?'
'You have a point but I would like a list of names anyway, just to give them the once over.'
'I've been expecting this, I was going to say no but any PI with half a brain would find out in the end. In an effort to prevent publicising my activities I've produced a list and it's headed - bridge and potential bridge players - just in case

someone other than you sees it. You will see that I have marked the majority with a hash mark which means we haven't been together for at least six months - I've been curtailing my activities.'

Zander glanced down the list of cuckold husbands and grinned, acknowledging how much Otis knew about the number and pleased that Heather Day was not one of them. It also crossed his mind that Morris was too smart by half.

'Are the men all friends of yours?'
'No, not really, more acquaintances; we know each other fairly well but that's as far as it goes.'
'I'm impressed, you obviously have a lot more energy than I do and I'm forty.'
'Don't tell the women but I'm forty-nine.'
'I'm even more impressed now. Where do you get your energy from?'
'I've only been foolin' around about five years; it's no big deal. Some of the women I see only two or three times a year.'
'There must be over twenty on this list. Who are your regulars?'
'I suppose the vicar's wife is the most regular. If I don't fix her up once a week I get phone calls, not aggressive but pleading.'
'All right, you've given me something to work on. You infer that all the men are wimps, but what about the women? Am I likely to get any hostility?'
'As long as you don't mention any of them to each other in relation to me, you should be all right. I should think a hunk like you would get propositioned.'
'Sounds interesting, but I don't think I want to poach on your patch.'
'Feel free, buddy. I'm being looked after right here.'
'I must admit you seem to be taking this light-heartedly. Have you forgotten there's a killer out there with your body as the target in his cross-hairs?'
'Yes, maybe you're right, but I've lived with risk all my life and it just makes me work harder.'

'Okay, well work hard at getting better and staying alive and I will look into the possibilities of a female killer stalking you.'

Morris seemed shocked by this. He straightened up and then winced as pain surged through his shoulder. Zander could not be sure but he thought that the shock was put on.

'You're not suggesting that this could be a woman?'
'Why not? If she has not actually got the gun she could hire one.'
'I've never gone for the aggressive sort of woman, more the gentle and simpering sort.'
'I wouldn't say Sal is gentle and simpering - more like hard-nosed.'
'Now you're way off base. Sal is sometimes outwardly outrageous and forthright, but when we are alone together she is gentle and loving.'
'We will see. I just wanted to know what your reaction would be. See you later.'

Zander turned and departed leaving Morris with a puzzled expression. The journey back to his sister's house gave him the opportunity to put together several scenarios, most of which involved the list of names. One point, which took up a considerable amount of thought, was that Morris was not surprised or shocked about the news of Manuel's death. Not even an act, he was totally unconcerned about the demise of one of his own farmhands.

Chapter 6 Sexual Encounter of the Lasting Kind.

Jenny and Stan Jones took Zander to the Beating Retreat at the army camp. They had drinks in the officers' mess before heading to the sports field for the spectacle. The regimental band gave a marching display followed by Beating Retreat and a march past and the Prime Minister took the salute.

George Galpen invited them back to the officers' mess for drinks and a curry supper. Zander was moving along the servery collecting his curry and as he picked up a popadum he felt something rubbing between the cheeks of his bottom.

'Whoops! I'm being goosed,' he said looking over his shoulder in mock surprise at Sal. 'Hello, Sal, nice to know you're there.'
'You let me down the other night. I was waiting for you.'
'I saw you sitting at the piano with young Nigel over there and I didn't want to intrude.'
'Oh, okay, but I was gonna get laid by you.'
'Did you get laid?'
'Yeah, and good too, but boy, I had to drag him singing from that piano. He's obviously fit and athletic, but not my type.   I like a stayer, not a "wham bam thank you ma'am."'
'Sal, you're so lady-like and your turn of phrase is dynamic.'
'I love your English accent, but now you're pissed at me because I ran off at the mouth.'
'No, not at all, just being flippant.'
'Oh, okay buster, perhaps later.'

Zander moved to the table where Galpen was sitting but he was headed off by the commanding officer.

'Adam, come and meet the Prime Minister.'

Zander was ushered to the large table with all the dignitaries.

'This is Adam Zander, Prime Minister. He's the chap that's assisting with the investigation of the murders,' announced the commanding officer puffing his chest out with pride and smiling as if Zander were royalty.

'How do you do, Sir,' said Zander putting out his hand.

The Prime Minister reached over without standing and they shook hands.

'Sit, Mr Zander.'

Zander pulled out a chair and sat opposite.

'Who was responsible for this murder?'

'It's difficult to say at this stage, Sir. There are several possibilities and pointing the finger right now would not convict anyone. The woman was obviously killed by the farmhand, but he wasn't ultimately responsible for it; he did what he did for some form of promise of payment or reward. Whether it was for the stash of hash or the flight money or for that matter something else, I don't think it was his idea.'

'We now have other killings and shootings. When is it going to stop?'

'I'm afraid I don't know, Sir, because I don't know why they are happening and I'm still stumped for a motive.'

The Prime Minister bent his head to his food as if Zander had been dismissed. Zander was about to get up when the person on the Prime Minister's right shook his head and gave him a piercing stare which stopped him. The Prime Minister looked up from his food with a mouthful of rice. He nodded his chin up, as if to say you may get up and go, so Zander stood.

'You may go. I follow you every step of the way,' stated the Prime Minister waving his fork in a shooing manner.

Zander then joined Galpen and sat down to eat his meal, which by now was now cold.

'He's obviously not impressed with my progress, George. I seem to be treading a lot of water and I'm not able to establish a sequence of events I've had several surprises but they are not turning into hard facts which is what I need.'

'I shouldn't worry too much about it, Adam. If he actually knew what you know about this case so far, he would be amazed at what you have been able to unravel. I know that from what little you've told me.'

'Thanks for that. I appreciate your support. I'm normally only treated the way he treated me by ignorant clients, and if I don't like it, I can tell them to piss off, but I can't do that to the Prime Minister, particularly when he is as anxious as I am.'

'You've confirmed my point exactly. Now why don't you relax tonight and have a fresh start tomorrow.'

'I will. This curry is delicious and spicy despite being only just warm. Is it local or army?'

'Army, Gurkha actually. We have several cooks from the Gurkha Engineer Squadron; the engineers came out to help with an earthquake disaster.'

They left the table and walked through into the bar where Nigel was about to sit down at the piano.

'He's going to play in the style of Richard Clayderman this evening. He feels jazz gets him more than he asked for. Mind you he tells me he's not complaining; he just wants to recharge his batteries,' said Galpen.

'I imagine Sal might be pretty demanding. Perhaps that sort of activity is what sometimes recharges me; on reflection, maybe I should seek solace in a woman, if I'm going to make progress in this case. Come to think of it I have several meetings tomorrow; maybe something will come of them?'

'Secret assignations, eh?' Galpen queried with a smirk.

'Yes, they are more or less; it's part of the investigation process though. I have an enormous number of wives to visit, none military, I'm pleased to say, but what some might call influential families all the same. I only hope I don't open up too much of a hornets' nest.'

As Sal sat down at the piano with Nigel, Galpen noticed a flash of desperation in Nigel's eyes and moved off to rescue him. Zander moved over and joined his sister and brother-in-law's group.

'I think I'm going to have an early night, Sis. I have a full day of interviews tomorrow.'

'Fine, we were just finishing up, weren't we Stan?'

'No, you don't have to come. I'll make my own way,' said Zander.

'Don't be silly, we'll come with you.'

Stan drove them back to the house where Mary opened the door and let them in. They went out onto the fly-screened veranda where Mary served them coffee.

'Sis, is there something local here that I'm missing? Is there some sort of impenetrable Mafia or an individual here that no outsider is likely to be aware of, or for that matter even know about?'

'I'm sure there is, and I would think your best bet is to speak to the intelligence officer over at the camp.'

'What sort of dummy am I? Why didn't I think of that?'

'The "wood for trees" as you always used to say when you were a young detective constable.'

'You're right; I've been running around chasing every lead when what I need to do is sit down and think this through.'

'Why don't you use the study? I will bring you a pot of coffee and I suggest you stay there until you have it clear in your mind. I wouldn't be surprised if you were still a bit jet-lagged. It always worked before when you used to use Dad's study.'

'You know me better than I know myself, don't you. Perhaps, I should hire you as an adviser?'

'No, you've had all the advice you need.'

'Thanks, Sis, I'll get started,' declared Zander looking over at
Stan who was fast asleep in the chair.

Zander went to his brother-in-law's study and sat at the large
rosewood desk. He turned the high-backed chair one complete
revolution taking in the framed pictures, the shelves with books
and numerous commercial pamphlets and publications and the
four quadraphonic speakers. He immediately looked for the
music centre and found it to the left of the desk at low level.
The bottom left-hand draw was open and filled with cassettes.

'I see you've found his horde of classical music,' said Jenny
as she came in with the coffee.
'I like the choice; *Elgar's Nimrod*, one of my favourites.
They are all hand-written. Did he record them?'
'No, his brother did, from the radio in the UK and sent them
to him for his birthday,'
'What a lovely idea.'
'Yes, we think so too.'

Zander put *Nimrod* on and poured himself a cup of black
coffee and inhaled the rich aroma as it wafted under his nose.

'Where shall I start? Elly murdered by Pancho - Why?
Martens accused; Pancho killed to keep his mouth shut; Morris
shot at (possible smoke screen); I'm shot at, (possible scare
tactics); and Manuel is killed. There's got to be a hit man in
this. All incoming flights will have to be checked. Motive - the
obvious one is the money but there's also revenge, but why
involve someone like Manuel and Pancho? Perhaps because
they were known to be greedy and dispensable? Pancho was
killed before I'd proved Martens didn't do it. There must be a
common denominator...'

Zander pondered these many points for several hours, and by
the time the coffee was finished he had convinced himself that
he knew who the culprit was, so then headed off to his room.
As he entered he saw a large tarantula spider scuttling across

the room. He backed out of the room and went through into the kitchen where he found an empty screw-top jar. Using a flat piece of card he scooped the spider into the large empty coffee jar, replaced the lid leaving it slightly loose to allow air in, not knowing how much air a tarantula needed. After a few minutes' reflection and observation he placed it on the dresser.

He quickly undressed and took a shower, pulled the sheets back and got into bed; they were cool and smelt fresh. Zander lay back and wondered if Medows would be interested in the spider; his imagination started to fail and he was asleep in minutes.

The following morning was a scorcher. The humidity of the previous day had gone and the sun was burning the grass. Zander sat down to an early breakfast, which was served by Mary.

'I'm off now, Adam; I'll see you this evening.'
'Okay, Sis.'

Mary made eyes at Zander, but he was having none of it. He shook his head and Mary's lips turned to a pout. He heard his sister pulling away in her car.

'Sorry, Mary. I've a lot of work today.' He drained the last drops of coffee from his cup and went to the phone.
'Morning, Sydney,' said Zander into his sister's telephone.
'Morning, Adam.'
'I've got a lead for you. I would like you to check the passenger lists of recent flights into the country. I believe there is a hit man here and he's about to leave; he was driving a green Dodge four-by-four. He's a black American. Have any flights gone out this morning?'
'Yes, the mail plane at seven this morning. It will be in Miami by now.'
'Well, he will most probably have been on that so perhaps the killings will stop now. All the loose ends have been tied

up now and the last piece in the jigsaw was the hit man. He shot Manuel and at me; that's my theory at this stage.'

'Who's behind it?'

'I think I know who it is, but I still need to prove it, which will not be easy, because all the witnesses are dead; the only one left, other than the culprit, is the hit-man and it seems that we've missed him now.'

'I have contacts in Miami so we still might get him, but you must tell me whom you suspect, Adam. I have to stop the killings, you must understand that.'

'Yes, I understand that, but as I've mentioned before maybe the killings are over, so we have plenty of time to get our man.'

'How can you be so confident? You must tell me what evidence you have.'

'I'm not confident enough yet and there is no further evidence; I only have the same as you do. The facts cloud things a little and you have to sort the wood from the trees and then you will come up with a solution. The motive for the first killing is the hardest to solve but I think I know why Elly was murdered, - either jealousy and or revenge. If I can fathom out or dig up some background on Elly and her recent associations, I think it will all come together.'

'But what about Pancho, the money and Manuel?'

'Yes, your point is well made, but class them as trees; you have to look to the wood. Look, Sydney, I must go. Let me know about the passengers and I'll be in touch. Cheerio for now.'

Zander put the telephone down and immediately picked it up again and dialled.

'May I speak to Mrs Day, please? Zander here.'

He could hear the flip-flop sound from the maid's shoes in the background as she went in search of Mrs Day.

'Good morning, Heather, how are you?'
'I feel wonderful and hunger for you.'

'That's a good start. Where and when?'

'Here and now.'

'Okay, I'll be there shortly,' he whispered putting the phone down.

'You go fool around with Missy Day?'

'It's none of your business, Mary; however, I am going to investigate her attributes,' declared Zander with a smirk.

'Oh, investigate – huh!'

Zander walked down the track to the Day house where he was met by a smelly mangy dog which snarled, snapped and made a lunge at Zander.

'Here, give him this,' called out Heather from the upstairs veranda, and a small strip of beef jerky winged its way towards him. He caught it and threw it to the dog which picked it up immediately and sloped off to the furthest corner of the large porch.

'Come up, Adam.'

The maid opened the door with a smile and a little bob of a curtsy. She directed him along a passageway between the veranda and what looked to be the sitting room. At the end of the passageway he walked through the open door into the library where Heather was waiting for him.

'That's a grotty dog you have out there, Heather.'

'Yes, he is unselectively fierce, liable to bite and he does keep uninvited people away. We can't get near him to clean him up and I've asked Arnold to shoot him actually but he hasn't got around to it yet.'

'A sedative dart from the vet followed by a bath and a medical might be more humane.'

'What a thoughtful person you are. I'll do that, thank you.'

'You look ravishing today, and with all that hostility gone you are a very congenial lady.'

'Thank you, you are so sweet, but Arnold makes my life a misery by just being around me. When we are on our own it's okay, but when others are present he is so jealous and I fear his violence. Anyway no more of that stuff. You can go now, shoo, shoo,' she said flapping her hand at the maid.

Zander looked over his shoulder and saw the maid standing in the doorway. She turned and left the library closing the door quietly behind her. The library had books on three sides of the room and the fourth side had a veranda that overlooked the river.

'What about the servants?' Zander asked.
'If they want to keep their jobs they will keep their mouths shut.'
'You've done this before?'
'No, never; I've thought about it but never had the nerve, then you turn up and I couldn't resist. We have two hours before someone is coming to do my hair.' As she walked towards him a waft of musk hit him.
'Mmm, that smells good.'
'Glad you like it, no need to shower first.'

She put her arms around his waist and thrust her lower body against him then leaned back and looked up expectantly.

He scooped her up in his arms and inquired. 'Which way?'
'Over in the corner,' she whispered pointing to a door.

They went into the bedroom where virtually everything was blue, as was her light cotton dress. Heather put her arms around his neck and kissed him deeply and passionately. He took his right arm away from her legs and her feet dropped to the floor. They were still kissing when she reached behind her back and pulled her dress zip down, and with a little giggle her dress was soon a circle of cloth around her feet she was naked.

Zander ran his hand over her beautifully smooth tanned body, and as he did so he felt his pulse start to race and the front of his trousers filling up. Heather unfastened his shirt buttons and they kissed again and using the tips of her fingers she gently titillated the bulge in his trousers. She moved her hand down lower and curled her fingers around the non-rigid area and caressed and massaged it. Zander was now swaying back from the hips and pushing against the palm of her hand.

Heather fumbled briefly with the front of his trousers until she had the belt undone and the zip down. The trousers dropped to the floor and he was left standing in his boxer shorts. She dropped to her knees, hooked her thumbs in his shorts and wiggled them down over his hips to his knees where they dropped to his ankles and he stepped out of them.

'Heather, please let's make love on the bed,' he pleaded.

She blew gently into the hair of his crotch and put her hands to the rear and gripped his buttocks. He grasped her hair in both hands and gradually prised her head away from his crotch and pulled her face to his and kissed her. She put her tongue deep into his mouth and put her hands behind his head and drew him down to the bed.

They rolled on to the bed and Heather parted her legs and Zander moved between them. She pulled her knees up and put the soles of her feet on top of his buttocks. Reaching under her right leg she grasped his rigid member and guided it into her. As he thrust forward she doubled up and when he drew back she threw her legs over her shoulders. He thrust forward and her legs bounced on his back. After several thrusts her right leg slipped off his shoulder but Adam quickly put his left leg over it and clamped it between his thighs. The pace quickened and he whispered in her ear that he was reaching his climax. Heather immediately thrust up hard against him and the rhythm became frantic and they pounded for some time until Zander made one final thrust and did not pull back but stayed fully embedded and they thrashed together. Heather tightened her grip on him and shuddered in climax.

They lay wrapped together for several minutes, until he shrank and eased himself out and lay beside her. Heather rolled over on top of him and kissed him passionately grinding her mouth against his.

'I could eat you that was so good,' she proclaimed pulling away from him.

'You nearly did. That would have been great for me but what about you?'

'I don't know, I've never gone all the way with oral sex, but I will if you want to.'

'Hold on, I've not got my breath back from this session and you're talking about another.'

Heather picked up a couple of towels from the dresser and threw one at him.

'Come on - shower time.'

He got up and followed her to the bathroom. They showered together, and after rinsing the soap from their bodies she turned the shower off and put a hand on either side of his face and pulled him to her and they kissed passionately until she started to breathe heavily. He broke free and lifted her into his arms and carried her to the bed. Positioning her well up on the bed and kneeling over her, he kissed her lips and moved slowly down her body, kissing her neck, breasts, and stomach and nuzzled her pubic hair.

'Let's do a sixty-nine,' she rasped.
'No,' he mumbled and moved his head back up her body.

Without warning she grasped his hair and pulled his head to hers, and at the same time gripped his manhood.

'Come on in,' she growled through gritted teeth.

She clawed his back and arched her pelvis up and stayed rigid as he pumped into her. Heather kissed his left ear as she unwound from her climax.

'God ...if only...'

Zander put his hand over her mouth. She realised it would
most probably be nothing more than brief sexual encounter;
nevertheless she wished it could be more.

'Shhh, Heather, let's make the best of what we have, which is
most probably just a couple of weeks. I think we have both
found something that was missing in our lives but we still have
to be sensible about it,' he pronounced removing his hand from
her mouth.

'You're just trying to ruin the most exciting day of my life.'

'We both have strings attached; mine are that I work in
England; yours are in the form of a husband. And before you
start, let's not wish his demise; there have been enough deaths
already since I've been here.'

'Yes, but let's "make hay while the sun shines" as you
English say.'

'I think I've made enough English hay for today. You said
two hours, which gives me just twenty minutes now to shower
- on my own - dress and get out of here before the curling tongs
and scissors arrive.'

'While you're doing that I'm going to look through the
diaries and see when we can meet again.'

'Okay.' Zander took a shower and was rubbing himself down
when Heather walked into the bathroom.

'Would you like me to do that?'

'No, thank you, I have to get dressed and out of here before
your crimper arrives. I doubt if I could resist you at close
quarters.'

'You do say the sweetest things. Will you be free on
Thursday of next week, Adam?'

'I have nothing planned at this stage and I should think I'll
still be here. Although, I'm close to solving the case, there is a
lot more to do. Do you know Jessica Bray, the vicar's wife?'

'Yes, she's a fastidious sort of person; she's in the bridge
club. She plays every week whereas I only play now and again.
Why do you ask?'

'I'm always asking questions; it's what I do. I have to interview several women over the next couple of days; most are in the bridge club or potential players. Jon Morris is a bridge player and somebody has been shooting at him.'

'What have the bridge ladies to do with that?'

'Nothing, I hope, but I have to start somewhere.'

'You think it might be one of the husbands?'

'What makes you say that?'

'He has a tendency to chase the ladies; he tried with me, but there was no chemistry, not like there is with you. I look at you and my pulse races,'

'I have a similar reaction when I look at you, and that's why if I don't finish dressing and get out of here, I'm going to be chasing you too.'

Chapter 7 Snakes

The dog started to bark and Heather gave a start.

'It's my hairdresser - she's early. Stay here until I come back. I will put her on the library veranda with a coffee.'

Zander finished dressing and went into the lavatory to relieve himself. He heard the door open as he was adjusting his zip.

'Are you ready, Adam?'
'Yes, I'm fine.'
'Good,' she snapped grabbing his head in both hands, she kissed him passionately and he responded.
'See you next week, about the same time, all right?' he whispered breaking away from her grasp.
'Yes, bye.'

Zander went out the front door, anxiously looking for the dog but relaxed when he saw it lying in the corner chewing a piece of jerky. He strolled back to his sister's and was met by Mary.

'You wan' lunch, Mister Adam?'
'No, I think I'll go out for a beer and a sandwich. Many thanks all the same.'

Zander picked up his briefcase and headed back out to the Bronco. He got into the truck and headed into town wondering where he should go, and he decided on the Majestic as he hit the first pothole in town. He went to the upstairs bar which overlooked the harbour. The fishing cruisers were just heading out to sea on the high tide; they were packed with rich tourists yearning to catch a big marlin or a big sailfish to go with the champagne.

'Slitz beer and a bacon club sandwich, please' Zander requested as he sat down on a barstool.

'Hello, Adam,' interjected a voice from behind.

Zander turned to see Nigel's beaming smile.

'Hello, Nigel, you seem pleased with yourself.'

'No, not particularly. It's just nice to get out of camp now and again, and I had a couple of tasks in town, so I decided to pop in for a bite to eat. How's the case coming?'

'Slowly, but I think I'm nearly there. The problem of course is proving it beyond reasonable doubt.'

'I hear you were shot at. Do you think you are getting too close?'

'That's a distinct possibility; however, I like to think it was only meant to scare me off. The culprit in all this thought I would give in after identifying Pancho as Elly's killer, but it's a little more complicated than that. I have several theories and they all point to different people in the equation. The strongest theory has had a bit of a setback because one of my suspects has become a victim, however, that could be a smoke screen. I had Manuel in the frame on a hunch; nothing stronger than that and now he's dead.'

'Who do you think it is?'

'As I stated to the Prime Minister - sorry about the name-dropping - I have several options for a motive. The likely reasons for the murder are money or revenge related to jealousy or perhaps drugs. The simplest explanation would be Elly was killed for the flight money and Pancho was killed when the money was taken off him. That's where things went wrong. Pancho didn't get the money. Now if Manuel killed Pancho expecting to find the money on him and became angry when it wasn't it's possible he went looking for the person who tipped him off and that got him killed.'

'That's as clear as mud, Adam. Where do you go from here?'

'Hopefully, there will be no more killings. I could be wrong but the last killing, which was Manuel, seems to have been carried out by a hit man. The only thing that makes me wonder about that is the cost of getting a gunman in. My present thinking is that things went wrong when Manuel didn't get the money.   The hit man was brought in to clean up the loose ends because the culprit was unable to shoot someone. Otherwise Manuel would have killed Pancho, taken the money and that would have been the last of it.'

'Why hasn't this person been arrested?'

'A lot of this is speculation, which won't convict anyone. I must have evidence, and as I've said, I must prove it beyond reasonable doubt. I'm convinced I know who it is but I just can't seem to get a breakthrough.'

Zander looked at his watch and jumped up quickly, taking the remainder of his club sandwich with him.

'Nice talking to you, Nigel, but I must dash. I've got an appointment in ten minutes. Cheers,' said Zander as he handed the bartender twenty dollars. He drove the short distance to the manse and found Mrs Bray was waiting at the door for him. He pulled up in the driveway and got out of the Bronco.

'Mrs Bray?' Zander inquired, realising why Morris would get involved with someone like Jessica. It flashed across his mind that she would make a good Doris Day look-alike.

'Mr Zander?'

'Yes, how-do-you-do?'

'I'm fine thank you. Look, I'm afraid this will have to be short as I have another appointment on behalf of my husband, a family bereavement.'

'Oh, I see, well there are only a couple of questions.'

'Do come in.'

Zander followed her through the door and into the air-conditioned living room, which was furnished with antiques, most of which were Victorian.

'What a lovely room,' declared Zander lowering himself into the chair that Mrs Bray had indicated. 'Because there is so little time I will get straight to the point. What is your relationship with Jon Morris?'

She was a little taken aback and gulped.

'What has he told you?'
'Let's say at this stage I haven't spoken to him about you. Just tell me the truth; I have no axe to grind as far as you are concerned.' Zander could see that she was agitated but he could also see her going through the process of formulating an answer.
'We're lovers,' she blurted.

Zander was not shocked, but nearly wrong-footed as he expected weasel words.

'That's what I thought so thank you for that. I now know we are going to get on.'
'My husband won't be told, will he?' she demanded back-peddling a little.
'No, not by me, and I see no reason why anyone else should know for that matter. Can you fire a gun?'
'Yes.'
'Do you have a gun?'
'Yes, a rifle and a pistol; all the ex-pats have them.'
'Are they here, and if so may I see them?'
'Yes they are in the gun cabinet in the study,' she said getting up. 'Please follow me.'

Zander stood and followed her down the long passageway to the other side of the house. The study was quite small about ten feet square and heavily furnished with rosewood furniture. The metal gun cabinet was situated in the corner of the room, masked by a bookcase.

'Have they been fired recently?'
'Nnnno, no I don't th-think so,' she spluttered hesitantly.
'You mean, *you* haven't fired them but somebody else might have.'
'Yyyes, yes.'
'Why do you need guns?'

'There are lots of burglaries here abouts, I'm not so good with guns particularly the pistol and if I had to use it my hand would most probably shake too much. However, a shot fired would most probably frighten off an intruder - well that's my theory, anyway.'

'Are you saying the locals would break into the vicarage?'

'Quite simply, yes.'

She opened the cabinet and directed Zander towards it. The pistol was lying on the top shelf together with boxes of ammunition. He picked up the .38 revolver first and then the .22 rifle. He opened the breach and sniffed them.

'They've both been cleaned recently.'

'Yes, my husband cleans them both regularly - the humidity you know.'

'Of course, thank you, Mrs Bray. Are you a good shot?'

'No, not really. I've been to the army camp for some instruction and that's when I found out I was useless with the pistol.'

'Do you know of anyone who might want to kill Jon Morris, besides your husband, that is?'

'My husband wouldn't kill anyone.'

'He might, if he found out someone was fooling around with his wife.'

'Let me scotch that straight away. My husband possibly suspects but I don't think he knows, and I haven't told him because I don't want to hurt him. He would understand anyway, because the thing is, he's impotent. This is a secret we share with our doctor - and now you. The only reason I'm telling you is I don't want you to start asking him questions along those lines. If you'd met him you'd know he could never hurt anyone.'

'I'm sure that's the case and I'm sorry, but I have to ask these questions. Two people have been killed and Mr Morris and I too have been shot at. He was hit but I wasn't, although I think he was meant to be and I wasn't.'

There was a gentle knock at the study door and Mrs Bray looked towards the door where the maid was standing.

'Your car here, Missy Jessica.'
'Thank you, Emily. I'm sorry Mr Zander I must go.'
'That's all right, Mrs Bray, I have no further questions.'

They walked to the door together and the maid opened it. Zander turned and shook hands with Mrs Bray.

'If you think of anything important that might have a bearing on the case, please give me a call at my sister's.'
'I will. Goodbye.'

Zander walked to the Bronco deep in thought. There is something about that woman that is not right. She has something to hide, of that I'm sure, but putting my finger on it is going to be the problem, he thought to himself. Zander arrived back at his sister's just before four o'clock; Spark met him at the door and nearly knocked him over in his enthusiasm to greet him. A thought crossed Zander's mind - 'the fifty thousand dollars! Did Morris catch up with the chap who owed him the money and ask him to clear the debt by shooting a couple of people?' Zander went to the phone and tapped in the number for police headquarters.

'Hello, Chief Inspector Kaba, please.'
'Kaba.'
'Sydney, good afternoon. Just thought I'd give you a call about those flight lists. Any luck?'
'Yes, there is a question mark against a man called Valence. Came in a couple of days ago; he's the man in the green Dodge. He hasn't handed the truck into the hire company and seems to have disappeared. I've put out an all-points-bulletin for him and the Dodge.'
'Okay, good. Do you know if Morris has a licence for a gun?'
'I'm sure he has.'
'It might be worth checking and then check his weapons. He could have been shot with one of his own guns. Everybody, it seems, has a gun or two and I don't suppose there would be

any difficulty in getting an untraceable gun. However, things have gone a bit haywire for the perpetrator in this case; therefore, in panic, a traceable gun may have been used. If any of Morris' licensed guns are missing he must be questioned relentlessly. I will leave all that to you and your boys. I will play the nice guy at this stage.'

'You think he's involved in his own shooting, Adam?'

'Possibly, and I think all weapons on the farm should be removed and the rifling checked.'

'That will take time, but yes, you're right, perhaps we should have done that in the first place. Of course, there are so many illegal guns in the country normally it's hardly worth bothering about and certainly it's never an immediate reaction, but under the circumstances we'll have a look at it now of course.'

'Okay, Sydney, that's good. I'll speak to you again soon. Bye for now,' he said and put the phone down.

'Dinner at eight, Adam; will that be all right?'

'Yes. Sis, thanks. I'm going for a nap.' Zander went to his room, undressed and lay on the bed and was asleep in minutes.

'It's seven thirty, Adam,' called Jenny after knocking the door.

Zander got up and went for a shower and as he emerged from the bedroom and he was met by the smell of roast beef.

'That smells great. Have you got Yorkshires to go with that?'

'Yes, and horseradish.'

The phone rang and Jenny answered it in the kitchen.

'It's Chief Inspector Kaba for you Adam.'

'Evening again, Sydney. What can I do for you?'

'I just thought I would let you know I got a court order to search Two Snakes and retrieve all weapons.'

'That was quick.'

'The judge walked in just after I'd finished speaking to you, so we went to the courthouse and got it fixed up. Morris was furious, but I am delighted; we collected forty-seven weapons. Six were not licensed, mainly from farm hands, but Morris had an unlicensed shotgun. All will be checked by forensics and a report will come to me as soon as possible.'

'That's good news, and can you give special emphasis on any .22 weapons. Was there a .22 pistol amongst them?'

'No, but there should have been. Morris has one on the license but it was missing.'

'May I suggest that the areas where Morris and Manuel were found be given another going over. I think we have our first break; our next needs to be finding that pistol. I thought I might have been barking up the wrong tree again.'

'What do you mean?'

'Well, I've always thought that Morris being shot was always phoney, but it's a bit difficult to appreciate how desperate a man has to be to let a hit man take a shot at him from two hundred yards and only wound him. It would also take a desperately daring or determined man, and having observed Morris for a couple of days now, I would say he is the latter and not so much the former.'

'You think he was shot at close range?'

'Yes. I think a cloth of some sort was put over his shoulder and the pistol held close to it and aimed to go through the flesh not hitting the bone. I think Manuel could have done that and then he was killed by the hit man when he was sent to the old poachers' shack.'

'Well, you've certainly got me thinking now, Adam, and I appreciate you keeping me up to date.'

'No problem. See you tomorrow.'

'Do you really think Morris did the killings?'

'No, but I do think he is responsible, and the dangerous bit is that he knows I think he did it. What will get him in the end is his arrogance. He's been wiping out all the evidence except circumstantial which he could most probably be convicted on, however, I'm convinced I'll get sufficient firm evidence to convict him. Goodbye Sydney.'

'Come on you two,' said Jenny as she put the roast beef on the table.

They were relaxing over a glass of port when Jenny reminded him of the snake lecture.

'I'll be late then, Sis. I'm going to drop in and have a pint with Fred Oxbee afterwards so see you later.'

Zander turned up at the education centre with only minutes to spare. There were about twenty people seated in the classroom and the desks were in pairs, a total of fifteen pairs in three columns of five pairs, and the front desks were empty. Medows introduced himself and explained that, in addition to his practice in the UK, he was an RAMC lieutenant colonel in the Territorial Army and doing a short tour as the CO of the hospital. In addition he had made a study of tropical medicine, and in particular snakes and their behaviour.

'The purpose of this talk is to explain the difference between poisonous and non-poisonous snakes. Hopefully I can give you sufficient information to allay your fears. A snake doesn't see a human as a meal, only as a threat, therefore, it rarely uses enough venom to kill a human; shock normally does that, and I'm sure you will be interested to know that 98% of victims of a venomous snake bite survive.'

Medows continued with his talk using slides to help identify the different types of snakes, pointing out the triangular-shaped head with the sacks of poison at the side of the head.

'As you might have guessed these covered cages contain snakes - local snakes. We will break now for a cup of coffee, and in fifteen minutes I will introduce you to them,' stated Medows with a wicked grin.

The coffee break over, they all took up their seats again while Medows shuffled through his notes.

'Is everybody sitting comfortably?' Medows asked over his shoulder as he turned and uncovered the cages and took out the first snake.

'This snake is non-poisonous, as are all the snakes you will be handling this evening. If you were to be bitten, you would need treatment, as there is a likelihood of infection because of the snake's eating habits. They prey on rats, mice, bats and the like.'

He handed the reptile to a person nearest to him and the snake was then passed around the room; Zander was at the back of the room and the last in the audience to handle it. The snake was extremely agitated having been handled by many people by then and it suddenly lunged at Zander's face. He stretched his arms away from him and slid his right hand along the snake's body to just behind its head. He squeezed firmly and let the tail go and it immediately wrapped itself around his right arm.

'Well done,' declared Medows as he walked to the back of the room. 'The black-tailed rat snake will give you a nasty bite and can give off a nasty smell. Adam's reactions were first class,' he proclaimed as he took the snake from Zander and put it back in the cage.

Zander was relieved the snake was back in the cage, but still had no hesitation when the four-foot python was handed to him.

'If you get a snake in your house or in the grounds, firstly don't panic. I would be grateful if you would give me a call. I will either come myself or I will send one of my pest controllers if I'm busy,' announced Medows as he passed the next snake to a person nearest to him. There were now four snakes circulating the audience. Medows finished his lecture having put the snakes away.

'There is a snake in each of these two jars. This is a deadly coral snake; its poison attacks the respiratory and nervous systems, and this is a king snake, which is not poisonous.'

He turned his back and placed himself between the snakes and the audience and switched the jars a couple of times masking the action with his body. Then he lifted the jars onto the front desk.

'Okay, ladies and gentlemen, which is the coral snake?' he asked pointing to the jars.   'Who thinks it's this one?'

All but three thought it was the coral snake; but in fact it was the king snake.

'I'm sorry but you got it wrong. It's easily done I must admit. Let me give you an analogy to help you remember. You will notice they are both black, yellow and red. If you always remember that red and yellow together spell danger, as in traffic lights - and the coral snake. The king snake has yellow bands bordered by black, and the coral snake also has a black nose. I leave you with the traffic light analogy and wish you the best of luck with your encounters.' Medows sat down as the audience applauded.

Zander then went to the sergeants' mess for a drink with Oxbee. The mess sergeant called Oxbee to the entrance of the mess and Zander was taken into the large atap area used for dancing where a local band was playing reggae.

'Fred, I need you as a sounding post, do you mind?'
'No, go ahead, Adam.'
'Thanks. How well do you know the vicar's wife?'
'You mean the one in town?'
'Mrs Bray.'
'A lovely lady - what I would suggest as a proper vicar's wife; friendly, caring and always helpful.'
'Do you think she could kill someone?'
'No, definitely not.'
'That's the impression I got, but I think she's involved.'
'Well she's actually a good shot. Not very good with a pistol but all right with a four-inch group with a .22 rifle.'

'Oh, really?'

'Yes, I was range officer when she had some practice with the wives' club.'

'I'm intrigued; she told me she wasn't any good.'

'I hate to say it but she's lying.'

'What about her husband?'

'I haven't seen him, but from what I hear he's no great shakes.'

The local band finished playing and the drum section of the regimental band marched in. They gave a marching and drumming display on the dance floor culminating in a finale where the lights were dimmed and all that showed were the illuminated strips on the drumsticks. The drummers beat out complicated rhythms with their sticks on the snare and side drums, and the sticks were twisted and twirled between taps. The audience was most appreciative and gave them a thunderous round of applause as they marched off.

'Thanks for the drink, Fred. I must be getting back.'

'I was going to fix you up with one of the local women. I think Weenie's here; do you want me to have a look around?'

'No more women for me today, I'm pooped. Besides I think I've found someone I'll stick with while I'm here.'

'Good for you. G'night.'

Zander drove back to his sister's in deep thought and was still pondering many things when he got into bed, but eventually sleep got the better of him and he slept soundly until Jenny knocked at the door the following morning.

'What time is it?'

'It's eight thirty, Adam and there's a call for you; it's Joe from Joe's Joint.'

'Okay, I'm on my way.'

He got out of bed and slipped his dressing gown on and padded down the passage to Stan's study.

Chapter 8 Hit Man

'Hello Joe, what can I do for you?'

'Yah know that green Dodge I mentioned to yah? I've seen it.'

'Where?'

'Crashed in the jungle about ten miles town-side of my place.'

'Have you told the police?'

'Nah, I asked myself, what are they going to do for me? Notting' whereas you might buy me some hooch.'

'You're right, Joe If it's the truck I'm looking for I'll buy the best bottle of whisky I can get.'

'Rum'll do.'

'Okay. Was there anybody in it?'

'I don't know. I was comin' into town early this mornin' with the boys, when one of them wanted the head. I saw the wheel tracks by the side of the road, so I pulled over. The boy had his crap behind a bush and I sent him back while I had a leak. Then I noticed the truck nosed into the jungle. I didn't want to hang around in case he'd been bushwhacked and they might still be around.'

'Okay. Where are you now?'

'At the gas station on the highway at the edge of town.'

'Wait for me, Joe; I'll be there in twenty minutes.'

'Okay.'

Zander showered, got dressed and drank the coffee that was waiting for him.

'Sis, would you call Chief Inspector Kaba on this number in about half an hour?' Zander asked passing a piece of paper to her. 'Tell him I've gone to a place ten miles this side of Joe's Joint to look at the green Dodge. Thanks,' he said without waiting for an answer.

Zander met Joe at the petrol station and gave him fifty dollars there and then which Joe accepted with a grin.

'I noo I done the right thing calling you.'
'You did indeed. Let's go.'

It took them another twenty minutes to get to the spot. The dodge could not be seen from the highway as it had turned back on itself. Zander took a machete from the back of the Bronco and followed Joe towards the Dodge, leaving the boys in Joe's truck.

'I'm going to have a look in the back window. Can you give me a hand with the tailgate?'

They dropped the tailgate and Zander climbed in and crawled to the back cab window of the opened back truck. The black driver was slumped down across the passenger seat and the windscreen was cracked where the driver's head had smashed into it. The glove compartment was open and a packet of cigarettes was resting on the shelf.

'Joe, I think I saw movement. Let's get in there,' he snapped passing the machete.

Joe started to slash at the bush along the left side of the truck.

'It's not him moving, Joe, it's a snake.'
'You're kidding me?'
'No, it's definitely a snake.'

Joe stopped immediately and jumped up into the back of the truck to join Zander.

'There - look - in the passenger foot-well under his right hand.'
'The snake must have killed him, Mr Zander.'
'No, I don't think so unless it was the shock that made him swerve off the highway and crash. That's a king snake, Joe, it's not poisonous.'

'No, Mr Zander, it's a coral snake and they're deadly. I've seen them many times before.'

'Well, I think we'll wait until Chief Inspector Kaba arrives and let him sort it out. The driver's dead, his open staring eyes confirm that, so there's nothing we can do. There are no windows open so the snake was most probably put in the glove compartment, then on reaching for the cigarettes the snake appeared, the driver panicked, drove off the road and crashed hitting his head on the windscreen and that is most probably what killed him!'

'He could have left it open when he was up on the ridge?'

'No, it's more likely that it was put there. Did you say he headed towards town?'

'Yeah, but he could have turned and gone by and I didn't notice.'

'You're right. Did any other vehicles pull up or leave your place while he was at your place?'

'Nah, I had a quiet day.'

'Let's go back to the highway; Chief Inspector Kaba is on his way.'

They walked back to Joe's truck where the boys were pretending to shoot at passing vehicles.

'I don't want to hold you up, Joe. You go on about your business, and I'll catch up with you later when I've finished here.'

Joe pulled away as Kaba arrived.

'Morning, Sydney. We've got a snake in the cab with Valence; it's a king snake - non-poisonous.'

'We'll soon have it out of there.'

Zander took Kaba to assess the situation.

'Firstly we need to get this bush cleared. On second thoughts, are you sure he's dead?'

'Look for yourself.'

No, hook up the Land Rover to the truck, Corporal, and drag it out. Then check and make sure he's dead.'

'The coroner is on his way, Adam. He was at Joe's Joint having breakfast.'

'While we are waiting for the coroner, just a quick question. What are these scaffolding poles sticking in the ground at the side of the road?'

'We've had these fifteen-foot posts installed at intervals of 25 yards on alternate sides of the highway on all straight stretches. They are to prevent planes from landing and taking off. As you know only the police and the armed forces are permitted to use helicopters and we can't afford one. The drug-runners were landing on the highway at night and the jungle farmers used to carry the bundles of marijuana on foot from the mountain fields.   They lit the highway with torches, and once the plane had landed they loaded the marijuana and sometimes other drugs and it would take off again within minutes. An accident would be staged as a diversion at each end of where the plane was landing to stop people seeing what was happening.'

'Have you caught anybody?'

'No, none that have been able to help us but we've been close. We've killed two farmers who were running away with sacks of marijuana which they didn't have time to load. There is still the odd plane that comes in, and we don't know how they do it but somehow they still use the highway.'

Zander wandered over to one of the posts.

'Looks fairly substantial to me,' declared Zander as he grasped the pole, but then he thought he felt it move.

He wrapped his arms around the post and heaved.

'Aren't these supposed to be concreted in?'

'Yes, they are. Why is there something wrong?'

'Yes, this one is loose,' stated Zander as he lifted it a foot and it came free. He dropped it to the ground with a thump and a clank as it bounced on the surface of the highway.

'What have you done?'

'Just lifted your post off its pin. The pole has been cut off at ground level and a close-fitting rod has been inserted. It looks as if when there is a plane due in, the farmers lift the poles off so that the plane can land and take off, and then they put the posts back on the inserts.'

'I wonder how long they have been doing that?'

'Most probably the day after you put them up.'

'I hope not; they cost a lot of money. Admittedly, the American Drug Enforcement Agency provided it, but short of rolling up the road and putting it away, I don't know what else we can do. We haven't got enough manpower to cover the roads, rivers and air to control it all.'

'Do you know who runs the operation down here?'

'We have our suspicions but no proof.'

'Anyone I know?'

'I don't think so, Adam. No, I'm going to have to tell my brother about this and he's not going to like it.'

'Your brother is in charge of drugs investigations?'

'No, he is the overseeing officer. Besides I'm going to be busy; we had another killing last night. The body was found two miles this side of Morris' place - throat cut.'

'Who was it?'

'Don't know yet, but in my experience someone with their throat cut has been surprised from behind. The last one was when a husband caught someone sitting astride his wife in what you might call a "compromising position".'

'But not in this case?'

'Could have been, but he was dumped. He'd stopped bleeding and he was in a crumpled heap just off the highway. It looks as if he was thrown or pushed out of a moving vehicle.'

The coroner arrived in a hail of dust and stones.

'What's the hurry, Sir George; he's dead and not going anywhere.'

'When I take my time, Sydney, you want me to hurry up, and when I hurry up you want me to slow down. I'll have you know I have three more corpses for autopsy back at the morgue and you are going to want answers on these two now. When is it going to stop?'

'We both thought it had, didn't we, Adam?'

'Yes, those other three aren't involved are they?'

'No, it was a street fight with possible drug involvement.'

Kaba briefed the coroner and let him get on with his work. They walked back to the roadside as the morgue ambulance arrived.

'You want to have a look at him, Adam?'

'Yes if you don't mind?'

'Feel free.'

Zander got into the back of the ambulance and pulled back the sheet covering the body, which was strapped to the stretcher. He gave a sharp intake of breath when he uncovered the body of Otis.

'That's it, Sydney. You've got to take Morris in for murder, or whatever you can hold him on.'

'It won't work. He's a person of great influence and he'd be out within an hour.'

'But why Otis?'

'Otis? That's the guy who helped you, isn't it?'

'Yes.'

'I didn't recognise him at the side of the highway; he was in a crumpled heap and covered in dust and sand. I'm sorry; I know you'd got to like him.'

'I wonder what he's done to deserve this.'

'Perhaps, Morris got him to plant the snake.'

'No. He couldn't have done that. Otis was with me. Either Valence left the vantage point and went to Morris' place where the snake was planted, or he went somewhere else first. I'm going to have to question Morris again. The other thing we need to do is check the track either side of the road from the site where Valence fired the shots to the highway. I didn't see a rifle in the Dodge, which means he may have dumped it somewhere. We need to find it.'

'Yes. You go and see Morris if you don't get anywhere, I will go and play the bad guy and maybe lock him up for a bit and see who gets him out. I will also get that track checked. Be careful, Adam, you might be next.'

Zander smirked as he got into the Bronco. He pulled away and his mind started to concentrate on the sequence of events. Had Morris actually killed anybody? Or had someone else always done it? Food for thought. And was he now in danger? Yes, possibly, but if he put up a smoke screen by pointing the finger at someone else, Morris might just think the trail has gone cold. The Bronco pulled up outside Morris' house and the nurse met Zander at the door.

'No housekeeper or maid?'
'No, they have time off.'
'It's awfully quiet around here. Where is everybody?'
'I don't know except Red has gone to Mexico for a vacation. Mr Morris is in the office.'
'Morning, Jon, how are you?'
'Fine. Still a bit stiff but back at work.'
'I'm pleased to hear that. Where is everybody?'
'Moving cattle to the new clearing. I'm just about to go and see how things are.'
'You heard about Otis?'
'Yes, I think it might be that gang of poachers he used to hang out with.'
'Oh! I didn't know about that,' said Zander scratching his head.
'Yes, there was a lot of bad blood when he refused to help them; I think they thought he might report them to the authorities. But I don't think he would, he was not that sort.'
'Well, that gives me something to go on, thanks. Now this other business, Elly, Pancho and Manuel. It all seems to point in one direction,' said Zander watching Morris's face tighten in anticipation. 'I'm afraid it all goes back to Martens.'

Zander saw the relief on Morris' face and continued without batting an eyelid.

'Did you know that he had another woman back in the U.S.?'

Morris looked stunned and shocked.

'You're kidding me'
'It's true. I haven't told Kaba yet but it seems he was about to leave Elly and that's what the row was about. He arranged for Pancho to kill her for the flight money, but it wasn't there because she had already stashed it away. Martens had already arranged for Manuel to kill Pancho and a flight for Manuel had been booked to Mexico. I can't explain the Manuel killing yet and I was hoping you might be able to shed some light on that.'
'Well, Martens was out this way after he was let out of jail, but I didn't see that as significant.'
'Is that why you didn't mention it?'
'Yeah, I thought Martens had been given the all clear.'
'Yes, I thought that as well. Okay, you've given me some more to think about, thanks.'

Zander drove back towards Joe's Joint as Kaba approached him. Zander flashed his lights and waved him down.

'Sydney, don't go and see Morris just yet. I've given him a false trail but only he and I know about it. What you can do is go and look up Otis' old poaching pals. I think Morris might have tipped them off by saying that Otis had been talking to you about their poaching and that he was dangerous, and then he sat back and waited for them to bump him off.'
'There are three of them; if they've done that they will swing for it. We've known about their activities for a long time and it was nothing to do with Otis. We are waiting for the organiser to come down from the U.S. He's the link man; we think we identified him after his last trip.'
'Okay. I'm going to have another word with Jessica Bray. She's a better shot than she admits.'

'You mean she's killed someone?'

'I don't think so but she's been up to something.'

'Well, surprise, surprise! Keep me informed, Adam, won't you?'

'Of course.'

Zander stopped off at Joe's Joint.

'How's it going, Joe?'

'Great, bud, great. Wanna beer?'

'Don't mind if I do.'

'I'll join yah. Do yah mind?'

'No, come on,' declared Zander waving Joe to his table.

'Bring your best bottle of rum - it's on me.'

Joe arrived at the table with two cans of Slitz, two shot glasses and a small purple and grey flagon of Appleton Reserve 12-year-old rum.

'Around here this is the crème de la crème.   It's so smooth you can drink it neat like a top-notch malt whisky.'

Joe pulled the stopper and poured two shots.

'Bottoms up, as you English say.'

Joe tipped the full contents of the glass in his mouth and swilled it around his gums then swallowed. Zander followed suit and after some smacking of lips, he felt the glow.

'That's some good stuff. It really is mellow and warming.'

Joe poured two more and Zander realised he wasn't going to last the day at this rate. As much as he felt like getting into a session and forgetting the investigation for a couple of hours, he knew he couldn't.

'Slow down, Joe. We have the rest of the day and I haven't eaten yet.'

'You want some grub?'

'I wouldn't mind.'

'You wan' a burger?'

'Yes, thanks.'

Joe ordered the hamburger and chain-smoked two cigarettes before it arrived. He poured himself another shot of rum and drained the glass straight away.

'Where do you come from, Joe?'

'Alberta, Canada, but I haven't been there in almost forty years, since I left the navy. I was in New York for nearly twenty years and then 'Frisco for fifteen or so, then Mexico and then here.'

'You've been around a bit.'

'Yeah, hey! You haven't touched your drink, Bud Somethin' wrong?'

'No, you go ahead; I have to finish my hamburger and I also have to drive back.'

Joe proceeded to decimate the rum, pouring the odd one for Zander. Customers came and went and Joe's wife had put the boys to bed.

'You closing up?' Joe's wife asked her husband.

'Nah, I'm gonna crack another one.' Joe's speech had become slurred and his eyelids had started to droop.

'I'll close the shutters up and you can finish when you're ready.'

'Okay, honey. She's good to me.'

Zander looked at Joe's wife; she was shaking her head as if to say not again.

'Joe, you said the guy in the Dodge had a burger and a coke to go but I didn't see any evidence of that in the truck.'

'Nah, he had a steak, sat here and ate it.'

'So there was plenty of time for someone to put a snake in his truck.'

'Yeah, plenty.'

'Did you see who it was?'

'Yeah, it was that guy Martens; he was here talking to the big fellah. Martens left and the other guy stayed to finish his grub.'

'Were they friendly to each other?'

'Yeah, sure. Big buddies.'

Zander looked past Joe and saw his wife shaking her head again, not in disbelief but in denial. Zander thought he would try another tack.

'Did Mr Morris phone here earlier?'

'Nah, I don't speak to him.'

Zander glanced at Joe's wife and saw she was now nodding her head. Joe had his head down staring into his drink and Zander mouthed the words "you speak me later" to Joe's wife. She nodded her head in acknowledgement. Joe was slipping away fast now.

'You all right, Joe?'

'Yeah, yeah,' he grunted without lifting his head.

'Bottoms up then.'

'Bottoms...' mumbled Joe slurping another shot of rum.

Zander filled it again and picked up his can of Slitz and called out, 'Cheers,' but there was no response from Joe except the steady purr of his breathing. Zander looked at Joe's wife and shrugged.

'Give me a hand to get him through to the back' Joe's wife asked.

They took an arm each and pulled him up out of the chair. He groaned a little bit and then started to sing something unintelligible. They laid him on the bed and his wife took his baseball cap off and his sandals.

'Let's go back out there,' she said pointing to the bar.'
'What was that all about?' Zander asked as he sat down.
'Joe was lying. Morris did phone here. I don't know what they talked about, but Joe disapproved and was on the phone for about fifteen minutes. Also he told you Martens was here, but he wasn't.'
'Why are you telling me all this?'
'Don't you want to know?'
'Yes, it's just that he's your husband and you seem to be saying he's involved.'
'I'm telling you because Otis was killed. He was my cousin. I hope Joe wasn't mixed up in it, but if he was then he must face the music. Otis was my mother's oldest sister's boy and we are a close family.'
'Does Joe keep snakes?'
'No, but there are plenty down in the orange grove. I could take you there tomorrow when it's light.'
'No, I believe you. Did Joe spend any time outside when that big American and the green Dodge were here?'
'Yes, he told me he was going to get some oranges from the grove.'
'Does Morris come here often?'
'Once or twice a month. He doesn't need to come here; he does a lot of things by messages and not just phone and radio. If you fall out with Morris, you've got trouble. He's a powerful man, Mr Zander.'
'Powerful enough to have you or me killed?'
'Yes, for about a thousand dollars they would be lining up to get the name.'
'Aren't you worried he will have you killed?'
'I've done nothing against him.'
'You have now; you've told me.'
'What! Are you working for him?'

'No, but you will have to be careful; he seems to be going on a killing spree but he's not doing the killing himself, he's just making the arrangements. As you say, they are most probably lining up at Two Snakes, now that the word is out.'

'Can't you do anything about it?'

'At the moment, no. We have no proof although I think he will be arrested shortly. The problem is, as I mentioned, he's not doing the killing so as long as he can talk, someone is likely to get killed'

Zander realised that perhaps he shouldn't have told her about the possibilities, because she now looked decidedly worried.

'Mr Zander, you're a healthy looking man and you've just scared the shit out of me. So, you wanna get laid?'

'Yes, most of the time, but I don't think now is the right time. I have a lot of things to do; besides I'm not so sure I could with Joe out the back.'

'Oh, shit to him. We haven't made it since before the last was born.'

'I don't even know your name and you're talking about sleeping together.'

'My name is Rosemarine, and I wasn't thinkin of doin' any sleepin'. I need to get laid.'

'Not by me, Rosemarine. I'm sorry if I gave you that impression but I'm otherwise involved . . .'

A loud bang cut short his sentence.

'That was a shot wasn't it?'   Zander said.

'Yes,' said Rosemarine as she got up and dashed to the door, followed by Zander.

'Where do you think that shot came from?'

'Down there, the other side of our orange grove,' she stated pointing into the dark.

'What's there?'

'Three families; they often fight over their daughters and sons.'

'You think that's what it was?'

'Yeah, sounded like a shot gun.'

'Perhaps you're right. I must get back to town; I will see you in the next couple of days.'

Chapter 9 Protection Assignment

Zander went back to his sister's place.

'Hi, Sis, everything all right?'
'Yes, what about you?'
'Not so good. Otis has been killed!'
'Oh dear, how did it happen?'
'I don't know yet other than his throat was cut.'
'How awful. Have you any ideas?'
'Yes, I'm more or less certain who did it and who caused it to be done.'
'Do you want to talk about it?'
'No thanks. Anyway, I need some sleep and a fresh start tomorrow.'

Zander took an invigorating shower before breakfast; he rubbed himself down with a towel and stood close to the down draught of the fan. He was still naked when Mary walked in.

'You wan' anythin', Mr Adam?'
'Just some clothes.'

Mary went to the wardrobe and selected a white cotton shirt and light grey slacks.

'Okay?' she replied holding the clothes up.
'Just fine, but what about some underwear?'

She handed him the clothes and went to the drawer for the underwear and looked over her shoulder knowingly.

'Not now, Mary, I have work to do. Would you like to get me some eggs and bacon with hash browns and toast, please?'

She screwed her face up in disappointment and left the
bedroom in a sulk. Zander dressed and brushed his short-
cropped hair.

'Morning, Sis.'

'Morning. Mary's getting your breakfast. Would you like
some coffee?'

'Please, black.'

'Any nearer to solving the Elly case? You seemed to be a bit
stressed last-night; was it not a good day for you yesterday?'

'It was a disaster. There were two more bodies, one of which
was Otis. I thought the killing had stopped but it seems the
perpetrator of all this mayhem is able to get people killed by
starting bad rumours or paying anyone with a gun or the
wherewithal to kill.

'I believe Otis was killed by his former hunting pals and the
Yank hit-man was killed in the vehicle accident as a result of a
fright after seeing the snake. I also think there is most probably
a price on my head as well. Killing me won't do any good
because Sydney Kaba knows more or less all I know.'

'Why don't you tell me who you think is responsible for all
this mayhem as you call it? Then I can tell all the ladies then no
one will come near you if they all know.'

'Thanks, but I still have to speak with many of your friends
and I don't want them to know they have been sleeping with a
killer.'

'Are you saying Jon Morris is the killer?'

'Is it that well-known that he sleeps around?'

'Yes, but few will admit that they are one of them, and before
you ask, I am not one of his bedfellows.'

'I wasn't suggesting you were.'

'Adam, you're my brother, and when I see that look in your
eye, I know what you're thinking.'

Jenny went through to the kitchen to fetch his breakfast.
When he had finished Zander took the Bronco to Jessica Bray's
place, and as he approached the door it opened.

'Mrs Bray is busy,' announced the maid.

'I will only be a couple of minutes.'

'Sorry, Sir, it's a bereavement and she can't be disturbed.'

'Okay, thank you. Please tell her I called and ask her to give me a call when she's free.'

'Yes, Sir.'

He suspected the vicar's wife did not wish to see him. He decided to visit some of Morris' other women, but he was unable to glean anything of significance during the visits. There was the initial denial, and then there seemed to be an abundance of shamed faces followed by the guilt when they eventually told him of their sexual escapades. The last person on his list was different.   Just as he was about to ring the bell at the security gate of his last call, he met the vicar coming out.

'Morning, Vicar, sorry to hear about the bereavement.'

'Bereavement?'

'Yes, I was told your wife was dealing with a bereavement.'

'Oh, oh yes, my wife, yes. I must go and see to that.'

'Can I help?'

'Yes, you could actually. Please refrain from hounding my wife,' he snapped.

'Mr Bray, you seem to forget, I'm dealing with several murders. I've been interviewing anybody who has been in contact with the victims or suspects and your wife was in the area, at, or about, the time Manuel was killed. I am not saying she is a suspect, but I would appreciate it if you were both a bit more charitable and helped me with my investigation. It would help if you could tell your wife to stop avoiding me, because I will get to her in the end, even if it means having her arrested.'

'There's no need to take that tone, Mr Zander.'

'I think there is, and perhaps now you realise that I'm serious, and if I don't hear from her shortly I will arrange for Chief Inspector Kaba and his men to visit the manse.'

Bray turned and left. The middle-aged lady standing in the doorway looked shocked.

'Sorry about that, Madam. As you might have gathered, I'm investigating several murders. Perhaps you could spare me a minute or two?'

'Yes, of course, please come in.'

Zander went up the flight of eight steps to the front veranda; it was an old colonial style veranda with a balustrade and fancy fretwork. They moved inside and sat in cane furniture in the air-conditioned sitting room. Mrs Platton appeared to be in her mid-forties; she had blond hair and had a good suntan. Her nails were manicured, her make-up precise and her hair was held back neatly with an Alice band.

'How can I help you?'

'By answering a few delicate questions, please.'

'I'm not so sure I like the sound of that - delicate? What do you mean by that?'

'I'll get straight to the point and forget the delicate bit. Are you having an affair with Jon Morris?'

'Why?'

'No, Mrs Platton, I'm the one asking the questions. I'm getting a little bit fed up with being given the run-around. Were you, or are you, having an affair? Yes or no?'

'Yes and no. Yes I was, but no I'm not now.'

'Well, thank you for that. I'm relieved that you have the courage of your convictions.'

'I haven't any convictions and I wasn't caught either. I just got fed up with being one of many.'

'You knew there were others?'

'Oh yes, several, but a few fell by the wayside when Sal moved down here. Initially she kept him on a tight rein, but then when he knew he was never going to get Elly back, he started putting it about again. But that was not for me. He was charming, delightfully physical and energetic and I enjoyed the sex. However, my husband got wind of it and started paying more attention to me, so I didn't need to be one of Jon's many.'

'Has he ever asked you to lie or cover up for him?'

'No, not that I can remember. Do you think he is involved in these murders?'

'I don't know for sure yet. I'm just going through a process of elimination. What does your husband do?'

'We run dive boats; I do the bookings and the office work and he takes the divers out to the reef and wrecks, and instructs them if necessary.'

'If I asked you who had the best reason to kill Elly, and was ruthless enough to do it, do you think Morris would come into that category?'

'Yes, and the vicar.'

'The vicar!'

'Yes, but this is only my theory though. He hates Morris, if vicars can hate, and I happen to think he would have done anything to get Morris out of the way, without getting himself implicated of course. But I don't think he would have pulled the trigger…'

'Well, you astound me! Why would he want to get rid of Morris?'

'Because Morris has been fooling around with his wife, and when the vicar found out, he went and told Elly. She was furious and that put an end to Morris' chances - Morris had been trying to get Elly back but she was having none of that. You might think I'm twisted, but I think he could have arranged Elly's murder to get back at Morris. As far as I know, Jessica is still fooling around with Jon.'

'Well, you've certainly thrown some new light on the matter. I think I had better start again.'

'I've always been outspoken; I tend to speak as I find. I'm not nutty I just see things differently from others.'

'No, I don't think you're nutty at all, and what you have said has a lot of merit and I will look into it. Do you have any other suggestions?'

'Yes, if you are visiting some of Jon's other ladies, be careful or you yourself might become the target of revenge.'

'What do you mean by that?'

'I hear you are hot in the sack and most of Jon's ladies are short of attention.'

'How did you know I was visiting "his ladies" as you call them?'

'We do have telephones here, you know. This might be a Third World country but it ain't that backward.'

'Yes, of course. I'm just surprised that you had been told. Is there anything else you would like to tell me?'

'Yes but it's a bit of a wild card. We run dive boats; we were approached to run drugs – they referred to it as "special cargo" – from the rivers to a ship out beyond the reef in international waters. The people who approached us did so anonymously. We have told the police because we want to be left alone to earn a decent living and we want nothing to do with illegal drugs.'

'What has this got to do with this investigation?'

'Just one of my ideas - Morris has boats and a light aircraft and he could have been approached by the same people'

'Do you think he would get involved in drug-running?'

'What I think doesn't really matter, but when you get to know someone like Morris, you realise he has no scruples at all. For what it's worth I think he would do anything if it suited him.'

'You certainly know how to put the cat among the pigeons. Is there anything else?'

'Another place, another time,' she gushed with a twinkle in her eyes as she stood up and took him to the door.

Zander walked back to the Bronco with his head in a spin. He sat for several minutes and mulled over what Mrs Platton had said. He did not dismiss it entirely but thought he should perhaps run it past Kaba. He started the truck and moved off and he was still so deep in thought that he nearly hit a cyclist who then shouted abuse at him. He wound the window down and apologised, and in that moment he decided that he would go to the police headquarters and talk with Kaba.

'Sydney, do you think it's possible? I mean to say, the vicar of all people?'

'Your instinct tells you it's unlikely, and I agree with that, but I think we need to check it out, although it sounds like gossip to me. The vicar is gentleness itself, and kind man whom I have known for many years.'

'Maybe the sun has got to him'

'What about the suspicion that Morris is involved in drugs?'

'We've looked into that and we know the approach is authentic because several people have told us they have been approached. The problem is, we're having difficulty monitoring it so the customs department covers most of it. It could be a crackpot making the phone calls, which we haven't been able to trace.'

'Is there a pattern? Do you know who has been approached and why?'

'I know the people who have been approached and mostly it's people who own boats or light aircraft.'

'If they've told you they've been approached, I suspect they don't want to get involved. What about the ones who have boats and light aircraft and haven't been approached or haven't told you if they have, because they have taken up the offer of shipping cargo?'

'You're going to think this is crazy, Adam, but we haven't looked at it that way. Come to think of it, there are a number of prominent people who fall into that category and we haven't heard a thing from them. I will get someone to draw up a list of owners and make some enquiries. Well, you've inspired me to look in another direction and, to use your expression, "thank you for that". Oh By the way, I'm in court today, all day.'

'Okay, Sydney, I'll see you later. Anything on Otis?'

'No, other than it was the cut across the throat that killed him and he had recently eaten iguana.'

'Now that isn't bunkhouse food is it? Maybe his old hunting partners had some as well?'

'Bunkhouse food is whatever is available, and we haven't found his partners yet but we will. Morris will be arrested this morning as soon as my men can get out there and serve the warrant.'

'I will go out this afternoon and have a look around while he's not there.'

'I shouldn't bank on him being in custody too long.
However, he might be in longer than he would like, because his
attorney is the defence attorney in court with me today.'

'Open and shut case?'

'No, it's a corrupt policeman, trafficking hard drugs.'

'Is Morris involved?'

'Not that we know of, but that doesn't mean a thing. Morris
wouldn't touch the stuff but he could still be the organiser. He
has all the communication equipment at Two Snakes as you've
most probably seen.'

'Yes, I have and I'm beginning to think I need some help
with me to give me cover if I'm going to wind up this case. Do
you have anyone that can shoot and is reliable?'

'Yes, I have several but I can't release them to you - I have
too many other things on the go. Why don't I try and get Oxbee
for you. I'm sure he's attended the close protection course
which will make him ideal.'

'That would be just the job, but can you fix it?'

'I should think so; I'll get the Prime Minister to speak to the
commander. I'm due to brief the PM and give him an update
on this case, because as you know he has taken a personal
interest. It'll take some time but if you let them know at the
camp what's happening, they will most probably release him to
you now'

'Okay, I'll go out to the camp now.'

Chief Inspector Kaba was as good as his word. Zander had
morning coffee in the officers' mess at eleven o'clock with
George Galpen. The intelligence officer dropped in to tell them
the commander had given Oxbee the all-clear and permission
to carry arms in aid to the civil power.

'Official all formal and correct then George?'

'No, not yet, but it will all be tied up in writing shortly. The
Foreign Office would be most displeased if they were not
notified formally but we've sent them a flash signal and
they've given us the nod. Oxbee is drawing a pistol and
ammunition now and he'll come here as soon as he's ready.'

'Thank you for your help - it is much appreciated.'

The mess staff sergeant entered the ante-room.

'Major Galpen, Sir. Sarn't Major Oxbee is outside, Sir.'

'Thank you, Staff. He's all yours, Adam.'

'Thanks, George,' and they walked to the rear of the mess where Oxbee was waiting.

'Morning, Fred. I hope you don't mind me getting you involved in this on a formal basis?'

'Not at all. I'm up to speed on protection duties so I know the score, and I could only carry a weapon if authorised anyway.'

'I don't need you just for your protection skills; I need you for your investigative ability as well. Right, let's go.'

Zander brought Oxbee up to date during the journey to Morris' place. A convoy of three police Land Rovers heading towards town passed them; Morris was in the middle vehicle sitting between two uniformed police sergeants.

'That's him out of the way for a couple of hours at least.'

'Bit high powered, isn't it?'

'Morris is a person of extreme influence as I'm finding out virtually by the hour.'

'Have we got a search warrant?'

'No, but that shouldn't be a problem. Morris gave me clearance to go where I like and everyone at Two Snakes knows that. The farm manager is in Mexico at present, so I don't know who is currently running the place.'

When they arrived, the housekeeper opened the door.

'I'm sorry but Mr Morris is out at the moment.'

'Oh! Is he out with the cattle?'

'No, he's gone to town.'

'I'll just pop into the office then because I need to make a phone call. Is that all right?'

'Yes, I suppose so.'

'I'm sure he won't mind.'

'Okay.'

They went into the office and the housekeeper went about her work.

'You have a look on those shelves and in those drawers,' announced Zander pointing to the left side of the office, "and I will check the desk and filing cabinet.'

Oxbee opened a wooden filing cabinet. It was slightly warped and the drawers were a little stiff, and as the drawer jerked open there was a dull thud as something dropped at the rear of the cabinet. He reached around the back and withdrew a pistol which was wrapped in a lightly-oiled cloth and the whole thing was in a plastic bag which had been taped to the back of the cabinet.

'It's a .38, Adam, similar to the one I drew this morning and it's fully loaded. I thought they had removed all the weapons from Two Snakes?'
'Your right, they should have, but they obviously missed that one. Got him!'
'Got whom?'
'Morris. I've just found Valence, the hit man, in his address book. So it looks as if the vicar is off the hook.'
'Surely there isn't an address?'
'No, just a phone number, and it's a Florida dialling code. I'll give it a try.'

Zander phoned the number several times but got no answer.

'I was hoping it might have been a home number. I'll phone Sydney.'

The phone rang for some considerable time and was eventually answered by a constable.

'Is Chief Inspector Kaba back from court yet?'
'No Sir, he gone all day.'
'Is Superintendent Kaba there?'
'Yes, Sir.'

'Would you put me through, please?'

'Kaba.'

'Good afternoon, Superintendent. Is Morris still under arrest?'

'Yes, we're waiting for his attorney so he should be out shortly.'

'You can keep him a bit longer because I've found another pistol together with evidence that he knew Valence, the hit man.   Ask him what he was doing with the hit man's phone number in his address book?'

'Is there anything else?'

'No.'

'Good. I suggest you leave Mr Morris' house now and stop going through somebody else's property because you are breaking the law. Goodbye,' and the phone went dead.

'I can't believe that man! He's just put the phone down on me, having informed me that I'm breaking the law. The fact that he has a suspect serial killer in his cells seems unimportant.'

'I've always thought there is something strange about that man but I can't put my finger on it.'

'Let's get on with the search.'

'There's lots of paperwork here.'

'We don't need to bother with that, unless it something to do with flights or shipping. He could be involved with drugs so, anything that looks like a timetable or is travel related would be interesting.'

Oxbee moved the portable safe and found another one in the wall behind it.

'I wonder if they checked the wall safe as well.'

'I doubt it. We'll have to get forensics back out here and give it the once over if it hasn't already been done. I've got a few more U.S. phone numbers. I'll try them later.'

'I'm finished here, Adam.'

'Let's go to the bunkhouse and see if we can find these hunters.'

It was late afternoon and there were only two cowhands in the bunkhouse.

'Good afternoon. I was wondering if you could help me?' said Zander.

'Depends'

'I'm trying to find out where Otis and his hunting pals get their meals?'

'Here or Joe's Joint or Lilly's.'

'Where's the cook?'

'Over there in the cookhouse.'

'Come on, Fred,' said Zander to Oxbee who was loitering and looking at pictures of naked women pinned to the wall.

'Let's go and have a word with the catering staff,' he declared with a smile.

The cookhouse was a tin shack at the rear of the bunkhouse and it had an open-sided eating area with an atap roof. The cook was preparing vegetables as they walked in.

'Hello, I'm Adam Zander. You know Mr Morris has given me permission to speak to his staff and that he expects you to cooperate'

'Yeah, what do you wan' know?' he replied with contempt.

'I just wanted to ask about the food you prepare.'

'Oh! Okay,' whined the large Carib with a look of relief.

'What is the most popular meal?'

'Rice and beans with beef'

'Do the hunters ever provide you with meat?'

'Why?'

'Look, I'm not interested in what the hunters shoot. Do you ever get iguana?'

'Yes, of course.'

'When did you last serve it?'

'About two weeks ago.'

'Where could I get bamboo chicken?'

'Lilly's or Joe's Joint.'

'Thanks very much for your help.'

Zander and Oxbee headed back to the Bronco.

'What was that all about, Adam?'

'The contents of Otis' stomach indicated that he had recently eaten iguana. Actually it was hardly digested, which infers that he was killed just after the meal. Do you know where Lilly's is?'

'Yes, out of the farm gate, turn left, and it's about two miles down the highway on the left. It's a brothel and eating house.'

'Oh really! Let's go and see.'

Chapter 10 Death at the Brothel

Lilly's was an atap-covered structure set back off the road; there was a bar at the front with a dining area in the back next to the kitchen, and there were several cabanas out the back where the girls lived and entertained their customers. The owner was a buxom Carib woman who helped the three girls tend the bar and tables, but she was not known for personally entertaining men in a cabana. There was a group of Hispanics sitting in the dining area with the owner and her cook who was a burly Mexican. The owner got up and approached them as they walked in.

'Ah! Mr Oxbee. None of your boys here.'
'Thank you, Lilly, but I'm not here for that. Mr Zander here want's to ask you some questions about your food.'
'Health inspector?'
'No, just trying to find out about Otis' last moments. He worked for me for a couple of days and now I'm investigating his death.'
'Oh, I see,' she uttered nervously. 'I don't know much.'
'What do you know?'
'He ate here the night he died.'
'Iguana?'
'Yes, how'd you know that?'
'Some people told me.'
'Must have been Miguel and the boys.'
'Who are they?'
'That's who he had supper with.'
'Are they his hunting partners?'
'They were but he stopped hunting some time ago.'
'What time did they leave?'
'About nine.'
'Any idea where they went?'
'No, they were arguing when they left here and there had been a lot of hostility towards Otis all evening - something about him telling the police. But he wouldn't do that. That would incriminate him. Besides, he just wouldn't do it.'

'Do you think they killed him?'

'I don't know. I don't want to get involved. Thinking out loud could get me killed and I've probably said too much already, but you seem to be such a nice guy.'

'I am, and I'm only trying to help get the people who killed him.'

At that point, a shot rang out and one of the girls slumped to the floor. Oxbee fired two shots and the gunman was hit in the face as he was loading his bolt-action rifle. He was sitting in the front passenger seat of the battered blue snub nose Dodge pick-up truck and the driver was covered in blood from the wounds inflicted on the passenger gunman.

'I've only winged the driver, Adam. I couldn't get a proper bead on him.'

Zander had crawled over to the girl to see if there was anything that could be done. The shot aimed at Zander had missed him by inches but had hit her in the side of the head.

'Okay, is there any more movement?'

'No,' snapped Oxbee taking a sweep of his arc of fire, 'other than the driver holding his shoulder.'

The Hispanics had left via the back door and one of them came back in with a shotgun and cautiously moved to the front of the bar. Oxbee swung round and pointed his pistol at the Hispanic holding the gun.

'Hey, I'm wid joo.'

'Okay, move to the left of the door and cover me when I go out the door.'

'Okay.'

Oxbee dashed to the doorway and then ran outside, covering the front of the truck with his gun.

'Help me,' cried the driver weakly.

Oxbee opened the door and dragged the hunter out. He yelled in pain as Oxbee roughly handled him up against the truck.

'Where's the other fellah. There's supposed to be three of you'

Oxbee's adrenalin was obviously running high as he growled his questions breathlessly. The driver didn't answer at first but Oxbee poked the pistol into his kidney and this immediately loosened his tongue.

'He chickened out; he wouldn't come.'
'How did you know we were here?' Zander asked.
'We saw you leave the cookhouse.'
'Did you think killing us would stop the investigation?'
'No.'
'Why'd you do it?'
'Money.'
'Who's paying?'
'Don't know.'
'How were you going to be paid?'
'Can I get my arm fixed before I answer your questions?'
'If you don't answer my questions you won't live long enough to get your arm fixed,' Oxbee growled angrily.

The Hispanic dragged the dead man from the cab of the truck and searched him.

'They bin smokin' wacky baccy, Mister,' he said holding up the remains of a joint.

Zander removed the eight-inch hunting knife from a sheath on the wounded man's belt.

'Big dispatcher, Adam.'
'Yes, and I wonder if there is any trace of Otis on here. Take your belt off.'

Using his good hand he unfastened his belt and pulled it out of its loops. Zander grabbed the sheath, as it became free.

'What's your name?'
'Miguel Olandee.'
'Did you kill Otis?'
'No.'
'Who did?'
'He did,' he retorted, nodding his head towards the dead man.
'That's convenient.'

The sound of police sirens could be heard approaching Lilly's, and when they arrived, a detective sergeant whom Zander had met got out of the Land Rover.

'What happened?'

Zander gave him a quick briefing and gave him the hunting knife in the sheath.

'Take this to the lab; there might be traces of Otis' blood on it. He says the dead chap killed Otis, but he doesn't carry a knife. There's one other; he's most probably at Two Snakes. I'll leave it all to you now. I need a drink - what about you Fred?'
'Most definitely.'

Lilly was sitting with the other two girls and the Hispanics. She looked ashen-faced and was in the early stages of shock.

'Let me buy you a drink,' pronounced Zander to the group gathered around the table. The Hispanics nodded and Lilly waved one of the girls towards the bar.
'Wad joo Wan'?'
'Bottle of rum and a large coke.'

The girl set glasses on the table for everybody and handed a quart bottle of Captain Morgan's rum to Zander.

'You pour,' said Zander handing the bottle to the girl.

Lilly didn't wait for anyone; she gulped hers down and gave a gasp as it hit the spot.

'Poor Emma, she had only just arrived from Honduras; she was trying to make some money for the family back home.'

'I'm sorry, Lilly; I had no idea this sort of thing was going to happen here. It's only thanks to Fred here that there are not a lot more dead people. I just don't know what made them think they could get away with it.'

'They were high on wacky baccy, which can make many things seem possible.'

'Yes, you're most probably right, Fred, but it seems senseless to me. If they were getting paid for it, we will more than likely have evidence to nail our perpetrator.'

'I doubt it. A slick attorney will trash the evidence as that of drug-crazed individuals out to get money to support their habit or getting revenge for informing on them and their illegal activities.'

'There's a lot in what you say and it's building all the time. There's going to be a point where there is so much against him that he won't be able to deny it.'

'But he will, Adam, he will.'

'We'll have to make sure we can prove he's a liar, then.'

Zander went over to the detective to see what the progress was.

'Everything all right?' he asked the detective sergeant.

'Nearly finished, Mr Zander. The coroner's ambulance will be here shortly.'

'Good; we're leaving now. Anything else you want from us?'

'No, Sir, unless you would like to drop in on Mr Morris and tell him what's happened to his men.'

'He's been released?'

'Yes, late this afternoon. He's to be charged with possession of illegal weapons. And they've arrested Mr Martens again; Superintendent Kaba arrested him after Mr Morris made a statement incriminating Mr Martens and intimated that you were following a similar line of inquiry.'

'That takes the biscuit! I set up Martens to take the heat out of the situation to see if we could get him to stop killing people who could incriminate him and he uses that to get Martens locked up. I'm just going to pop back in the bar and use the phone.'

'Mr Zander seems angry, Mr Oxbee?'

'Yes, Mr Zander and Chief Inspector Kaba have been working on a theory and now it's backfired.'

'Sydney, what's going on? Why has Martens been arrested?'

'Sorry, Adam, but Morris made a statement to my brother which pointed at Martens and he inferred that you believed that Martens was responsible anyway, so he had him arrested.'

'Doesn't your brother know that Morris is our prime suspect?'

'Yes, but he ignored that and went on his instinct.'

'Well, I'm sorry but your brother is a bloody fool. He's never got over the fact that I proved Martens was not involved.'

'My brother has a tendency to be a bit single-minded.'

'A bit single-minded! I won't say any more because he's your brother, but if I get the chance to tell somebody in a position of authority about your brother, I sure as hell will.'

'I understand - and this is going to make you even angrier. My brother has forbidden me to release Martens. The other problem is Morris arranged an attorney the first time but he has withdrawn his support now and told Martens to sort it out himself.'

'That's great! Is there some sort of public defence attorney here?'

'No, only for locals. Martens will have to employ his own attorney, but with no funds I'm afraid he's stuck.'

'All right. I'm on my way into town to see him - there's no block on that is there?'

'No, but please avoid my brother. He's gloating because he thinks he has got his man.'

'I'll give him "got his man." No, I won't give him the satisfaction; I'll get someone to help me get Marty out.'

'Okay, whatever you like. How are you after that shooting incident? Must have given you a bit of a scare.'

'Yes, just a bit. The only thing that has really got to me is that, that young girl has been killed by a pot-crazed waster.'

'Yes, I know, but in a Third World country like this sometimes life comes cheap.'

'Well, perhaps it shouldn't.'

'You're right, and that's why I do what I do, to try to make Vanmalla a better place to live.'

'Point taken. Okay, look, I should be at HQ in about two hours. If you could be there I would appreciate it. I don't really want to get into a tussle with your brother.'

'Before you go, Adam, we have found Valence's rifle; it had a telescopic sight and a clip of ammunition and it's with forensics now.'

'That's good news. I'll see you later,' said Zander and put the phone down.

He walked outside as the two bodies were being put into the coroner's vehicle.

'Fred, I've thought of a way we might be able to get Marty out of jail. I think I will have a word with the vicar about revenge. As I mentioned earlier, he hates Morris and if by helping Marty out of jail he gets one over on Morris, he will have some self-satisfaction and do us a favour at the same time.'

'This will highlight his penchant for revenge against Morris and you already have your suspicions, Adam.'

'Yes, but they're not suspicions anymore. I know it's Morris but I now have to prove it.'

During the journey to the manse they went over the case against Morris and came to the conclusion that there was insufficient evidence to charge him. They also had to be careful that Morris didn't turn his lawyer on them for harassment. The maid let them in when they arrived at the manse.

'Good evening, vicar. I'm sorry to bother you at this time of night but I'd like a word with you about Morris,' said Zander.

'I have nothing to say about that man. You are most probably aware that I dislike him and I can very easily lose my reasoning where Morris is concerned. If you get me going I shall have to say a special prayer and seek forgiveness.'

'It's nothing like that vicar; I don't want an opinion on the man - I have nearly enough to hang him.'

'You do!' Reverend Bray exclaimed, then he suddenly realised he was rejoicing in someone else's downfall and his face went sullen.

'I know how you must feel, Vicar,' said Zander.

'I don't think you do'

'Well, let's put it this way, I have as many reasons to see him hanged as you have for disliking him.'

'Yes, I suppose so. In your line of work I suppose you meet an awful lot of nasty people'

'Yes, but I also meet some truly good and helpful people.'

'Talking of helpful, Mr Zander, how may I help?'

'You obviously know Marty Martens. Well he's been arrested again, and this time for all the murders so far, and he's in jail as a result of a statement made by Morris. The problem is, Morris has withdrawn his support, which means Marty no longer has a lawyer and I get the impression that Morris has put the word out, and perhaps the frighteners, so consequently there are no legal volunteers.'

'I'm only too happy to be of assistance. My attorney will, I'm sure, be pleased to help. I haven't used him much but he is a Christian man with a sense of fair play, and if he smells a rat he'll be there like a shot.'

'Thank you, Vicar. Would you like to contact him and tell him about Marty?'

'Yes, I'll do it right now. Would you like a cold beer?'

'Please,' Zander and Oxbee chorused.

He went out of the room, and a couple of minutes later the maid came in with two cans of Slitz with chilled glasses.

'My attorney is phoning the police now and will meet us there in fifteen minutes,' said the vicar as he returned to the room.

'That's more than good of you and I'm sure Marty will be grateful for the sight of some friendly faces.'

'Well, if we can't get him out, it won't be for the want of trying.'

'Is Mrs Bray here?'

'No, I'm afraid not, she's helping to run the beetle drive in the community centre.'

'Oh! Okay, perhaps some other time.'

'Yes, are we ready?' Bray demanded looking over the top of his spectacles to see if the beer glasses were empty.

They drained their glasses and followed the vicar out into the drive.

'I'll take my own car and see you there.'

The lawyer had arrived before them and was already talking to Martens, and the desk sergeant would not permit anyone else to go through to the cells. The lawyer came out of the cells for a couple of minutes to have a word with Zander, and as they talked Chief Inspector Kaba arrived.

'Ah, Sydney, may I confirm a few things with you?'

'Yes, of course.'

They went into a huddle. And had a quick discussion.

'Sydney, would you arrange to have Mr Martens released on the grounds that there is insufficient evidence to hold him?

'I'm afraid I can't do that; I have to get Superintendent Kaba in to do that. The lowest ranking officer able to release Martens is a Superintendent.'

'Please do that, would you?'

Twenty minutes later Superintendent Kaba arrived. Sydney had left earlier, not wanting to get involved with his brother.

'What's this? Some sort of delegation?'

Zander nearly bit his tongue off in an effort not to react. The vicar's attorney put his case to Kaba who had to concede that, under the circumstances, there was insufficient evidence to hold Martens, so Kaba authorised Martens' release. Kaba signed the release order leaving the desk sergeant to do the remaining paperwork, and he stormed out. After the release process they all went outside, thanked each other and said goodbye.

'You shouldn't need me again, Marty, but if you do here's my card.'
'Thank you, but I can't afford to pay you.'
'You don't have to; that's been taken care of.'
'I don't know about you lot but I'm going to the Majestic for a couple of beers' Martens declared.

The vicar made his excuses and left, and the remaining three went to the Majestic where they settled themselves at the bar and Zander ordered the drinks.

'Adam, who paid the attorney?' Martens asked.
'There's no need for you to know that. Just put it down to experience.'
'I'm not so sure I can do that, but I'll leave it there for now.'
'Good. Fred is going to get us some company in a minute.'
'I don't think so; it's a bit quiet tonight.'

Zander looked at Martens who was looking rather dejected.

'What's the matter?'
'I'm going to have to leave the country and go back to the U.S.'

'Why?'

'Because I've been fired. I have nothing here and without a job I have no income, and I have nowhere to stay, how can I live?'

'You might have difficulty with the case still being investigated. When did you lose your job?'

'When they picked me up. Kaba had great pleasure in passing on the message from Morris.'

'There must be something in law that says that is not allowed. You are arrested on the evidence of your boss and he gets the police to tell you you're sacked? That can't be right. What do you think, Fred?'

'I agree with you. It does sound a bit like rough justice. I don't know enough about the local law, other than it is based on English law, but I would say it is morally wrong if nothing else.'

'Didn't the lawyer mention Morris pointed the finger at you?'

'No, I just gave him a rundown on what had happened so far and then he went and spoke to Kaba.'

'Let me have that attorney's card; I'm going to give him a quick call.'

Martens fished out the card and handed it to Zander who went to the phone in the lobby. He looked over his shoulder while listening to the attorney's explanation and saw what he thought was Elloween going into the bar. He finished his telephone conversation and went back into the bar where Weenie had joined the company.

'Hello, Weenie.'

'Hi, Adam,' she replied giving him the glad eye.

'Well, Marty, not that it will do you any good, but Kaba is most probably on the take and the attorney suspects he has been for some time. But you wouldn't be able to prove it using that incident as evidence; however, if combined with several similar incidents of Kaba doing Morris' bidding, there could be grounds if the evidence could be corroborated.'

'So what you're saying is we don't pursue?'

'In short, yes.'

'Perhaps I'll go and blow him away myself,' proclaimed Martens.

'Don't talk like that, even jokingly. If we were called as witnesses to that statement, we would have to commit ourselves.'

'I don't know if I was joking or not, it just came out. I must have been thinking it subconsciously. Has this beer gone to my head or something? I don't usually use words like that.'

'Did you leave the bar while I was on the phone?'

'Yeah, Fred and I we went to the latrine.'

'There was another guy here when I came in,' said Weenie.

'Where'd he go Weenie?' Zander asked.

'He went over that way,' she stated pointing to the left-hand corner of the dance floor.

'Let's go and have a look over there,' uttered Oxbee.

'Let me smell your beer, Marty.'

Martens slid the can over to Zander who took a good long sniff.

'It's not straight beer that's for sure. Let me smell the other can.'

'That's empty; I finished that one when I got back from the latrine.'

Zander sniffed the empty can then his own and then Oxbee's.

'They have all had something put in them. Would you say that's baking soda, Fred?'

'Could be, which means crack cocaine. I wonder how much they put in?'

'With the size of the can opening probably no more than a small rock I should think.'

'It shouldn't be fatal then, Adam.'

'No, you're most probably right, but get him in the lavatory and wash his mouth out, Fred.'

Oxbee departed for the lavatory with Martens in tow while Zander took Weenie with him to the table on the edge of the dance floor and had a walk around.

'He's not here; there are two cans at that table over there.'

Zander picked up the cans and sniffed.

'These are okay,' he declared heading back to the bar.
'Bar-keep, have you got a minute?'
The barman approached Zander cautiously.
'Yes, Sir?'
'Did you serve someone while we were away from the bar?'
'Yes, Sir. One guy had two cans and he went over there,' he burbled pointing to where they had just come from.
'Did you see him interfere with our drinks?'
'No, Sir. I went down that end of the bar to get the beers and when I came back he paid and left.'
'Okay, thanks.'

Martens was starting to giggle.

'I think it's getting to him.'

Zander reached out across the bar and grabbed the barman.

'What did he put in the cans?'
'Not'in', Sir,' he whined with his eyes nearly popping out of his head.
'You're lying! Tell me what he put in the can or you're crocodile bait,' growled Zander as he lifted the slim young barman up off his feet and halfway over the bar.
'I didn't see not'in', Sir.'
'This is your last chance. What did he put in the drinks?'
'Okay, okay. He put a small piece of white stuff in each can.'
'How big?'
'Little,' he spluttered, holding up his little finger and putting his thumb near the top.

'You sure?'

'Yes, Sir.'

'Okay, sorry I shook you up. Have a drink on me,' he declared putting a ten-dollar note on the bar.

'I think we'd better take Marty home, Adam.'

'You're right, Fred, but there's no one to look after him'

'He can stay with me,' chipped in Weenie.

'That's a good idea. Fred, you take him in his truck with Weenie and I'll follow and pick you up in the Bronco. Remember what you told me about parking at Weenie's.'

Chapter 11 Spiked Drink

'I'm all right guys, I just feel a bit light-headed.'
'Right, you're going to the doctor's in the morning.'

Zander helped him upstairs to Weenie's room.

'I don't think he's going to need you for anything other than nursing, Weenie.'
'Okay, Adam. You wanna stay and look after me - I need looking after too.'
'No, not tonight. Here's fifty dollars if you'll give him breakfast in the morning. And if anything else comes up, I'll give you another fifty.'
'Okay, Adam.'

Zander woke to a knock on his bedroom door and the first thing that went through his mind was that Mary wanted some attention.

'Yes,' he moaned.
'Adam, it's Jenny. Sydney Kaba is on the phone, and it sounds urgent.'

Zander jumped out of bed, put on his dressing gown and jogged down the passageway into Stan's study.

'Morning, Sydney, what time is it?'
'6.30. I've just had a report that Martens has been arrested out at Two Snakes. He was attempting to kill Morris. They've put him in the local police post and he will be transferred down here when the day-shift comes on.'

Zander explained about the previous night.

'That might be significant, Adam. I don't know of a drug that has that specific effect although many drugs affect different people in different ways, but LSD can certainly bring the worst out in some.'

'We think it might have been crack cocaine.'

'It could have set him off; we will have to wait and see.'

'Are you going out to see Marty?'

'No, but I'm going to Two Snakes to see Morris. He's been grazed, but nothing serious. Of course as you know he's angry because we took all his weapons away from him even the one that you found and then we let Martens out and Morris has nothing to protect himself. That other pistol that you found was his last chance to protect himself.'

'Yes, point taken, but Marty might have blown his chances of being cleared.'

'That's more than likely. He's really muddied the water now. He won't get out of jail this time; he will be charged with attempted murder.'

'This means we will have to work harder to prove that Morris was responsible for all these murders. Do you have such a thing as a crime of passion in this country?'

'No, but mitigating circumstances would help. If he was using a weapon that was registered to him and he used it in self- defence, he would have grounds for acquittal.'

'That's good enough for me. See you in town later. I would like to speak to Morris once you've had a word with him.'

'Okay, Adam, speak to you later.'

Zander put the phone down and walked back into the living room.

'Coffee?'
'Please, Sis.'

Zander talked over the situation with his sister who suggested that Morris might have picked up another weapon after he was released from jail on the weapons charge.

'Where would he get another weapon though?'

'Adam, a man with his influence would just have to turn up at a homestead and ask for the loan of a gun and they would

151

fall all over themselves to get it from under the bed and give it to him.'

'Yes, I suppose you're right. Guns are out there in great numbers, both legal and illegal. But what on earth was Marty doing out there in the early hours of the morning?'

'From what you were saying about yesterday and last night, I should think he woke up with a thick head and thought to himself "I'm going to sort this out once and for all," collected his gun which was most probably in his truck and then drove out to remonstrate with Morris and it all went wrong.'

'Well, it certainly went wrong and you are definitely thinking a lot clearer than I am. I'm going to have a shower and shave and see if I can get my mind in gear.'

Zander drained his coffee cup and padded off down the passageway to his bedroom.

'Sorry about the early wake-up call, Sis,' he called over his shoulder.

'That's all right; I'll put your breakfast on.'

Zander waded into a full English breakfast and finished it off with a cup of Earl Grey tea. Mary came in and cleared the table and was just leaving when the phone rang.

'I'll get it," called out Zander. 'Hello.'

'Adam! I'm so glad it's you, this is Heather. I didn't want to leave a message. I was going to make up a story about having some new evidence but thank goodness I don't have to; you know how messages get misinterpreted Adam, please come and see me.'

'Yes, of course I will, as agreed next Thursday.'

'Are you able to make it tomorrow morning?'

'No, not at this stage, but if things change, well, possibly.'

'Good, I'll be waiting. Give me a call first. He shouldn't be here.'

'Okay, bye Heather.'

Mary was standing in the doorway watching Zander with an expression of disapproval on her face.

'What did I do?' he retorted hunching his shoulders.
'Nothing,' she declared with a pout.

Zander shrugged and got up from the table.

'Where's Miss Jenny?'
'Gone to the office with Mr Stan.'
'Ah, now I know why you've got a monk on. We're alone and you think I'm going to see Miss Heather. Well I'm not.'

Her face lit up immediately only to turn like thunder when Zander told her he was going to the police station.

'Bye, Mary.'

There was no response, so he went down the steps to the Bronco and was greeted by Winston the gardener.

'I've done a service on the Bronco, Mr Adam.'
'Thank you, Winston,' and then in a whisper, 'Why don't you go and service Mary?'

Winston's head shot back in disbelief but Zander winked and patted him on the shoulder, to which Winston responded with a big toothy grin and a nod of agreement.

'If you say so, Mr Adam.'
'I say so, Winston.'
'Thank you, Sir.'

Zander drove off while Winston called Mary down to the utility room. His reception was frosty at first but she soon gave in to Winston's advances. Meanwhile, Zander went and picked up Oxbee and briefed him on the night's happenings.

'I think the first port of call, Fred, is Weenie's place.'

'You're right. What the hell was she doing, letting him go out in the early hours of the morning?'

'She wouldn't have had much choice if he got physical'

'No, but she could have phoned.'

'You're right; I just hope he hasn't done anything to Weenie'

'No, I don't think he would hurt a woman.'

'Perhaps you're right, but these drugs do strange things to people. That said, he took shots at Morris.'

'Allegedly. In fact so would I if I had been treated like that.'

'Point taken; my attempt at devil's advocate is not working is it?'

Zander and Oxbee went up the steps to Elloween's room and were met by an elderly man, who looked as if he had just got out of bed.

'Wad yah wan?'

'I would like to speak to Elloween please.'

'Down there,' pointing over his shoulder with his thumb like a hitchhiker.

'Let me do the talking, Fred.'

'Fine by me.'

Zander knocked on Weenie's door.

'You in there, Weenie?'

'Yeah, comin'.'

'What's up, Weenie?'

'Nothing, why?'

'Where's Marty?'

'He woke up about four this morning; we had sex, and he left.'

'Where was he going?'

'He say he go home.'

'Was he all right?'

'So, so; he had a headache, which I tried to soothe away, but that turned him on. I expect you know the rest.'

'Is that all there was?'

'Yeah, do I get my fifty bucks?'

'Yes, okay, Weenie. Was he still drunk or acting funny?'

'No, we had good sex, his load come quick. I didn't, but I pretend.'

'Here you are,' Zander declared as he peeled off five ten-dollar notes. 'Did you let him have a gun?'

'No, I don't have gun.'

'Okay, see you later.'

'So, he wasn't drug-crazed, Adam.'

'No, it looks like we've been barking up the wrong tree.'

'He obviously went out to see Morris, but why? They were no longer friends or boss and employee. It wouldn't be revenge; although Marty said he would kill him I don't think he would actually do it. I know Morris had pointed the finger at him but that's no reason to get yourself charged with attempted murder. So why?'

'We're going to have to ask him, Fred. He won't be in town for another hour or so let's go and have another word with the vicar and see if we can utilise his lawyer again.'

As Zander turned on to the main road he saw Superintendent Kaba go by in the opposite direction.

'Do you think that Kaba senior is on the take, Fred?'

'It certainly looks like it. When you get to his rank and seniority, there are not many who will question your integrity.'

'They don't get paid that well so how does he get to drive around in a Pontiac like that?'

'Perhaps he is on the take or has independent means.'

'I think we are going to have to put the word to the commander so that he can have a word with the PM.'

'I don't think he would want to get involved in that sort of thing, Adam, unless it affected the military in some way.'

'You're right again; I've not got my thinking-cap on straight today - maybe I drank some of that drugged beer last night.'

Oxbee just laughed.

Adam and Fred went to the vicar's manse and got his agreement to use his lawyer. They then proceeded to Police

155

Headquarters and the desk sergeant took them to the cell where Martens was being held; the vicar's lawyer was already there.

'That was quick - we've only just left the vicar.'

'Ah! I phoned the attorney from the Police Post so he was here to meet me,' pronounced Martens.

'Morning, gentlemen. I'll have him out of here in a couple of hours,' stated the attorney as he left.

'What happened, Marty?' Zander asked.

'I went out to see Morris to find out why he was trying to get me locked up. I've done him no harm.'

'What about taking his girlfriend?' Zander said.

'I didn't do that - he'd already lost her and he knows it. I think Elly found out something about him, which she didn't like.   She was just looking for some way out and found it, whatever it was.'

'You mean Elly left him and he didn't know the real reason?' Zander asked.

'Exactly. If I ever brought the subject up, she would just cut me dead. She would not discuss it under any circumstances. The rumour was that it was the vicar's wife; Elly knew about the other women but it didn't worry her. That might have been the excuse but not the real reason.'

'Why didn't you tell us this before?'

'Because, like now, there is nothing to tell. I don't know what happened.'

'But it would have indicated that there might be a motive,' stated Zander.

'But there isn't, is there?'

'No, I suppose you're right. Well, what did you find out before you tried to kill him?' Zander asked.

'I didn't find anything out because I didn't get to see Morris. The nurse let me in and she told me Morris was in the shower, and asked me if I would like some coffee. I thanked her and she ushered me into his office and gave me a pot of coffee. She said it had just been made for Morris and she would make another pot for him. The next thing I know is, I wake up handcuffed, and that's it. I've been accused of attempted murder.'

'You obviously think the coffee was spiked?' asked Oxbee.

'It had to be. I remember taking a gulp of coffee and then nothing until I woke up in cuffs.'

'It looks as if Morris has arranged to have himself shot again, Fred. What do you think?'

'Could be, and if that's the case, the nurse is bound to be in on it. I think if we have her arrested on suspicion of administering knock-out drugs to Marty, we might just be able to get something out of her.'

'That's quite possible.'

'Are you going to get me out of here?'

'The short answer is no. We can't yet because they haven't cleared the story and it was your gun they found. However, your lawyer reckons a couple of hours,' said Zander.

'Okay, but my gun was in the glove box in my truck.'

'When the gun was picked up, it had just been fired and Morris has a flesh wound to his right arm. They've removed the bullet from the bedroom wall.'

'If I intended killing him why is it he is still alive? I couldn't have missed from where I'm supposed to have shot him from, and how did he stop me from killing him?'

'You were overpowered by the nurse and she knocked you out using a book as a club.'

'I've got no bumps or bruises.'

'Apparently she chopped you in the side of the neck with the book.'

'This is all mighty strange; I had no intention of killing Morris. Why don't you see if there are any fingerprints on the glove box other than mine? Another point is that I'm left handed so if my right hand-print is on that gun, then it could prove that it was a plant. I couldn't hit a house with my right hand and I did not take that gun out of my truck.'

'Okay, I'll get that done. Adam, are you staying here? If so I'll get someone to come with my bag of tricks and pick me up.'

'Yes, that would be fine; I would like to go over a few things with Marty. Perhaps you would like to check with ballistics as well.'

'Okay, I'll leave you with Marty.'

Oxbee turned and left the cell, and Zander sat on the chair opposite Martens who was sitting on the bed.

'Marty, what on earth possessed you to go out to see Morris?'

'I thought I might be able to persuade him to stop all this killing. There is no doubt in my mind now that he is behind all this. I don't know the motives, but I know it's him.'

'I just wish you had evidence, Marty.'

'Me too, but we have little chance of that with me locked up. He thinks he's home and dry.'

'I think the best thing we can do is let him think that. I hope arresting the nurse won't jeopardise that. On second thoughts I'll get Sydney to question her when we have some more information from ballistics and Fred has checked the fingerprints.'

'I don't think Morris knows her that well, Adam. She only came in after he was shot the first time.'

'Maybe she didn't know him, but she does now. She was in bed with him the morning after the shooting.'

'He does have a way with women. He seems to be able to charm almost all women.'

'Do you think the nurse teamed up with him to knock you out?'

'He most probably doctored the coffee and she delivered it, not realising she was getting involved. When he told her what she had done, she had little option. Perhaps it was entrapment or maybe she wanted to do it because he made her some promises. As a wealthy man he has plenty of scope for soliciting help.'

'Well, we've covered the speculation and facts of which there are few, and it all points to another set-up, and you're the target, Marty. I'm afraid I'm going to leave you now but your lawyer will have you out of here soon, I'm sure. I'll see you later, and this time, when you get out, stay away from Morris.'

Zander went through to the duty sergeant.

'Is Chief Inspector Kaba in his office?'
'No, Sir.'
'Thank you,' Zander turned to leave as Kaba walked in. Sydney, my friend! The very man. Have you questioned the nurse yet?'
'No, other than the initial questioning carried at the scene by the investigating sergeant there has been no formal statement or questioning.'
'Good, I think we need to let Morris think he is no longer a suspect until we have something more concrete.'
'Okay, do you think this will stop the killing?'
'Yes exactly. There is no one other than Marty who Morris would want to eliminate. If we question the nurse he might see that as a threat and bump her off.'
'Okay, but we're going to have to question her eventually.'
'Yes, I accept that, but when we do, she will most probably be locked up at the same time as him as an accessory. Anyway, Fred has gone off to check Marty's truck for fingerprints. Marty thinks someone took the pistol out of the glove compartment and might have left their prints while searching.'
'He could be right because ballistics have confirmed that the bullet was fired from Marty's gun, but there were no prints on it other than Marty's, but of course they could have been put on by wrapping his hand around the trigger and pistol grip while he was unconscious.'
'I agree, and there is another point though; check to see which hand the prints came from. He's left handed; also check if there is any residue on his hands after firing the weapon. I think this is significant and I believe it will show this was a plant.'
'That is certainly an important factor; just let me do some checking.'

Kaba went to the desk sergeant's phone and phoned the coroner's department.

'Good morning, Sir George. That preliminary report on Martens, do you know if it was his right or left hand prints on the gun and did we check for residue on his hands? We did - good, and the outcome? Thank you very much indeed, Sir George,' he said and put the phone down. 'Right-hand prints and no residue,' declared Kaba with a beaming smile.

'That's enough to have Marty released don't you think?'

'Most definitely. I will speak to the public prosecutor and get him released. I don't want to ask my brother.'

'Have we enough to arrest Morris though?'

'No, I don't think we have. There is too much uncorroborated evidence at this stage and if we arrest him now and he is released again, his attorney will be on us for harassment. I don't want to move until I can nail him. If we can link the nurse to the truck or better still, link Morris to the truck, then we are getting somewhere.'

'That would be the icing on the cake but that would only get him for perverting the course of justice.'

'You are absolutely right, and I want him for murder and I want to see him hanged. It's coming together and we just have to be patient. I don't want one of his slick attorneys getting him off on a technicality. I will make a point of being there when he takes the long drop,' said the chief inspector with a considerable amount of venom.

'I'm not so sure I want to see the hanging but knowing justice has been done will be enough for me. The motive is what escapes me right now, but I have an inkling that it was something Elly found out - or maybe he's a psychopath. I have many theories but they all seem to lead up blind allies.'

'In my opinion, Adam, motive is not too important at this stage. We know who is responsible and a motive is an aid to finding a suspect. We have Morris and it's only a matter of time before we get him.'

'Yes, but if we are to convince a jury we need to have a motive that fits with the evidence. He didn't commit all the murders, Sydney.'

'No, but all those who have committed murder are either dead or in jail as in the case of the hunters.'

'Have we been able to get anything out of those two?'

'Not much, they haven't admitted they killed him but they admit to having been tipped off that he was going to talk to the police about their illegal hunting activities.'

'I don't suppose they are going to tell us who tipped them off.'

'No, they just heard about it on the grapevine.'

'Have you got that list of boat and light aircraft owners who didn't come forward about being approached?'

'Yes, there are about twenty. I'll get you a copy.'

Zander scanned the list and noticed Morris was on it and so was Arnold Day.

'Did you notice Arnie Day on the list Sydney?'

'Yes, we've questioned most of them; all have reasonable excuses for not informing us. Some deny all knowledge but we know that is not the case. Leave Morris alone for the time being; we have enough to be going on with as far as he's concerned.   However, we haven't questioned Arnold Day about the approaches yet.'

'I'll look into that for you, Sydney, if you don't mind.'

'Okay, if it gets difficult let me know.'

Zander phoned Heather.

'Heather, would you like to have lunch with me?'

'Yes, of course, I would love that. Where?'

'What about the Majestic today?'

'Yes, that would be wonderful.'

'All right, see you at one if that's okay.'

'Yes, see you at one.'

Zander went to the records department within the police headquarters to have a look at the files on Day. There was a lot of inconclusive and circumstantial evidence arising from explanations he had given the police during his many interviews.   He had two boats and a light aircraft but the movement records were sketchy. Zander finished looking at the records and then phoned and booked a table at the Majestic.

'Okay, Sydney, I've one or two things to do. Let me know about the truck dusting, won't you.'
'Yes, of course.'

Zander went out to the Bronco which was parked in the police compound. There were numerous trailer-mounted patrol boats, cars, Land Rovers and motorcycles parked in the compound due to lack of funds to operate them. The police sentry let him out and gave him a smart salute as he drove off.

He made a point of arriving at the Majestic ten minutes early to ensure the table was in a secluded area of the dining room. He ordered a drink and sat at the bar and looked out over the harbour, keeping an eye on the road outside. He saw Heather arrive and park her car so he put his drink down and went into the reception area to meet her.

Chapter 12 Heather's Relationship

'Hello, Heather, lovely to see you; you look stunning.'

'Thank you, Adam. What brought this invitation on?'

'I just felt we ought to have a talk before I carried out some formal business. I need to have a talk to your husband about his business, mainly the export element.'

'I know nothing about the business other than he exports furniture from our factory.

'Let's go through to the dining room. What would you like to drink?'

'Dry martini, please.'

He ordered Heather's drink, picked up his own and walked through with her to their table. He held the chair for her as she sat down and then the waiter arrived with her drink and the wine list. Zander ordered a bottle of wine and then took the menu.

'I'm famished. I'm going to have the rack of lamb. What would you like?'

'I think I'll have the lobster.'

'Good choice,' declared Zander as he summoned the waiter.

He said nothing until the waiter had moved away.

'Heather this is a bit delicate. I hope you are not involved, but do you think Arnie has anything to do with drug-running?'

Heather looked suitably shocked.

'No. You astound me. What possessed you to say such a thing?'

'I have information that he has been approached by some unsavoury people with regard to his light aircraft and boats.'

'Well, he has never mentioned it to me. Mind you, he never mentions anything to me anyway, only when I ask and that's rare. I asked the other day if he could supply some details of furniture that was available for a friend in the States, but he said he was too busy. I know he's not that busy because the maid told me that her cousin, who's a carpenter, had been laid off.'

'Do you think he has moved into some other commodity?'

'Like drugs you mean?'

'No, not necessarily, but perhaps vegetable or oranges; bananas or other fruits?'

'Yes, come to think of it there're about fifty mango trees at the back of us and he had a team of men up there picking them a couple of weeks back. But other than that I wouldn't know.'

'How many did they pick?'

'I don't know exactly but there were five or six truck-loads.'

'Well, it's good of you to tell me that. Is there anything else you can tell me?'

'No, we never discuss business. I've never been involved in it at all.'

'If this turns out the way I think, it will mean he's going to go to prison.'

'For shipping mangoes?'

'No, it's not the mangoes; it's what goes in the crates with the mangoes.'

'Are you saying he sends drugs in the mango crates?'

'That is a distinct possibility.'

'That can't be right.   He wouldn't do a thing like that.'

'Has he spent more time at the office than usual recently?'

'No, but he has had a few more fishing trips than usual - particularly four and five-day trips.'

'Does he bring any fish back?'

'Well, yes, but he doesn't bring them to the house. He usually sells them to the market or gives them to the local orphanage or something like that.'

'Is that what he tells you?'

'Yes, well, I wouldn't know any different, I've only ever been fishing with him once and I got so bored I didn't go again.'

'But you go to the cayes most weekends?'

'Yes, but he often leaves me there and goes off for the day fishing and picks me up in the evening or sometimes the next day.   I enjoy lying about in the sun and doing a bit of snorkelling.'

'Where does he go?'

'I've no idea. Sometimes he goes for tarpon; sometimes for marlin or swordfish, and he has brought the odd barracuda back for the barbecue. That's normally pre-planned and we have guests out on those occasions.'

'Do you know the men he goes with?'

'Yes, they've been going fishing together for years.'

Zander slid her a piece of paper and a pen.

'Would you jot down some of their names?'

'Yes, of course, but for goodness sake don't let him know you got them from me. He would kill me.'

'He won't do that and he won't know where I got the names. Could you also put a "B" for boat and an "A" for aircraft against each name if they own either or both.'

'They all have boats and seem to take it in turns because Arnie sometimes leaves ours at the island and goes with someone else. I see it as totally innocent - just a bunch of guys going fishing.'

Zander cast an eye over the list and he could see that all the men on Heather's list were also on Sydney's list, but only one had admitted being approached. The rest were in the "denied all knowledge" category.

'I think Arnie has a lot of explaining to do, Heather. Please be honest with me; have you been involved in this at all?'

'No, I have not.'

'You do realise I'm going to have to speak to him and you know better than I do how fiery he can be. When is the best time to approach him?'

'In the evening after dinner, as long as he hasn't had too much to drink'

'This is obviously going to affect you. Will you take steps to protect yourself?'

'I don't know how I can. If he went to prison I wouldn't know what to do. Business-wise he has managers in the factory, but Arnie deals with all the sales and exports.'

'We'll cross that hurdle when we come to it and I will give you as much warning as possible. If he tries to do a runner because you have warned him, I shall be less than pleased.'

'There's no chance of that. If he has sunk that low then he must face the consequences. Ten years ago I would have defended him fiercely, but not now. It's more or less over between us and he knows it. He still puts up some resistance, as with Nigel the other evening, but that was just pride. He still frightens me.'

Their meal arrived and they began to eat.

'Do you really think he is involved in this drug thing?'

'It looks that way from the information I have. I'm not sure how deeply he is involved; he might just be ferrying the drugs out to a ship beyond the reef or he could be packing it in crates and sending it by ship or flying it to Mexico or one of the Caribbean islands. Of course all this is pure speculation, and until I speak to him I don't know for sure.'

'Will you be able to get to see me before next Thursday?'

'Maybe, but what with the Elly van Dam case and now the drug-running case, I'm kept pretty busy.'

'Not too busy to have lunch with me.'

'I would enjoy having lunch with you at anytime and today I wanted to let you know what I was doing and find out your feelings.'

'I have mixed feelings; I don't know whether I want him locked up or left alone, Adam, I really don't.'

'I'll come and see Arnie soon. That won't be much fun for you but it has to be done.'

'We're not going to the cayes this weekend.'

'I will drop in as soon as I can, maybe before the weekend.'

'Okay, I don't think he has any plans to go out after dinner at all this week.'

They finished their meal and Zander saw Heather to her car. He then went to the Bronco and as he climbed in he got the impression he was being watched from a large Pontiac about two cars away. He pulled away from the kerb and kept an eye on the rear view mirror. Zander was getting used to the hard-packed sand streets and had become quite adept at dodging the potholes; however, he found this rather difficult while watching the mirror at the same time. He headed for the vicar's house in the hope of catching the vicar's wife at home. Zander pulled up outside the manse and was surprised to see the maid at the doorway by the time he reached the entrance.

'I'm afraid the vicar is not in.'
'I'm looking for Mrs Bray.'
'Missy Jessica has gone to see Mr Morris; he has been shot again, so he needs some help.'
'Thank you very much, goodbye,' declared Zander

He retreated to the Bronco looking each way to confirm that there wasn't a shadow. He recently had the feeling that someone was following him but had not seen anybody. Zander decided to go back to his sister's.

Jenny answered the phone.

'No, I'm afraid Adam's not here at present. Can I take a message?'
'There's been another murder on the Morris property.'
'Okay, I'll get him to call you when he gets in. Goodbye.'

Jenny went down to the utility room to see Mary and find out where her brother was and when he was likely to be back. The sound of a vehicle approaching sent her back up to the house and when she looked out of the window she saw the Bronco swing into the drive. Zander leapt up the steps two at a time and his sister opened the door, as he was about to put his hand on it.

'Hi, Sis, you look worried.'
'I am. There's been another killing out at the Morris place. Would you call Sydney; he's in his Land Rover on the way to Two Snakes. If you phone headquarters they will patch you through.'

167

'Thanks.'

It took Zander a couple of minutes to get through to Sydney and when he eventually got connected the reception was appalling. The only intelligible information to come out of the distorted conversation was that Red Hodson had been killed and his body had been found in the jungle near the new grazing meadow.

'Sis, would you make me some coffee and sandwiches to take with me. I'm going to pop through to my room and have a quick wash and change and then I'm off to Two Snakes.'
'All right.'

Zander threw his clothes in a heap on the floor at the end of the bed and stepped into the shower. The water was refreshing and even more invigorating when he turned the showerhead to rapid massage. He dried himself and dressed in light slacks and shirt and walked back into the dining room as his sister came out of the kitchen with his packed meal.

'Thanks, Sis, see you later.'

Zander took the quickest route by going into Malla and taking the Capitol Highway. He saw the coroner's vehicle at Joe's Joint, so he pulled in.

'Hello, Sir George, are you on your way to the murder scene?'
'No, I'm on my way back from a suicide. I didn't know there had been a murder.'
'Red Hodson, Morris' farm manager, has been killed; his body has been found up at that new meadow they have just stocked.'
'I'd better go on up there; they've most probably called my assistant but Sydney prefers it if I do the crime scene work.'
'I can understand that; he has a lot of faith in your reports.'
'It is good of you to say that and is much appreciated. Most of the time this is a thankless task but don't get me wrong - my

assistant is a perfectly capable person and I know that when I get there he will have covered all the essential aspects. I'm not a one-man band, and although I'm the coroner and the medical examiner, I'm also in charge of forensics, ballistics, pathology and of course scene of crime work.'

'You're obviously always busy.'

'Yes, that's what happens in a Third World country like Vanmalla with little or no money. I must admit that this last spate of deaths is more than we normally have in a whole year.'

'I only dropped in because I saw your vehicle and I didn't know if you had been informed or not. Obviously not. I'm going to head for that clearing now, and not to Two Snakes. I think that might just complicate matters.'

'Right, Zander. I'll see you at the scene.'

Zander turned around in the potholed car park of Joe's Joint and went straight onto the highway. The journey to the clearing was uneventful except that he noticed a police Land Rover parked at the entrance to Two Snakes, but he resisted the temptation to stop and ask what was going on. There were two policemen standing at the entrance to the clearing and the taller of the two walked over to Zander when he stopped.

'Hello, Mr Zander. Chief Inspector Kaba is expecting you - he is over there to the right, about a hundred yards past his Land Rover. He asked if you would park behind his vehicle and walk through, following the tape to where you see the policeman.'

'Thank you, yes, of course. The coroner is right behind me he will need to be told to do the same.'

Zander pulled up behind Kaba's Land Rover and walked through the secondary jungle to the scene.

'Hello, Sydney, what's happened?'

'He's been shot in the back of the head but all the indications are that he wasn't shot here. The assistant coroner is working on it now.'

'I've just seen the coroner and told him about Red. He's going to follow me up.'

'That's good. His assistant is all right but I get the impression he is not as thorough as Sir George is. He might be one of the old colonialists but he's downright efficient.'

'Any idea how long he's been here?'

'Several days; the body has started to decompose and is flyblown.'

'Is it all right if I take a look?'

'Yes, it's not a pretty sight but you are welcome to… Oh, here's Sir George now. You can go up with him and you'll get the handover brief as well.'

'Thanks.'

As they entered the thick jungle, they saw an overgrown path leading through it, but they took a parallel path which the police had made to allow for access without destroying tracks and any evidence on the overgrown path... The assistant coroner briefed them both and then uncovered the body.

'As you can see, maggots and other insects have caused a lot of damage but no scavengers have got to him yet.'

Zander was reasonably prepared for the sight of the body when the black plastic sheet was pulled back, but not the stench.

'Phew, that's putrid.'

'Exactly. One of the disadvantages of being a coroner in the tropics. Bag him up; there's nothing much more we can do here. Has the area been searched?'

'Yes, Sir. There was nothing material found. The cowhand who found the body came this way for a call of nature and discovered the body. There is one other set of footprints other than the cowhand. They are deep prints obviously from someone carrying the body. There are also tyre marks in front of the Chief Inspector's Land Rover, up to about fifteen yards from where the body was found. They are taking plaster casts now of the tyre marks and footprints. Whoever dumped him didn't expect the body to be found so soon. Given a couple more days the scavengers would have got to it and it would have been spread far and wide,' said the assistant coroner.

'How did we know it was the farm manager?' asked the coroner.

'The cowhand recognised him and went back to Two Snakes and told the assistant farm manager who then reported it to the police post, Sir,' said the assistant.

'That will be all for now. We will discuss other matters at the mortuary.'

Zander walked back to Kaba.

'He's in a bit of a mess, Adam, don't you think?'

'Yes, but what do you think he's done to lose his life?'

'My guess is he found out something he shouldn't have. I'm sure he told me he was going away on holiday. That could mean that he thought he was going to get paid off and sent back to the States to keep him quiet. It's turned out the same as all those others who crossed. Morris - they ended up dead.'

'That said, Sydney, I think we should throw caution to the wind now and get that nurse out of the way or she might end up dead too.'

'Yes, I think you're right. Let me radio HQ and see if it was her prints on the truck.'

Kaba called headquarters and found there were several sets of prints in addition to Marty's but none of them belonged to Morris. There were two sets that could belong to women or children.

'Any luck, Sydney?'

'Not yet. We haven't got a record of the nurse's prints. So we can use that as a reason to arrest her if she won't come in for her own protection and keep her away from Morris. We did find a set of Sal's prints though, which is a new twist.'

'I should say so! I think we should question Marty before we say anything to Sal.'

'Yes, I would agree with that. She rarely goes out to Two Snakes these days, and now that Martens has been sacked, she has no reason to contact him let alone travel in his truck.'

'Yes, you're right, but I do want to speak to Sal about her role in the company. I have a funny feeling there is a lot more to Sal than meets the eye.'

'Like what?'

'I don't know yet; I'm still thinking about it. I like her a lot and I don't really want her to be involved in it.'

'We don't choose the players, Adam; they put themselves in the frame.'

'I know that. Is your radio connected to the military net?'

'Well, put it this way, we can re-tune to speak to them on the command net. During operations we carry a second radio, but it's easier for me to contact our headquarters and let them go through direct on the command net. Why; what did you want?'

'Would you ask them to speak to military operations and get Fred on the radio to me?'

Kaba spoke to his driver and had the message passed and within ten minutes Oxbee was on the radio.

'That was quick, Fred. Were you waiting for the call?'

'No, I was in Sir George lab, they came and got me.'

'Will you have a word with Marty and find out if Sal has been in the Truck and if so why? If his explanation seems reasonable, leave it at that but if it sounds contrived, speak to Sal.   But I don't want you speaking to her unless it is absolutely vital - I'm saving her for another day.'

'Okay, Adam. Out.'

Zander turned to Kaba.

'That's that set up.'

'Do you think we should tell Morris about Hodson or do you think he will have found out from his assistant farm manager?' Sydney asked.

'He should know because I believe he is responsible and he might even have done this one himself. We need to find out

172

when Hodson was killed and once we get that information;
we'll be able to check what alibi Morris has. I do think he
should be told formally though; perhaps you could do that and
pick up the nurse at the same time.'

'Yes, I'll go to Two Snakes now. It's all finished here.'

'Try and get the nurse on her own and tell her that her life is
in danger and see if she will go with you voluntarily. If not, use
the prints as a reason and arrest her. I'm going to have another
try at seeing the vicar's wife. See you later.'

Zander moved off down the track and then on to the highway
and after about ten minutes he came to a clearing at the side of
the road so he pulled over to have his coffee and sandwiches
and to think things over. His mind wandered off the case and
he started to think of his next meeting with Heather and a hot
flush came over him. Zander decided it was time to move on
and see Jessica Bray. He pulled up outside the manse and was
met by the vicar.

'Hello, Adam, what can I do for you?'

'I was hoping to have a word or two with Jessica?'

'I'm afraid she's not here at the moment. Can I help you?'

'No, not really, I wanted to ask her about her shooting
prowess. Is she a good shot?'

'Well, I don't know exactly. I do know that she goes to the
ladies' shooting club. It's encouraged out here - most
households outside the camp have a gun of some sort in the
house, and burglary is commonplace. As to how well she
shoots, that is another matter - taking horses to water and all
that.'

'Point taken. I will speak to her later. Bye for now.'

Zander drove round to the police headquarters to see Oxbee
and during the journey he pondered on how the vicar's attitude
had changed.

He asked at the desk for Oxbee.

'He's in the forensic department, Sir,' replied the Desk Sergeant.

He went through to the small forensic department, which also housed ballistics and came under Sir George's control.

'Any news, Fred?'
'Yes, I've had a word with Marty and he confirmed he gave Sal a lift into town the other day.'
'I'm glad about that, as I haven't made up my mind how I'm going to approach her as yet. What about the other prints?'
'One set, possibly female but not yet identified.'
'I think Sydney is bringing the nurse in for her own protection so we can check her prints then. I'm sure they're hers,' said Zander.
'It would make sense. With Hodson dead she is most probably next and if she knows more than just about the Martens incident, then we're in with a shout.'
'I've been trying to see the vicar's wife for days now, Fred, and she's always out or unavailable. Have you seen her?'
'No, but I know she has the hots for Morris; that's the inside story from the army wives' club.'
'Mrs Bray is not the only one; there's a list longer than two netball teams. I get the impression she thinks she is special and if she knew there was any serious competition, I think she might get agitated. She most probably accepts the wife back in the U.S. and perhaps Sal down here. I don't think she had any time for Elly although she had more or less finished with Morris when Mrs Bray started to get interested. I'm only surprised Morris hasn't been killed by one of the jealous husbands or at least beaten up.'
'You have obviously gone into greater detail than I thought.'
'Yes, quite a bit and I'm going to go into a great deal more tomorrow. I'm going to have a look around Hodson's place; Sydney's boys had a look today but found nothing of significance. They've sealed it off but I'm sure there's a link between him and those illegal skins.'

Chapter 13 Drug Flight

Zander phoned Kaba.

'Sydney, I'm going out to have a look over Hodson's place first thing in the morning. Is there anything in particular you would like me to look at?'

'Yes, go through his files see who he knew. See if you can find out what he was doing before he came down here.'

'Okay.'

Zander drove back to his sister's.

'That you, Adam?'

'Yes.'

'Dinner in an hour - that all right with you?'

'Yes, fine, I'm going for a shower.'

Zander took his shower and went back through to the dining room.

'Evening, Stan, how are you?'

'More importantly, Adam, how are you? I haven't seen you for days.'

'Doing pretty good, under the circumstances but I find it difficult to come to terms with all these killings. I know I've often commented in the past about terrorist organisations. "We know who they are, why don't we send in the Special Forces and wipe them out", but I know the rule of law must prevail or we end up being the same as the terrorists or worse. In this case I sometimes feel like taking the law into my own hands.'

'Surely you wouldn't do a thing like that?' Stan said.

'I heard that, Adam Zander, and if your father could hear you talking like that, he would turn in his grave,' said Jenny.

'Yes, Sis, I know, but you must admit this is getting out of hand.'

'Maybe, but I don't want you being hanged for murder.'

'There's no chance of that; anyway if I was to do anything, they wouldn't know it was me, I can assure you of that.'

'Would you like to take your seats please, dinner is ready,' said Jenny.

Jenny joined them at the table and Mary served crayfish tails with a thousand-island sauce followed by beef Wellington, and afterwards they had coffee.

'Adam, would you like a whisky?'

'No thanks, Stan. I'll get a nightcap when I get back if that's all right.'

'Okay,' said Stan.

'That was a lovely meal, Sis, but I must go and see Arnie Day. Oh! I know what I was going to ask you; you know when they were picking those mangoes at the back of Arnie's place, how many truckloads of mangoes were there?'

'I think Mary said six or seven. It was a lot anyway. Why?'

'Hey, I'm the detective and the one who asks the questions. It must be a family trait.'

'Don't go getting yourself into trouble with him.'

'Strictly business. See you later.'

Zander arrived at the Day's house just after eight. He was surprised not to be met by the snarling dog and then noticed it in the corner of the entrance, chewing a bone. He knocked on the door and the maid answered.

'May I speak with Mr Day, please?'

'Do come in, Sir. I will speak to Mr Day.'

She was gone only a minute and returned with a beaming smile.

'Mr Day will see you in the library, Sir. Please follow me.'

Zander was immediately aware that the maid was behaving as if she had never set eyes on him before, and this amused him.

'Mr Zander, Sir,' announced the maid, and she then made a bob curtsey and left.

'Evening, Zander. Have a seat; what can I do for you, old boy?'

'As you know I'm investigating the killing of Elly van Dam.'

'You think I have something to do with that?'

'No, not at all. But I've come across a lot of boat and light aircraft activity and I was wondering if you get involved?'

'What do you mean get involved?'

'Do you transport items in you boats or aircraft?'

'Sometimes. I shift perishable fruit across the country and sometimes over to Mexico.'

'Do you ever take things to the Turks and Caicos Islands?'

'No, it's out of range of my aircraft.'

'They could make it if they island hopped, though, couldn't they?'

'I doubt that, but I suppose it's possible. What are you getting at?'

'I've been getting information that certain aircraft and boats are making trips out beyond the reef with cargo and dropping it off close to or onto a ship that is waiting.'

'Am I being accused of smuggling?'

'No, not necessarily, but perhaps one of your aircraft pilots or a crewmember is doing it without your knowledge'

'Well that's possible but highly unlikely.'

'Surely someone would have picked that up, fuel hours of flying or sailing - that sort of thing,' suggested Zander.

'Who for instance?'

'Well, there you've stumped me. I would think one of the auditors or accountants or someone who keeps an eye on costs.'

'I doubt that they are that meticulous, old boy. I mean to say, they could be covered up as fishing trips, couldn't they?'

'What - the aircraft?'

'Yes, even the aircraft. It could be said that they were being used for spotting large fish like tarpon or marlin prior to or during a fishing trip.'

'Well, I suppose they could. But the reason I say this is because the aircraft and boats have been recorded doing just that,' said Zander.

'Who's been doing the recording then?'

'Now that would be giving away investigative secrets because the local police and customs department are linked to the U.S. Drug Enforcement Agency.'

'Yes, I seem to remember someone mentioning it.'

'Yes, I'm sure you do. Have you been approached with a view to carrying some special cargo?'

'No.'

'That's strange because I've been told otherwise.'

'Well, whoever said that was lying.'

'More or less everybody with a boat or aircraft has been approached, and that includes you.'

'No, you have been misinformed. I have not been approached.'

'Are you playing word games with me, when you know that perhaps you personally have not been approached but someone in the company has?''

'No. When I say no, I mean no.'

'Good, I'm glad you're so certain because that gives me another line of questioning. What about the people that you go fishing with. Are any of them involved or have they been approached?'

'I've no idea and if they have they haven't mentioned it to me.'

Zander decided to try bluffing.

'Did you not pull up along side a ship outside the reef the last time you were out fishing on one of your friends' boats?'

'I think we pulled alongside for water. We had run out of water - yes, that was it; we had run out of water.'

'Whose boat was that?'

'I can't remember.'

'But you can remember that it was water that you pulled along side for. Isn't that the agreed reason that you should give if questioned, amongst your friends that is?'

'That's nonsense. I just happen to remember that.'

'Well, what about crates of mangoes. Do you transport them to ships?'

'Yes, of course we do.'

'Now you're adamant that you supply ships yet when I asked you earlier you said, and I quote, "Sometimes I shift perishable fruit across country and sometimes over to Mexico." No mention of delivering to ships there. Had it slipped your memory?'

'No, it's local and I didn't think you meant local.'

'You know exactly what I meant, and you say, "Yes of course I do", but have you reported this activity to the customs department?'

'There is no need to; there is nothing illegal about exporting mangoes.'

'No, there is nothing illegal in itself but it is illegal if you don't declare it and produce a manifest.'

'There is no need for a manifest for the odd crate of mangoes, is there?'

'I'm afraid that's where you're wrong and you know it. I've looked at the records and you've been formally told to notify the customs department every time you despatch a crate of mangoes.'

'You've done your homework. But I haven't been shipping any mangoes. As I mentioned we only went to get water.'

'Yes, on that occasion perhaps, but within that last couple of weeks you have shipped mangoes so what I would like to know is have you declared them?'

'I haven't shipped any.'

'What happened to the mangoes that were recently picked at the back of your house?'

'They were sold locally.'

'Good. Then you will have invoices for the transactions.'

'Well, yes, I should think so.'

'You only think so but don't you know for sure. Who is responsible for sales and exports in your organisation?'

'I am. I deal with all that sort of thing.'

'Then why aren't you sure about the local sales?'

179

'I am sure about the local sale, but I think they were sold to the market and they don't use paper - it's a cash transaction. That's it, it was a cash transaction.'

'Do you remember the trader involved?'

'No, I'm afraid not.'

'So, now the tax man will be interested because you have no documentation.'

'Well, we do these little deals sometimes.'

'How many crates did you get from those trees?'

'Not many; they're not cultivated they're just wild.'

'That's different from what I hear. I got the impression there were several truckloads.'

'Whoever told you that has got it wrong.'

'Maybe, Mr Day, but you are being less than honest with me. I know you know more than you are telling me, and do you know how I know?'

'No, but I'd like to know.'

'I get my information from many sources. I suppose you've heard of satellite tracking. Well in certain areas all shipping is tracked and when a ship is sitting outside the reef in international waters, the satellite can pick up every visitor to that ship. They can also see trucks travelling along the road and there is not much you can do about it. So, when I say I hear differently, I really mean it. Your fishing trips have been monitored for months so why don't you come clean and tell me all about it?'

'There's nothing to tell - we just go fishing.'

'Where did all those truckloads of mangoes go? Were they packed with cannabis and then loaded on to a ship?'

'I don't know what you're talking about.'

'Thank you for your help, Arnie. I'm going to have a word with the rest of your fishing pals - yes, even the one who reported to the police that he had been approached by someone wanting him to carry special cargo.'

'Albert won't tell you anything.'

'Why? Has somebody stopped him from talking since he first told the police? Your saying he won't tell me anything indicates to me that he actually knows something and is being prevented. I wonder who is behind that?'

'You're bluffing.'

'We'll see when I've spoken to the rest. Would you like to give me a list of the people you go fishing with?'

'Why should I?'

'If you've nothing to hide, why not?'

'All right, if that's what you want.'

Arnie took a piece of paper from the drawer of his desk and a pen from the rack and proceeded to write the names down.

'I was going to ask you to indicate who has an aircraft but having had a quick glance at the list I already know that. Thank you for the information. I'm sure it will help during the case when the court is told that you cooperated with the investigation.'

Zander looked Day straight in the eyes and was immediately aware of the fear. He then looked at his face as a whole and it was white and drawn; Arnie Day was a worried man.

Zander made his farewell and walked back to his sister's to have a nightcap with his brother-in-law.

'Hello, Stan, am I in time for that nightcap?'

'Yes, what would you like?'

'Whisky, water and ice please.'

Stan went to the ornate built-in cocktail cabinet in the corner of the dinning room and poured himself a rum and Coke and a whisky for Zander.

'Plenty of ice, Adam?'

'Please, and top it up with water, thanks.'

'I'm afraid I've gone native; the rum gets to you after a bit. I'd been a confirmed scotch drinker until I'd been here about a month, then I tried a rum and Coke and stuck with it. I suppose one of the reasons was the indifferent water, and for that matter the ice is made with the water. Of course we buy bottled water but it's not the same.'

'I find if I have too much rum, Stan, I end up smelling of the stuff for a couple of days afterwards. It's as if it comes out in the sweat,' said Zander wiping his brow with the palm of his hand then smelling his hand.

'Yes, you're possibly right. I've known people say that about garlic; the body exudes it with the perspiration. How did it go with Arnie?'

'Not that easy. I know you only have a small speed boat, Stan, but have you ever been approached about running special cargo?'

'No, we don't use it that much. We use it to go up the river occasionally and sometimes out to the cayes with the children when they are on holiday from boarding school, but we are not boating people. I've heard that some have been approached and they were more than upset about it.'

'Have you heard what sort of approach they got?'

'Basically they were asked if they were prepared to take a special cargo to a ship outside the reef. If they were interested they had twenty-four hours to phone a number in Florida and leave their name and number and the type of boat, and then they would be contacted. After the twenty-four hour period the phone number was disconnected. I suppose they checked the authenticity of those individuals that called in, and then contacted those that they thought had not been set up by the police and customs department.'

'So, the police and the customs got people to phone in and try and set them up?'

'Oh yes, but they didn't get to find out about it until near the end of the deadline. Next they phoned people they thought might have been approached and were prepared to go along with the scam, and then either get them to phone the number themselves or the customs people used their details and phoned the number for them. I don't know if they got anybody set up but I'm sure these people vetted any replies and anticipated that the later calls might have been suspect.'

'What a strange way to start up an illegal drug-shipping network.'

'Yes, I suppose so, but when you think about it, the law of averages says if you approach enough people you're going to get some that will take up the offer, which is more than they started with.'

'Yes, you're right, but I'm just surprised at the approach. Who would have thought they would have the brass neck to do that?'

'Yes, but when you consider the reasoning, it might have been a genuine effort to muddy the waters. If they actually asked boat owners to transport bananas, mangoes, oranges or whatever to a ship outside the reef, the authorities would monitor that. In a country like this monitoring an activity like that would take all personnel in the customs department and a considerable number of policemen and administrators. That in turn would overstretch them to the point that the real activities of the moving of the drugs could continue unobserved.'

'Yes, I think you're absolutely right. If they've put up a smoke screen like that and the special cargo carriers are being told to accept the flak because they've done nothing wrong other than transport fruit, of course they are right to a certain extent; however, aiding and abetting drug-smuggling is a serious offence, and if people like Arnie have been taking crates of mangoes out to these ships as a cover for other activities, they will be in just as much trouble anyway.'

'Somehow I don't think that's the case. These gangsters have some enterprising attorneys backing them. This is not just some ad-hoc flash-in-the-pan organisation. They knew the police and customs were clamping down on the light aircraft flights so they are trying to distract the attention.

'Well, they've started the flights again because Sydney was mentioning it the other morning. They are quite ingenious; they've sorted out the inconvenience of the fifteen-foot poles by cutting them off at ground level and inserting a snug-fit pin for the pole to drop over; they then take them off and lay them down while the plane comes and goes.'

'They seem to have it buttoned up. What d'you think can be done about it?'

'I think the first thing I'm going to have to do is get Sydney or the customs to arrest Arnie for taking mangoes out to these ships, which I think he's been doing. It might mean that we could only get him for shipping fruit out without a manifest, but if we get him in a cell, we will then see who pops out of the wood to defend him. Then if we arrest somebody else on the same charge and see who defends him, we can do some background investigations on the lawyer and I think there will be a link with one of the drug cartels. If not we arrest another one, and so on, even if it means arresting all Arnie's fishing pals. I don't think it will come to that because I think Arnie will come clean. I got the impression when talking to him earlier he was keeping his powder dry.'

'What do you mean by that?'

'He knows more than he's saying because he is confident he's done no more than take a few mangoes out to a ship. He will most probably say he took them out as a gift or goodwill gesture and think he's on safe ground. We have to come up with a plausible reason to arrest him as a result of those crates of fruit.   We need to put the shits up him to get him rattled.   I don't know enough about customs and excise, and in particular export rules, to suggest anything, but I'm going to get Sydney on to it first thing in the morning.'

'Saying that, Adam, I'm going to have to go to bed.'

'Yes, me too. See you tomorrow, Stan, and thanks for the stimulating conversation. It's got my mind racing to such an extent that I most probably won't be able to sleep.'

That was not the case; within minutes of getting into bed Zander was asleep. He woke before dawn and couldn't get back to sleep so he decided to set out early for Two Snakes. It was still dark when he left and he hadn't gone more than six miles on the Capitol Highway when he came across a roadblock. Zander was three cars back from the barrier. He got out of the Bronco and walked up to the barrier.

'What's going on?'

'There's been an accident just around the corner. A timber lorry has turned over on its side,' said the policeman.

Zander thought of drug planes.

'How long is it going to be before they clear it?'

184

'They say about another twenty minutes.'
'Thanks, I think I'll go back to town.'

Zander drove back towards town and as he did so he heard the purr of a light aircraft engine. Zander then knew that he was right; that was a drug plane and the roadblock was manned by a policeman. He decided he had to go and see Sydney. He continued his journey to town. The early-morning traffic was having difficulty negotiating the potholes in the main street as a torrential downpour had flooded the streets causing vehicles to splash water over each other making driving difficult. Dashing into the police headquarters Zander got a little wet as he caught the tail end of the storm.

'Is Chief Inspector Kaba in yet?' he asked the Desk Sergeant.
'Yes, Sir, Mr Zander, Sir. He's in his office.'

Zander went down the corridor and up the short flight of steps to Kaba's office on the mezzanine floor. He was about to knock the door when Kaba opened it.

'Morning, Sydney. Is driving in bad weather - in a tropical storm and poor visibility - part of the driving test out here?'
'We don't have a driving test.'
'Oh! That shuts me up. Did you know there was a drug collection by plane this morning?'
'No. Where?'
'At about the six-mile stone on the Capitol Highway.'
'Are you sure?'
'Yes, the operation had all the hallmarks we discussed including a convenient accident at this side - a timber lorry overturned, so I was told. I was on my way to see Hodson's place but didn't make it so I came straight here There was a policeman manning the roadblock.'
'Really, did you get his name?'
'No, but I got his epaulet number. It was 2244.'

'We don't have any four-digit numbers starting with two; all two-thousand numbers have been allocated to the fire service.'

'It was obviously phoney, then; I think you're going to have to do something about it, Sydney.'

'I don't know what I'm going to use for manpower. I'm going to have to turn it over to the customs department again, but I hate handing over control to them.'

'Well, I don't think you have control at present - I think the drug-runners have.'

'We are certainly not making much of an impact.'

'I went to see Arnie Day last night and I think he's hiding something. I know he's taking mangoes out to the ships but is there anything we can get him on?'

'There might be on the customs side. Why?'

'If we arrest him for evading something or other on the export side, we could get him in a cell and see who defends him. I think approaching the boat and aircraft owners was a scam to tie up your resources monitoring those movements, while they started the flights again moving the real drugs.'

'I will put customs and excise onto it right away. Thanks, it's a good angle.'

'Thank my brother-in-law; it was his idea.'

'I will next time I see him.'

'I will leave that with you, Sydney; I'm going to have a word with Sal Klug.'

'Okay, Adam, see you later.'

Zander drove the Bronco across town to Morris' office; he had to be careful because driving was still hazardous. There was no space outside Morris' office so he parked outside the Majestic and walked back and headed straight for Klug's office.

He knocked and walked in. Her office was next-door-but-one to Morris' and it had windows that overlooked the harbour, which impressed Zander.

'Your office is better than the boss's Sal.'

'I like sunlight; Jon doesn't.'

'Have you got a minute or two?'

'Yeah, sure, come on in. What can I do for you?'

'I would just like to find out what you do as far as the company in concerned. Do you have a position in the company?'

'You mean without mentioning promiscuity, yes, I'm the Business Manager. I look after administration, transportation and shipping, and I sometimes hire and fire people.'

'Do you have anything to do with Two Snakes?'

'Administration; I also organise the maintenance contracts and pay the wages.'

'Do you physically pay out the wages?'

'No, I authorise the collection of the money from the bank, confirm the totals and then release the pay packets. They are then handed out on Friday afternoons.'

'Do you book flights?'

'Yes, private and company. I book private flights and get the company discount.'

'How often does Jon go to the States?'

'Every month or so. He combines visiting his family with business and he visits our office in Miami. He also meets new and potential customers who want to buy our pork, beef and ice cream.'

'Is there much that goes by ship?'

'Yeah, all our meat and livestock.'

'You ship meat to the U.S.?'

'No, most of our meat goes to the Caribbean countries and some to Mexico. However, the business is conducted in the States. Why does this interest you?'

'If you ship a lot of cargo, it's a good cover for other things.'

'Like what?'

'Don't tell me you don't know what I'm talking about.'

'I don't know what you're talking about.'

'Well, Sal, if you had said... "Oh! You mean drugs"... I would have believed that you genuinely didn't know anything about it. However, now I know you know something about it.'

'I do not. I have nothing to do with drugs and nor does the company.'

'You're lying to me and I will prove it.'

'You won't 'cos it ain't true.'

'Well, you won't mind then if I take all the logbooks relating to all the boats and light aircraft, will you?'

'You can't do that; you need a warrant, Adam.'

'Only if you say I can't have them, and you've just stated you're clean so, there should be no objection.'

'I'll have to clear it with Jon. He's not going to like it.'

'Well, that's tough. I would like to see all the fuel accounts and cargo manifests for everything that has been moved by this company in the last year. I also want a list of all dates, times and full details of all trips out of the country by members of the company. And I mean all, even if it's a cowhand visiting his mother in Mexico.'

'You can't do this.'

'Oh, but I can and if you are saying no, then I will be back with a warrant and a team of auditors.'

'What's got into you? What have we done wrong?'

'Nothing, I hope, but I have a sneaky feeling that not everything you do as a company is legitimate.'

'What makes you say that?'

'Have you ever shipped endangered species animal skins to the U.S.?'

'No.'

'You know damn well you have because I've spoken to the hunters and they send their skins to you and you send them to the U.S. with your cowhides, which are going for processing.'

'I know nothing about that.

'So if I speak to the taxidermist in Texas where you send your entire annual collection of wild and endangered animal skins, you won't object?'

'Where did you get all that crap?'

'It's not crap, Sal, and by the expression on your face when I mentioned Texas, you know I know what I'm talking about.'

'You might know what you're talking about, but I don't.'

'Yes you do, and if you don't start talking fast I will tell Morris you told me. You might get what Elly got for knowing the same thing?'

'Elly didn't know about the skins.'

'Ah! So you do know about the skins.'

'Well, yes, but it's only small scale; we do about a hundred a year.'

'Well, if just ten of those are puma skins, you are contributing to the destruction of a species.'

'Bullshit, it's only a few.'

'There are only a few pumas left and with the trade you supply, you will eventually destroy the wild life of this world.'

'What the hell's it got to do with you? You're supposed to be investigating a murder, not snooping around our company.'

'If you remember, Morris gave me free rein to go anywhere.'

'He didn't expect you to go looking into this sort of thing.'

'I'm sure he didn't. He didn't know my reputation but he tried to employ me and buy me off at the same time. You say Elly didn't know about the skins and you're most probably right but she knew about something else because that's what got her killed.'

'That was nothing to do with the company. That was a greedy cowhand.'

'You might say that but you know it's not true. You know what she knew, and more, so if I were you, Sal, I would seriously consider my position. The shit is going to hit the fan shortly and some of it is going to land on you.'

'Bullshit, you're bluffing. You've nothing on me.'

'You can think what you like, Sal, but I'm about to wind this thing up, and remember, it was the U.S. Embassy that asked me to investigate this case. If I tell them about your skin trade, you're in hot water and you will have difficulty explaining those one hundred skins. If I throw them a curved ball, like, Valence's flight was booked through your company and he's a hit man, what do you think that would mean?'

'I'm not going to say any more until I've spoken to Jon Morris.'

'I'm sure you will, but just be aware I know about your little game and it won't be long before everybody knows. Now may I have those logbooks and the fuel account?'

'No, you can't. Get a warrant.'

'I might just do that and turn this place upside down.'

Chapter 14 Vital Written Evidence

As Zander walked out of the office he could virtually feel the knives in his back. It did not worry him though because he had got what he wanted and that was an admission that they were making illegal shipments. He went back to police headquarters to see Chief Inspector Kaba.

'Sydney, good afternoon.'

'Hello, Adam. You seem exceptionally cheerful.'

'Yes, I've just got Sal to admit that they ship skins to the U.S. illegally.'

'It's not illegal to ship skins.'

'It is when they are from endangered species.'

'She admitted that?'

'Yes, I bluffed her. I remembered Otis saying there was a taxidermist in Texas so I plucked that out of the air and threw it at her and she took the bait. Rather than admit shipping drugs, which I'm convinced they do, she indignantly admitted shipping only one hundred skins a year.'

'Well, there won't be any more of them moving for a bit. She will put a stop to that if that's what's been going on.'

'Oh, yes they've been doing it, and they will stop it because it's small change, but she won't be able to stop the drugs because of the demand. They might change the schedule but it will keep moving until we stop them. I also told her I would most probably be back with a warrant to see all her logbooks and fuel account.'

'How are you going to get a warrant?'

'I was hoping you could arrange that.'

'I don't think I can, not at this stage. I would need evidence and facts to put before a judge to get a warrant; it's a serious accusation.'

'Are you saying you are going to do nothing about it?'

'No, I'm not. All I'm saying is these things take time. You admit you bluffed her and that's the first thing their attorney will recognise and they will stonewall.'

'They will stonewall until they've tied all the loose ends up you mean?'

'Yes, that's right. The other thing that might have slipped your mind is that we are dealing with ruthless people and you've just stirred up a hornets' nest. I would be careful, Adam; I think you should have Fred Oxbee with you all the time. These people mean business.'

'Thanks for the warning, but, the simple fact that you have given it surely shows that there is sufficient concern on your part to do something about it. Why don't we go in there and look at everything; people are getting killed left, right and centre. Surely we have a legitimate right, in fact a duty, to investigate this company?'

'Yes, we have, but if I want to keep my job, we have to do it by the book, so we need a little more substantial evidence and information. I have also been advised that another agency is looking at many aspects of this company and that I should not jeopardise their investigation. Klug's confession to moving some skins is hardly reason enough to turn them over. I doubt we would find much anyway as it is most probably kept separate from the legitimate side of the business. The fact that you have given them the tip off will ensure that any incriminating evidence will be secreted, and that probably happened before you left the property.'

'I still have difficulty in understanding your reluctance to investigate.'

'It's not a reluctance to investigate the company. There are mitigating circumstances and you must accept that they will be investigated but we have to get it right. If we go in there, even with a warrant, we won't find anything that will stick. Their legal team would have us tied up with harassment charges within minutes. They have some powerful people on their side so we need to be absolutely one hundred percent correct when we go in, and mark my words, we will be!'

'Well, thank you for that. You've convinced me you're right and I was being head-strong.'

'You know I'm right, and I'm also getting low on manpower. However, I will get the customs department to look into the shipping and skins activities. This might be a Third World country, but we still have laws and rules.'

'I'm sorry, Sydney, you're right; I did get a bit carried away. I'm going out to Hodson's place and have a mooch around.'

'Take Fred with you. The army have been good enough to assign him to you so use him; you need to watch your back.'

'Okay.'

Zander phoned Oxbee and went to the camp to pick him up.

'Sorry about this, Fred, but I've upset the apple cart and Sydney thinks Morris will try and have me bumped off. He most probably won't be as friendly towards me as he was when we first met.'

They drove out to Two Snakes and during the journey Zander made a point of checking the area where he was told there had been an accident. There was no evidence of an accident whatsoever but there were signs that a plane had perhaps landed and taken off because the yard-wide strip of sand on either side of the road for over a hundred yards was blown flat and clear compared to the rest, which was littered with foliage, footprints and tyre marks.

'Did you know about these drug pick-up ploys, using planes, Fred?'

'Yes, we get called in when they get wind of one. We've never caught anyone but we've directed the police on the ground and we've found several fields of marijuana, which have been virtually impossible to get to except on foot. We sometimes helicopter in a section to "slash and burn". It's dangerous work and all the workers have run off into the jungle by the time we have landed. They have this habit of firing pot-shots at the troops as they cut down or pull up the plants and burn them.'

They continued the journey to Two Snakes and had great difficulty getting past the gate guard who had been instructed by Morris to let in only the police.

192

'I work for the police," said Zander. "Go and get that policeman standing over there in front of Mr Hodson's house.'
'You can go to him but nowhere else.'

Zander accepted that and proceeded to the house. The policeman unlocked the door to give them access.

'What are we looking for, Adam?'
'I don't know. I just want to shuffle through some of the papers. There has to be something that ties him in with skins or drugs. I'm convinced he knew about it, and that's why he was killed.'

They searched each room on the ground floor but found nothing in the office and yet they looked at virtually every piece of paper.

'That surprises me, Fred. There is no mention of skins and there is nothing in his diary. Another thing that I think is strange is that there is no personal mail.'
'Maybe he keeps it somewhere else.'
'Yes, let's go upstairs.'

Zander went into Hodson's bedroom and there in the corner was a small roll-top desk.

'I think we might be lucky here, Fred.'

Zander rolled up the desk and rifled through the papers.

'This looks interesting; it's a letter to his mother, but on second thoughts it's most probably the first draft as there are lots of amendments to it. This last sentence is a clincher, listen:
- *"Mom, if I die unexpectedly, send this tape to Mr Zander. It's mighty important you do this. His address is on the package. You can listen to it if you wish but not until I'm dead because it might upset you."* Bingo! This is all we need. Her address is here. I wonder if she has been informed. I'm going

to phone Sal. No, perhaps not; would you phone her, Fred, and just ask her if Red's mother has been told and does she have a phone number?'

Fred looked at the company phone list next to the phone and tapped out Sal's number.

'Hi, Sal, it's Fred Oxbee. Has Red's mother been told about his death? She hasn't. Oh, I don't suppose you have her number, do you. You do - I would be grateful if you could let me have it. I'll wait.'
'She's gone to get it from his file.'

Zander grinned.

'Thanks, Sal, you're a darling,' said Oxbee and hung up.
'I'm going to phone from here, Fred. We can't miss out on this.

Zander tapped in the number and a female voice answered.

'Is that Red Hodson's mother?'
'No, this is Red's sister. Mom is not well.'
'My name is Adam Zander. I'm afraid I have some bad news for you. There is no easy way of saying this but your brother has been murdered.'

There was a gasp at the other end of the phone.

'I'm sorry to have to break this news to you this way; your mother has some vital information that Red sent to her recently.   We were just going through his effects down here at Two Snakes and found a copy of a letter he wrote to his mother.'
'Would you give me a minute; I'm just going to get Mom to go and lie down.'

Zander put his hand over the phone.

'Luckily his sister was there, Fred. It sounds as if his mother is unwell.'

'Mr Zander, this is Judy again. I've seen the letter you mentioned but Mom hasn't.'

'Have you listened to the tape?'

'No.'

'Then I suggest you don't, of course you can if you want but I think it might have information that might upset you. What address did he put on the package?'

'Police Headquarters.'

'Would you be able to send it express air?'

'I'll do better than that; I'll bring it myself in the next couple of days. I'll get my sister to come here; she can look after Mom and I'll get a flight as soon as I can.'

'If you let me know what flight that is, I will meet you. If you phone the police and ask to leave a message for me they will see I get it. I'll give you the number. Okay, see you in the next couple of days, Judy. Goodbye.'

'She has the number in the letter, Fred.'

'Red seems to have it all tied up. I just hope the information is what we want.'

'I don't think he would go to all this trouble without having substantial information. He might have been blackmailing Morris and knew he was in danger or maybe he just had some suspicions.'

'Let's hope there is something to nail this lot.'

'Me too. Let's go and tell Sydney the good news.'

They went into Joe's Joint on the way back to the police headquarters and found Rosemarine was busy serving tables and Joe was serving at the bar.

'Afternoon, you guys. What'll it be?'

'Beer for me, Joe, please. You, Fred?

'Coke, please.'

'No rum in it?' Zander queried.

'No, I'm watching your back remember.'

'Yes, Okay. Two cheeseburgers please, Joe. That all right for you, Fred?'

'Yes, just fine.'

Rosemarine went behind the bar and stood behind Joe. She looked straight at Zander and mouthed, "You come lay me Adam."

'Would you do a rush job on the burgers please, Joe, we're in a bit of a hurry.'
'You got it, Bud.'

They carried their beers to a nearby table.

'I saw that, Adam. You lucky bastard. We walk in the place and the best looking woman this side of the city asks to go to bed with you. How do you do it?'
'With a great deal of charisma and practice. No, Fred. Joe collapsed drunk the other night and I helped her carry him back to the bedroom. I then asked her about Morris and got some favourable answers, and after that she then propositioned me and I had great difficulty refusing but I did.'
'I bet you did.'

Rosemarine delivered the burgers to the table.

'Adam, please come and see me. I have some more information for you.'
'Can't you tell me now?'
'No, I get laid first or no information.'
'Okay, Rosemarine, in a couple of days.'

She moved away and Oxbee sat open-mouthed.

'I can hardly believe what I just saw and heard. She deliberately let you look down the front of her blouse so that you could see she had no knickers on and then gives you the come-on and all you can say is "maybe in a couple of days". You must be nuts. I would have been tempted to do it there and then, but for the fact that I'm a faithful and happily married man.'

'I've been busy and she is not the only fish I have to fry.'

'Maybe not, but she's just about the best looking woman there is around here.'

'Joe, are you going to join us for a beer?' called Zander.

'Don't mind if I do.'

Joe came round the bar and sat at their table.

'Anything happening that you want to tell me, Joe?'

'Ain't not'in hap'nin' 'sept old Red bought it.'

'Who did it, Joe?'

'If I noo an' told yah, I'd end up like him.'

'You must have some idea. Come on, who'd you think did it?'

'Same as done the rest.'

'I'll come back in the next couple of days to see if you've found anything out.' Zander stated.

'Okay.'

They finished their burgers and headed back to town and the police headquarters.

'Sydney, we've had a break.'

'That sounds good, Adam. I've been bogged down with paperwork for ages; I can't seem to get on top of it.'

'Paperwork is one of the reasons I left the force.'

'I don't blame you. What have you got for me?'

Zander explained the situation about the tape and the cloud hanging over Kaba seemed to lift instantly.

'We deserve some luck and it couldn't get much better.'

'It could if Morris confesses.'

'Now you're talking miracles.'

'Any result on the fingerprints?'

'Yes, they belong to the nurse. She has refused to talk; Morris has provided an attorney. Before he arrived I explained that we could release her but she would end up like Hodson for knowing too much. She says she needs time to think. So I've

197

given her forty-eight hours; I'm in no hurry now it's almost buttoned up.'

'Yes, with Judy's evidence I think we'll soon have him locked up. Have we heard from Hodson's sister yet?'

'Yes, she's arriving on the midday flight on Monday.'

'Good. Fred and I will meet her and bring her here straight away.'

'I'll book her into the Majestic for a week, which should give her time to arrange things.'

'Thank you. I was wondering - do you think we should do something about Sal Klug?'

'Like what?'

'Perhaps bring her in for her own protection?'

'I don't think she's in danger, Adam.'

'If you say so. I'm going to have an early night Sydney. I'll see you tomorrow.'

'Okay, see you tomorrow.'

Zander dropped Oxbee off at the camp.

'I'll pick you up just before eleven. I have a few things to do first thing in the morning.'

'All right, see you in the morning.'

Zander parked the Bronco in the carport and went into the house.

'Hi, Sis.'

'Hello, Adam, are you in for an evening meal?'

'Yes please. I have a phone call to make - is that all right?'

'Yes, Stan's in the shower, which is where I'm about to go.'

'Me too after I've made this call.'

Zander went into Stan's office picked up the phone and tapped in Heather's number.

'Hello, just returning your call. I'm glad you answered. I was wondering if you would be available for interview tomorrow morning at nine? You will? Good, see you at nine.'

Zander put the phone down and went through to his room where he showered and changed. When he went back into the dining room Stan was holding a cold beer for him.

'How's the case going, Adam?'

'I think it's just about tied up. We have some evidence coming in from Texas on Monday and then it's a matter of sifting through all the facts, making an arrest and then laying some charges.'

'You make it sound easy.'

'No, it's not that. I don't know what this evidence is that's coming in from Texas. I know it's a tape made by Hodson to be passed to me in the event of his death. That makes me think the killer is named. That being the case, he should be locked up shortly after we have had time to decipher the information.'

'You're that sure?'

'I've been sure for many days, just unable to prove it. In the UK he would have been in custody and undergoing intense questioning long ago and then perhaps some of these people needn't have died. The trouble is this person has so much influence that honest hard-working policemen like Sydney are afraid of getting it wrong. I can understand that, particularly when some in the police force are less than honest.'

'Are you saying there are corrupt policemen obstructing this case?'

'Yes, and it's a bit too close to home for Sydney.'

'Surely not his brother?'

'I think so but please keep that to yourself, Stan. I'm sure it will become clear when the sequence of events is brought to light and Morris' company is investigated.'

'How long do you think it will take?'

'I've no idea; there is an outside chance that I might set up business here until such time as the case comes to court. I've been told there might be some form of reward from the U.S. Embassy if I solve the case. They might not like what I've dug up but I'm sure they will do the honourable thing when the time comes.'

Jenny entered the dining room with a steaming dish of vegetables and set it in the centre of the table.

'Would you like to take your seats and Mary will bring the rest in.'

'Adam is thinking of setting up in business here.'

'I won't be a burden, Sis; I'll get a place of my own.'

'There is no need for that straight away; perhaps later if and when you get yourself established.'

'You're always practical and down-to-earth; you never cease to amaze me, Sis.'

'Well, this might surprise you also. Your assignation,' - and she pointed over her shoulder towards the Day's - 'has been noted and is being talked about by certain people,' Jenny whispered pointing down below.

'I hope that's not the pattern of things to come, gossip, I mean.'

'If you put yourself in these situations they will talk about it.'

'Well, I'll give them some more to talk about tomorrow because I'm going there again.'

'I don't mind, Adam. I'm sure you're good for each other and I can't see anybody that matters getting hurt. I don't particularly like him - I think he's an oaf, however, the local circle might get a bit shirty about it if it ever gets that far.'

'Morris has been putting it about for years and got away with it.'

'Yes, but he's been here several years; you're a newcomer.'

'Do you think I should stop seeing her?'

'No, you're both consenting adults but just make sure she knows what sort of flak might ensue. What do you think, Stan?'

'I agree; just be careful of any backlash if he gets to find out.'

'I have an appointment there in the morning.'

'Be careful, that's all I'll say. If you intend staying a little longer and continuing the relationship, it might be worth looking for your own place. We have a bachelor pad at the side of the office block. We use it when we get long-stay visitors

from the States. I'm sure a short-term lease could be sorted out
if that's what you want.'

'Thanks. I'll talk it over with her tomorrow.'

They finished the meal and went to bed. Zander pondered the
consequences of staying on and getting in deeper with Heather
and the thought pleased him and he slept soundly.

Zander was up, showered, dressed and having his breakfast
by eight o'clock. After he had eaten he made a quick phone
call and proceeded to the house next door to see Heather.

The dog greeted him like a long lost enemy. Heather leaned
out and threw down a piece of jerky which Zander gave to the
mangy dog, and, as before, it went off to the corner to enjoy his
titbit. Zander went upstairs and Heather met him at the door.

'We are on our own. The vet is coming at eleven to sort the
dog out and give it some more jabs, but until then we have the
place to ourselves.'

'We have to talk, Heather.'

He had hardly finished talking and she was all over him. She
was kissing him vigorously and he contemplated pushing her
off and doing the talking first, but he couldn't help but respond
in kind. They eventually broke for breath.

'I hope you're not going to say what I think you're going to
say.'

'What do you think I'm going to say?'

'You're leaving.'

'No, the opposite, in fact. I'm thinking of setting up business
here. I'm sure there are one or two openings.'

'Adam, I don't believe what I'm hearing. Have all my recent
dreams come true? Or is this another dream?'

'Are you aware that the servants are already talking about us?
I would suggest this could mean it won't be long before Arnold
finds out.'

'I feel like saying I don't care, but of course I do. I don't know how he's going to react. He can be violent as you saw at your sister's. Oh, my God, what am I to do?'

'If I got my own place, that would stop the servants seeing anything because we could meet there. There are of course other people who might start to tittle-tattle but perhaps we could confront that if it occurred.'

'Of course, that's the answer. No one need know.'

'It's not foolproof but it's a stepping stone.'

'Problem solved. Let's make love,' purred Heather grabbing both his hands and walking backwards through the library to the bedroom.

She pulled him into the bedroom, spun him around and kicked the door shut. Heather was wearing a light-pink flower-patterned dress, which she slipped off her shoulder and it was around her ankles in what seemed like one movement. Zander started to take his shirt off.

'No! Please don't, let me,' she pleaded.

She pushed him back against the wall and kissed him as she undressed him. She unfastened his belt and let the slacks drop. Hitching her thumbs in the waistband of his boxer shorts she eased them part-way down his thighs. Bringing up her right foot and putting it between his legs, she pushed down with her foot taking the shorts with it and when they reached the floor he stepped out of them. Heather had her left hand at the back of his head while the right hand unfastened the buttons of his shirt which she pushed off his left shoulder; he shook his arm out and the shirt hung from his right shoulder which Adam shrugged and the shirt dropped to the floor.

They manoeuvred each other to the bed. The back of his legs bumped against the bed and he stopped, only to be pushed over gently by the continual forward motion of her body. She went down with him and they rolled to the centre of the bed, with Heather ending up on top; he tried to roll over but she pinned him down to the bed. She put her right hand between their

202

bodies and grasped his manhood, which pulsed with desire and need as she guided it into her. She sat up astride him with her knees forward and her hands on his shoulders. Heather shuffled her torso backwards and forwards and he responded by thrusting upwards and gripping her waist. They got out of rhythm with each other so Adam pushed her hands off his shoulders, reached up and wrapped his arms around her neck, and in a crocodile-like roll he ended up on top.

He thrust forward from the hips to achieve full penetration. She moaned as Adam eased his weight up off her and continued with a steady rhythm, which she soon matched. His fingers found the hardened centre of her breast and he lowered his head and caressed this swollen peak with an erotic movement of his tongue. She sensed there was a build up down below as did he. Their breathing quickened and the perspiration had started to build up between their bodies as there was the odd squeak as air escaped. Their rhythm was at fever pitch when the phone rang.

'Shit! Ignore it,' she snapped.

The shrill ring of the phone made him jump and he shuddered into a premature ejaculation and then he collapsed in despair. The phone stopped after two rings.

'That was some bloody good timing. I'm sorry, Heather, that just set me off.'
'That's all right. Could you go just a little longer to help me?'
'Of course.'

The urge had gone and he had difficulty in continuing but he did and Heather thrashed as he increased the tempo. He was starting to get exited again as she climaxed.

They showered together and were caressing each other when they heard a truck pull up and the dog started barking.

Heather hastily left the shower and threw a towel at Zander as she put on a towelling robe and went to the front veranda.

'Put it over there. My husband will sort it out when he returns,' she shouted to the delivery man.

She went back into the bedroom where Zander was partly clothed.

'Sorry about that; it was a delivery of timber. Arnold's going to build a roof over the slipway to keep the sun off the boat. This morning has been a disaster. Well, not quite; we did make it in the end, but the sooner you get your own place the better.'

'Heather, you took the words right out of my mouth. I will put the wheels in motion today.'

'When can I see you again?'

'As soon as I get myself established in town. I'm going to be busy for the rest of the week.'

They heard the delivery truck pull away and she walked to the door with him and handed him a piece of jerky as she kissed him goodbye. He fed the dog and looked back over his shoulder; the expression on her face was that of someone deep in thought. He went back to his sister's and decided to stop for coffee.

Chapter 15 Shoot-out at Joe's

'Is Stan in his office today, Sis?'

'Yes, but not until after lunch.'

'Would you like to give him a call and see if he could arrange that bachelor pad he was talking about last night? I'm going to be tied up the rest of the day and would like him to get the wheels in motion as soon as possible.'

'You've obviously decided that you are going to stay. I'm delighted; however, I'm not so sure about your motives.'

'Business and pleasure, dear sister. I'm convinced there is a role for me here as an investigator, particularly in the field of drugs, corruption and perhaps even gun-running. I think it will involve me touting my abilities to some international organisations, however, that said, with this case under my belt and maybe the thanks of the Prime Minister and the Americans, it should look good on my CV.'

'Well, you've certainly been doing your homework on the business side.'

'And the pleasure side,' said Zander with a smirk.

'Aren't you playing with fire?'

'Yes, and the bachelor pad will hopefully stave off the barbecue for a little longer.'

'Are you serious?'

'Never more serious.'

'Are we talking matrimony here?'

'Put it this way, it's not out of the question as far as I'm concerned.'

'I think we'd better leave it there, before we get too deep.'

'Okay, I'll see you later. I'm picking up Fred then I'm going to have another look at Hodson's place.'

Zander suddenly felt a fine tremor in the pit of his stomach in anticipation of the future. He drove to the camp at Batdove, where Oxbee was waiting for him.

'Morning, Fred. I want to go and have a word with that hunter that killed Otis. I don't know what I'm looking for but I just feel I should question him.'

They arrived at the police headquarters and went to Sydney Kaba's office.

'Morning, Sydney. May we see Olandee?'
'Yes, I'll take you through. Oh! The forensic department has told me that the eight-inch knife that you confiscated had traces of Otis' blood on it. Olandee has been charged with murder.'
'Good.'
'Okay, Miguel. Who promised to pay you for killing Otis?'

Zander asked as soon as they saw Olandee in his cell.

'Nobody. I just got mad 'cause he was gonna talk to the police. We don't do much hunting, but when we do, we get paid well.'
'How'd you get paid your money?'
'Usually cash notes in a package.'
'Where did you get the packages?'
'I picked them up from the farm manager's office most times.'
'And the other times?'
'Red - he bring it over with another order.'
'You got your orders through Red Hodson!'
'Yeah, all of em.'
'Where did the skins go?'
'They were cleaned, packed in salt and went to the killing yard in down town Malla.'
'Why didn't we think to look where the skins went from, Fred?'
'Because it's nothing to do with Morris, I suppose.'
'We searched his office in the house we couldn't find any records.'
'There in the stockyard office, where the cattle are picked up from.'

206

'Thank you for your cooperation. You know that Otis didn't tell the police, and he wasn't going too either.'

'I do now. I was mad and high on drink and wacky baccy. I didn't know what I was doin' anyway.'

'Well, the court will have to decide your fate now.'

Zander got the policeman to let them out.

'Do you know where this killing yard is, Fred?'

'Yes, it's down at the docks.'

'Is it a slaughterhouse?'

'Yes, killing yard is a local expression. A Mexican-based company runs it.'

'Let's go and have a look.'

The day's killing had finished by the time they got there and the butchers were preparing meat for the local market. They spoke to the manager and arranged to go the skin store which was   a concrete-block building with skins packed one on top of another and about three feet deep.

'Don't they go off in this heat?'

'No, they're salted; there might be some deterioration but we ship them before that get too bad.'

'Do you get stock from Morris' farm?'

'Yes.'

'And skins?'

'No skins, we kill and skin.'

'Okay, thanks.'

Zander and Oxbee made their way back to the Bronco.

'We're not going to get anything here, Fred. Let's go and have another look at Hodson's place.'

They drove to Two Snakes and had no problem getting in this time. They went to the bunkhouse and asked where the stockyard was. They found it located to the rear of Hodson's house. It was a series of pens and passageways, all interlinked and gated. There was a vehicle track around the outside, which led to the main gate and the stockyard office was located at the far side near the main gate but obscured from it by several mango trees. The assistant manager was in the office.

'Did you know that Hodson was shipping endangered animal skins to the U.S.?'
'Yes.'
'Have you shipped any?'
'I haven't been asked.'
'Would you if you were asked?'
'Probably - I don't want to lose my job.'
'Where do you come from?'
'Mexico.'
'Where do you keep the records of the skins?'
'They've been taken.'
'Who took them?'
'Don't know; the drawer is empty.'

Zander and Oxbee had a rummage around and Zander eventually found a small notebook down the side of a cabinet.

'This look's like it, Fred,' remarked Zander as he flipped through it. It stopped being used about eight months ago. I think it must have fallen down the side of this cabinet and Red most probably started another notebook. We have enough here; we'll take this with us.'

Heading back from Hodson's they decided to call in at Joe's Joint; it had just turned 7 pm. and the sun had just set creating an orange glow over the horizon.

'Hi, guys,' called out Joe as they walked in, 'what kin I git yah?'
'Beer for me; you Fred?'
'Coke, please.'
'Comin' right up.'

Zander and Oxbee moved to a table at the back of the bar, and sat next to each other facing the entrance. There were only two other people in the bar and they were at a table in an alcove at the end of the bar.

'Adam, there are two small-time gangsters over there to the right of the entrance. One is called Arturo; I recognise the other one but can't think of his name. Arturo is a known drug-dealer; and he's been arrested on suspicion of murder on two occasions. The first time he got off on a technicality and the second time it was circumstantial evidence and he didn't have an alibi - he was still in custody and had been charged with murder. He suddenly remembered where he was when the old lady got her head smashed in and her money and valuables stolen. He said he'd been drinking and had had too many, and his three friends came forward to say that he was with them. His lawyer inferred he had had an alcoholic blackout so because there was only circumstantial evidence, the case was dismissed.
'We've had a soldier court-martialled for being caught in possession of drugs and he stated that he got them from Arturo but he denied it and since we have no jurisdiction over civilians, it was passed over to Superintendent Kaba for a follow up.'
'What came of it, as if I didn't know?'
'You guessed - nothing. We've also had reports that he's made lewd remarks to wives of British Servicemen - overall not what you would call a good character.'
'Come to think of it, that car outside is like the one I thought was following me the other day.'

Joe brought the drinks to the table and when he was between Oxbee and Arturo, there was the sound of chairs being pushed back aggressively and a clatter as the chairs hit the floor. Oxbee had his pistol out but two shots were fired before he could get a sighting on either of them. Both Joe and Zander were hit.   Oxbee fired three shots; two hit Arturo and one hit his partner in the side of the head as he dashed for the door.

209

Oxbee knew Arturo's partner was dead when he saw the blood splatter at head height on the doorpost. Arturo was still twitching with blood seeping out of the two holes in his chest Oxbee saw that Arturo was no longer holding a weapon so he sprinted across the bar to check him.   He was dead by the time he got there.

'What the hell was that?' Oh, my God!' Rosemarine exclaimed.'
'Give me a hand - quick,' shouted Oxbee.

She ran out from behind the bar and took some bar towels with her. Zander was sitting up holding his left shoulder with his right hand. Joe was out cold.

'Is it bad, Adam?'
'No, I don't think so, but it hurts like hell though. You'd better see to Joe.'

Rosemarine was cradling his head; his eyes were closed and Oxbee felt his neck for a pulse.

'He's got a good strong pulse. Ah! He's been hit in the side just above the pelvis. I hope it hasn't hit a vital organ. It looks like it went straight through but there's a bit of a mess at the front where it came out. Help me roll him onto his good side; we must keep the wound uppermost. Put a towel on the back and hold it with your hand, and one on the front and put your knee against it, and keep that pressure on; use alternate hands. Where's the phone?'
'Right-hand side of the bar, underneath the counter,' informed Rosemarine.

Oxbee tapped in the police headquarters number and asked for Chief Inspector Kaba who then came on the phone. Oxbee explained what had happened and asked him to get an ambulance and a doctor to Joe's Joint; he put the phone down and went back to Zander.

'Sydney was working late so he's on his way with the team, and he's going to arrange for a doctor and ambulance. Now let's have a look at that shoulder.'

Zander took his hand away from his shoulder; the blood had already oozed through his fingers. The bullet had gone right through the fleshy part of the outside upper arm. Oxbee took a bar towel and put it over the wound.

'I'll get my first aid kit from my bag of tricks in the Bronco.'

He was back in minutes.

'Can you move your fingers, Adam?'
'Yes, and my arm but I just have this burning sensation in my shoulder.'

Oxbee opened the kit and took out the scissors. He snipped the shirt and peeled it away and then cleaned the wound with a sachet of sterilising liquid. Placing two thick pads of gauze on it, one at the entry point and one at the exit, and using white elastic bandage, he taped Adam from his shoulder blade at the rear to the centre of his chest under the chin. He had just cut the tape when he heard a vehicle pull up, and shortly after that Dr Mark Smith walked in. He assessed the situation and went straight to Joe.

'I'm sure that's tiring holding that pressure, but well done. You can ease up now while I have a look at him.'

He removed the towels and pulled the shirt up under his arm and the trousers down over his hips.

'He's going to be all right; the bullet went in below the liver and kidney.'

Joe started to come round.

'How do you feel, old buddy?'

'What happened?' Joe asked weakly.

'You've been shot in your right side. I'll give you an injection for the pain and an antibiotic and I'll put a dressing on, but then we need to get you off to hospital as soon as possible. That wound needs to be cleaned out properly and any internal damage put right. The pressure has stemmed the flow of blood but there could be some internal bleeding but you'll be all right for now,' he declared moving over to Zander.

'What about you?'

'I'm all right. It went through the muscle at the top of the arm. Fred has put a dressing on it.'

'Okay, I won't disturb it but I'll give you some injections like I did for Joe. I think the best idea is for you to go to the hospital as well and get it cleaned up properly and dressed,' he pronounced as he leaned over and gently manipulated the arm.

'That's obviously painful; it doesn't seem to have clipped the bone and the muscle will heal but you'll have to restrict the movement for a while. What happened here, Fred?'

'These two tried to kill Adam. I know this one; he's a small-time gangster. As soon as I heard the chairs move I knew there was something on. I couldn't see properly because Joe walked in and he was between them and me. When he was hit he fell forward and then I had a clear shot at both of them before they could get a shot off at me. Their first shot hit Joe, and as he fell they could most probably only just see Adam so he was only winged.'

'I owe Joe a few more drinks, I can see that.'

'I'll keep yah to that, buddy,' spouted Joe.

'That's no problem, Joe; I'll put one in for you.'

Rosemarine smiled and winked at Zander and he smiled and winked back.

'I could do with one now.'

'No, you can't have anything, Joe; you're going to need anaesthetic.'

'Just a little one.'

'No, I'm sorry, you must have nothing.'

There was a roar of engines and a banging of vehicle doors and the ambulance men ran in with a stretcher followed by Sydney Kaba.

'You're a fine one, Adam. I told you to be careful.'

'I was careful, Sydney and if it hadn't been for Fred, I'd be dead. I hadn't a clue about those two until Fred explained. He knew them as soon as he saw them and was on his guard. It so happened that Joe got in the way and for a split second Fred couldn't see them but as soon as he could, he killed them both.'

'I'm sorry I got in the way.'

'Don't worry about it. You most probably saved my life because you got between them and me as well. I think the bullet that hit you Joe went through the corrugated tin behind me.'

Kaba went over to the bodies.

'Arturo has been hit twice - once in the neck and once in the chest and his partner was hit in the head.'

Joe was put on the stretcher and taken to the ambulance. Rosemarine went over to Oxbee and gave him a kiss and a hug - he was startled to say the least.

'That bastard raped me when I was fourteen. He's where he belongs, in Hell,' pronounced Rosemarine.

'Are you going with Joe, Rosemarine?' Zander asked.

'No, unless they can wait. I will have to get my sister and her husband over to look after the boys and this place after what's happened.'

'I'm in no hurry to go to the hospital. Fred and I will wait here until they arrive. Phone them and explain and then you go in the ambulance with Joe,' said Zander.'

'Oh, thank you.'

She made the phone call and checked on the boys.

'They're still asleep. My sister will be here in ten minutes.'
'Off you go then.'

She gave a little wave and giggled childishly as she went out the door.

'Sir George is on his way. You're a fantastic shot, Fred. Aren't you glad he was with you, Adam?'
'Well, I can't think of a better place for him to have been.'
'I could, Adam - about a foot to the right of Joe. Then I could have had them as soon as they pulled their weapons rather than after.'
'Perhaps you're right. I'm just glad to be alive.'
'Well, I went for Arturo in the head but he was still on his way up from the crouched position so he got hit in the neck. He swung the pistol in my direction so I aimed for his chest. The other one had fired his shot, which is the one that hit Adam. He was on his way to the door when he turned slightly to look back and I hit him in the side of the head.'
'I'm more than grateful to you, Fred; Arturo has been a thorn in my side since I was a kid; he was always in trouble. I think he's done two short stretches in prison; one was for assault with a weapon, and one was for burglary. He won't be a problem anymore, thank goodness.'

Zander got up off the floor where he had been sitting with his back against the wall and he groaned a little as the movement sent a pain across his shoulder.

'I'll be off now. I'm sure it's only superficial, Mr Zander.'
'Thank you for responding so quickly."
'I was on my way back to town when I got the call over the radio. I'm happy to be able to help. Goodnight, all.'

Dr Smith went out the door as the coroner arrived.

'Are you all right, Zander old boy?'

'Yes, thank you, Sir George. It's those two you want.   Fred killed them protecting me so, between the two of us we should be able to give you all the information you need.'

'Good, I'll just give these the once over.'

He went to the one near the doorway first and bent over him.

'This one stinks of marijuana; he was most probably high.'

'I'm glad it didn't improve his aim or one of us might be dead.'

'Yes, did you see where the empty cases went, Fred?'

'Yes, mine anyway. Here they are,' he said removing them from the pistol, 'theirs - I don't know.'

'This is going better than I expected; I'll be in bed by midnight. I'll do the preliminaries when I get back and a full post-mortem in the morning. Is that all right with you, Sydney?'

'Yes, Sir George, that'll be fine.'

The bodies were being put in the bags when Rosemarine's sister arrived. She was an attractive young girl with a strapping great husband; he was not as tall as Zander but not far off, and his stomach was a big as his chest, and he must have weighed about twenty stone. The introductions were made and he started to close the shutters down.

'Right, I'm off then, Sydney. See you tomorrow.'

'All right, Adam. Get yourself sorted out first. And well done, Fred. Not only have you saved two people but you've also disposed of two undesirables.'

'Only doing what I was asked to do.'

'Well, I'm going to organise a big party when we get this lot locked up. Sydney, what do you think?'

'Start planning the party; I don't think it's far off.'

Oxbee took Zander to hospital where they removed the dressing, cleaned the wound and gave him some more injections.   Oxbee then drove him back to his sister's.

'Fred, you'd better come in with me. I want a word with Jenny. I want you to take the Bronco tonight and pick me up tomorrow when I call you. I should be all right in the morning but they've pumped so much stuff in me I'll most probably feel as if I have a hangover.'

Jenny was very concerned when she heard the story and told Zander in no uncertain terms he was to go to bed and not get up until he was totally fit. Zander protested but to no avail. He was given a cup of tea and some of the tablets provided by the hospital and packed off to bed.

Zander woke to a knocking at the door.

'Who is it?'
'It's Jenny. Are you well enough to come to the phone?'
'Yes, I'm on my way.'
'It's the Prime Minister's secretary.'

Zander picked up the phone. 'Hello.'

'Hello, Sir. The Prime Minister has asked me to pass on his good wishes, and if you are well enough he would like to speak with you today. The Prime Minister is departing on a five-day overseas visit today and would like to meet you at the airport at noon. Would that be possible?'
'Most certainly, I will be there. And please thank the Prime Minister for his good wishes.'
'I will. Goodbye.'

The phone clicked and Zander put down the phone, and explained the conversation to his sister.

'You can't go, Adam, you must stay in bed.'
'I'm fine, Sis, just a bit sore and stiff; I'll be all right.'
'Well, if you say so. I'll put some breakfast on for you. Here, take your tablets with this cup of tea.'

Zander did as he was told and Mary followed him to his room and helped him wash, shave and get dressed. He had a leisurely breakfast and read about the incident in the local newspaper, including some editorial hostility towards foreigners getting involved in law enforcement. Zander phoned Oxbee.

'Fred, would you pick me up at twenty to twelve. I have to meet the Prime Minister at the airport.'
'Yes, of course.'
'I see we got a bit of flak in the papers.'
'Yes. The Defence Commander was furious; he phoned the Prime Minister. I think the leader of the opposition is stirring things up with the press. I believe that will be reversed tomorrow and we will be thanked for helping on the case at the request of the Prime Minister.'
'That's all right. I'm not worried about the hostility; I've had worse.'
'I think you might be missing the point, Adam. Some people take umbrage at foreign interference and they could declare open season on one, Adam Zander. Without the retraction and PM's support, you could be dead by the end of the week.'
'You'll just have to stop them, Fred.'
'I had enough exercise last night. I've spent most of the morning explaining what happened and had to fill out so many forms, and the commander has had to inform the Foreign Office. The British High Commissioner is coming to camp this evening and wants to see me for a quick chat so I don't want anymore escapades like last night if we can help it, thank you very much.'
'Okay. You saved my life last night and I shall be eternally grateful, but today it's back to work.'
'Right. I'll pick you up as requested.'

Zander put the phone down and walked through to the kitchen.

'Jenny, would it be possible to have some sort of party here to celebrate the closing of this case.'

217

'Yes of course, but the officers' mess might be better; it's larger and has better facilities.'

'You're probably right. I'll phone George Galpen.'

Zander sat down and produced a list of people he thought should attend the party and decided to stop at one hundred.

'Do you know, I've come up with such a big list, I didn't realise I knew so many people.'

'If you've listed that many, there will be at least another thirty by the time Sydney and Fred have added a few names.'

Zander was about to pick up the phone to Galpen when it rang.

'Zander.'

'Are you all right?'

'Yes, Heather, I'm fine.'

'I'm coming over to see you,' she said and put the phone down.

'Sis, Heather's on the way.'

'I'll put the kettle on.'

Zander was surprised by her casual reaction. Heather arrived and Zander went to the door and let her in. He had no hesitation in kissing her and now it was his sister's turn to be surprised. They had coffee and talked until Fred arrived to collect him.

'Where is there at the airport that you could actually have a meeting with a Prime Minister?'

'The control tower I suppose but I don't really know. We'll park the Bronco and wait at the main entrance; he will most probably arrive in his Bentley with police outriders but we will just have to wait and see,' said Oxbee.

The entourage duly arrived and the Bentley stopped next to them. The car door opened and the Prime Minister invited

218

Zander to join him; his ADC, driver and the security man were
asked to leave.

'Okay, Zander. Who is doing all this killing?'
'Morris, Sir.'
'Jon Morris?'
'Yes, Sir. He will be arrested as soon as we get some final
evidence from Texas.'
'Explain.'

He gave a brief explanation and saw the intense expression
on the Prime Minister's face change to one of fury.

'How certain are you, and do you have sufficient evidence?'
'Absolutely certain, Sir, and yes we do have evidence. If I
might add - and you might not like this, Sir, - but I believe
Superintendent Kaba is corrupt and Morris has him on the pay
roll.'
'I hope you realise what you are saying.'
'I do, Sir, and I have told Chief Inspector Kaba of my
concerns.'
'What did he say?'
'He said I must do what I feel is the proper thing to do.'
'Good for him. You have evidence?'
'Only circumstantial at this stage, Sir; because of these
killings I haven't had the time to put it together.'
'All right, but get it buttoned up. The reason for our meeting
today is two-fold. Firstly to enquire after your health, and
secondly, to offer you a position. When you have Morris
locked up and had time for your wound to heal, I would like
you to consider taking up a post working directly for me.'
'What sort of work would it involve, Sir.'
'Well, I don't think you will be very popular, but I would like
you to investigate corruption within government, and that
means all departments: Customs; Civil Service; Armed Forces;
and the Police. In fact - everything. Don't give me an answer
now, just think about it.'
'I don't have to do much thinking, Sir, other than how I will
go about it and what I will need.'

'I'm glad you are being positive. I have been getting regular reports on your progress and I'm impressed. We will discuss it further when I return. Thank you, Zander,' the Prime Minister said with an upward lift of the chin indicating the door.

Chapter 16 Dubious Activities

Zander got out of the Prime Minister's car and walked towards Oxbee.

'You look dumbfounded, Adam, what's up?'

'You don't want to leave the army and join me in private practice do you, Fred?'

'I don't think so; I don't really know. I've never thought about it; I'm a career man. Why?'

'Just think about it and I'll brief you on the way to see George Galpen.'

They drove into camp and went straight to Galpen's office.

'George, would you be able to arrange for me to speak to the intelligence officer and perhaps the operations officer? I want to know what they have on drug-running, gangs, corruption and that sort of thing.'

'Yes, of course. I'm just about to go to lunch. Come on, I'll introduce you to them both.'

'There is another point; on the conclusion of this case, I want to hold a party. Would it be possible to hold it in the officers' mess?'

'How many were you thinking of?'

'About a hundred.'

'Yes, the mess could handle that; we would have to set up a bar in the ante-room, but yes I'm sure that would be all right.'

'Thanks, I will pay for everything, staff included.'

'Okay, we can sort that out later. Let's go for lunch.'

Zander had lunch and went back to the operations room for a formal briefing. Arnie Day, Sal Klug and Morris appeared on the list of those suspected of being involved in dubious activities. And, to his surprise, Superintendent Kaba was there as well.

'Is any action being taken against any of these characters?'

'No, Adam. These are our observations. Our military attaché at the High Commission will brief His Excellency who will, given the opportunity, inform the Vanmalla foreign secretary.'

'Thank you for your cooperation; it's all a bit too diplomatic for me.'

There was no comment just a smile. Zander walked to the Bronco which was parked in the VIP car park outside the headquarters.

'Pushing your luck parking here, Fred, aren't you?'

'No, if the NAAFI Manager can park here, so can we.'

'Okay, let's go and see Sydney.'

They went to Kaba's office on the mezzanine floor and again he was snowed under with paperwork.

'Any news on Valence's rifle yet, Sydney?'

'Yes, it's the one that killed Manuel and shot at you.'

'What about the one that hit Morris?'

'No, not the same.'

'I thought so. I'm sure that was self-generated, perhaps Manuel.'

'Yes, possibly, but we now know that Morris didn't kill anybody.'

'Up until now, I never really thought he had. However, I think he might have actually pulled the trigger when it came to Hodson.'

'We've yet to prove that.'

'Give me time and I'll have his accomplice locked up as well.'

'What have you got planned for today and tomorrow, Adam?'

'I'm going to see Joe at the hospital.'

'And Hodson's sister?' Kaba stated.

'I'm picking her up tomorrow lunchtime.'

They arrived at the hospital just as a tropical storm started so they made a dash for the entrance and had their heads down; when they lifted them, inside the entrance Superintendent Kaba was standing in front of them.

'Where you goin'?' Kaba demanded.
'To see a patient,' replied Zander reluctantly.
'He don't wan' to see you.'
'Okay, we'll go.'

Oxbee was surprised by Zander's response.

'Good. Go - now.'
'When it stops raining.'

Kaba stomped off into the rain.

'I thought for a second that you were actually going to do as he said?'
'No chance - just humouring him.'

The ward was on the first floor and consisted of twenty beds, ten on each side. They saw Rosemarine sitting by Joe's bed. The ward sister stopped them at the entrance to the ward.

'Where do you think you are going?' she demanded.
'To see Joe.'
'I'm afraid he is not permitted visitors.'
'Who said so?'
'The superintendent of police.'
'My name is Zander and I'm with the police.'
'I'm sorry - no visitors.'
'Rosemarine,' called Zander.

She looked up and ran to Zander.

'Mr Zander, that big policeman was here, and now Joe won't speak.'

Zander brushed past the sister but she grabbed his shoulder and he spun around.

'If you want to survive, lady, you will shut your mouth and get out of my way,' growled Zander as he jabbed his finger at the sister's face.

She backed off and went to her office.

'Follow her, Fred, and keep her off the phone.'
'How yah doing Joe?'

Joe looked at Zander and smiled weakly.

'Come on, buddy, what's the problem. Is it the food?'
'Superintendent Kaba sent Rosemarine for a glass of water and then told me that if I didn't keep my mouth shut about that snake, I was crocodile bait.'
'What about the snake?'
'I put it there. Morris phoned me and told me he would clear all my debts if I did it, and kill my kids ifin I didn't.'
'Now you're endangering yourself by telling me.'
'I know you'll look after me, like when I told you about the Dodge.'
'Would you feel safe at your joint?'
'Yeah, I got the brother-in-law there.'
'Okay, I'll arrange it.'

Zander went back to the sister's office and phoned Sydney Kaba and explained what his brother had been up to. They arranged to have Joe taken back to Joe's place and for Dr Smith to get a nurse too. Zander went back to Joe's bed.

'It's all arranged, Joe, they'll be here to collect you shortly and I'll try and get out to see you tomorrow.'
'Thanks bud. I noo I could count on you.'

Rosemarine went all dewy-eyed and then started crying with joy.

'I'm off; see you later.'

He went to the Sister's office.

'Come on, Fred, let's get out of here.'
'Where're we going?'
'To see my brother-in-law, Stan.'

They pulled up outside Stan's office.

'Any joy with the place next door?'
'Yes, it's yours if you want it. Let's go and have a look.'

It was on three floors with the bedroom at the top with an en-suite bathroom. The sitting room was on the first floor with the kitchenette and there was an office and another sitting room on the ground floor.

'This will be just great, Stan. What sort of price are we looking at?'
'About $1500 a month.'
'I'll take it. When can I move in?'
'If you come next door, our property manager will get you to sign the contract and it's all yours.'
'That is fantastic. I've been offered a job with the Prime Minister, which I will now take.
'I'm pleased for you.'
'Were you serious about me working for you, Adam?'
'Yes, Fred, I was and I am. The job involves locking up people like Superintendent Kaba.'
'I'm going to give it some serious thought - thank you for asking.'
'Good. I'm finished here; I'll see you at home, Stan. I'm going to have an early night. Drop me off will you, Fred, and then collect me tomorrow to go to the airport.'
Zander phoned Heather and told her about getting the house and the job she was extremely excited. He put the phone down just as Jenny called him for dinner. Zander decided to relax

and sit and have a good read and he had hardly finished the first chapter when the phone rang.

'Phone for you, Adam. It's Heather,' said Jenny.
'Hello, Heather.'
'Adam. I'm very worried; I've just heard Arnold have a blazing row over the phone with Superintendent Kaba.'
'Are you free to talk about it if I come over?'
'Yes, Arnold has stormed out.'

Zander went next door to see Heather and she met him at the door having already given the dog a titbit. They went upstairs to the library veranda where Heather poured two whiskies. Heather was visibly shaking when she handed the drink to Zander.   He saw the fear in her eyes and responded by wrapping his arms around her and holding her close to him.

'Tell me what happened and don't worry, I'm here to protect you.'
'Ahh thank you. I'm so worried - he threatened to kill him.' she stammered nervously. 'It might sound strange me being worried, but he's still my husband.'
'All right, calm down; it sounds as if it was quite frightening. Now sit down and tell me all about it. When did it happen?'
'About ten minutes before I phoned you. The last thing he said to Kaba was... "If you do I'll kill you". He then slammed the phone down and went out banging the door. I then phoned you.'
'That could have been an over-reaction to the bombastic Kaba. I've felt like saying that to Superintendent Kaba on more that one occasion.'
'But you don't know Arnold; he is likely to do it. I've mentioned to you before he frightens me when he's angry.'
'Obviously he frightens you. Let's hope he doesn't carry out his threat. What was the rest of the conversation?'
'I didn't hear the start of it. He was in the study at the time and it wasn't until he raised his voice that I knew he was still on the phone. It was something like: *"you told me all I had to do was make the deliveries on time as directed by you and*

there would be no problem. What do you mean people are asking questions? I've done nothing wrong and you know it. Don't you dare say that I've been aiding and abetting drug smuggling. You've been smuggling the drugs, you bastard, so don't try and implicate me; if you do I'll kill you." That's as much as I can remember.'

'How do you know that it was Superintendent Kaba on the phone?'

'Because the maid answered the phone and when she called Arnold she said who it was.'

'He didn't say where he was going?'

'No, he just stomped out and slammed the door.'

'Did he take his gun?'

'No, but he didn't have to; he has one in the truck.'

'I don't know if I should go running after him and be accused of over-reacting to what was no more than a ferocious argument, or ignore it and be accused of not reacting at all. I'll phone Sydney and see what he thinks because there is an investigation required here whichever way we look at it.'

Zander phoned Sydney Kaba and was satisfied that his brother often flew into a rage and said things he didn't mean. It was nothing new and nothing to worry about. Zander explained this to Heather and it seemed to calm her a little but she was still concerned.

'Make love to me, Adam.'

'No, this is not the time or place, and if Arnold came back, in the mood he's in, I hate to think what might happen. I'm sure Arnold will be back shortly and behave as if nothing has happened.'

'All right, if you say so.'

Zander left Heather and walked back to his sister's and was deep in thought trying to understand the implications of what had happened. Zander sat down to dinner with his sister and her husband.

'You're looking worried, Adam. Is it anything you want to talk about?'

'No, Sis, it's to do with the investigation. There has been a turn of events which is concerning me. I feel I ought to do something about it, but I don't know what and that makes me feel helpless.'

'Ah well, perhaps a couple of stiff whiskies and a good night's sleep might help.'

'I'll take you up on that.'

'Good. Stan, do the honours would you, please.'

After several hours of chit-chat about nothing in particular Zander went to bed and had what his sister promised.

'Adam.' Jenny said after knocking the door.

'Yeah.'

'Sydney Kaba on the phone for you; says it's urgent.'

Zander's mind raced back to the previous evening and his heart started to thump as he quickly put on his bathrobe and went through to the study.

'Sorry to call you at this time, Adam, but there has been another murder.'

Zander's heart sank. 'Who - and where?'

'Mrs Platton; at her house. I'm on my way there when I've finished speaking to you. It's eight o'clock now so see you there at about nine.'

'Yes, okay Sydney.' Zander put the phone down. 'That's all I need. Here was me thinking that Arnie Day had gone and done something stupid and it looks now as if Morris has had Mrs Platton bumped off.'

'Why would he do that?'

'I don't know yet, but would you make me a quick sandwich and a cup of coffee and could you run me into town I need to call Fred and get him to meet me at Mrs Platton's.. I'll have a quick wash, get dressed and be there in a minute.'

'Yes, of course to both.'

Zander went over in his mind the conversation he had had with Mrs Platton and remembered that she had her own suspicions and was not afraid of speaking her mind. He went through to the kitchen, gulped the coffee and took the sandwiches with him.

'Okay Sis, let's go,' he said as he went out the door putting a sandwich in his mouth.

It took them just over twenty minutes to get to Mrs Platton's house and he saw Sydney on the veranda as he arrived. A uniformed policeman opened the security gate for him.

'Mornin', Mr Zander.'
'Morning to you.'
'Hello, Sydney. Who discovered her?'
'The husband - he's over there and he's distraught, to say the least.'
'How did it happen?'
'It looks as if she answered the door and was shot at close range in the chest; killed instantly. Sir George is looking at her now - she's just inside the door.'

Zander went and had a look at Mrs Platton.

'Was it a contact shot?'
'No, I don't think so. There are scorch marks and obviously residue so, it was close. I'll know more when I get her to the lab.'
'Thanks, Sir George,' said Zander as he wandered back to Sydney Kaba.
'Do you think this is Morris' doing, Sydney?'
'Possibly, but we mustn't jump to conclusions.'
'No, you're right, but she was outspoken and veracious and had some strange ideas, one of which was that Morris was running the drugs.'
'Did she tell you that?'

'Yes. Was there anything taken?'

'No, Mr Platton doesn't think so.'

'Had she made any complaints to the police?'

'Other than being approached about special cargo I don't think so. What makes you ask?'

'I get this feeling that your brother might be involved.'

'Really, in what way?'

'Well if she had made a complaint about the approach, who questioned her?'

'I don't know.'

'I'll ask Mr Platton.' He walked to the far end of the veranda where Mr Platton was slumped in a bamboo armchair. 'Has your wife spoken to the police recently?'

'Yes, someone came out a couple of days ago and had a word with her. She had a tendency to be a bit outspoken and mentioned at some function or other the other day that people running drugs, like Morris, should be locked up. She was told that she should stop spreading rumours or she could end up in court.'

'Who said that?'

'His brother,' said Platton pointing at the Chief Inspector.

'Thank you, Mr Platton,' said Zander and went back to Sydney. 'Your brother has been doing Morris' bidding again.'

'I don't really know what I'm going to do about it.'

'Who's his boss?'

'I suppose it's the Police Commissioner or his assistant; I'm not really sure.'

'Do you want me to deal with it? I think I might know how to get him to cooperate.'

'How!'

'I won't tell you at this stage and then you can say you know nothing about it.'

'All right. This is very embarrassing; I know you're going to find out something bad about him. I've felt there has been something wrong for a long time.'

'I won't ask you about it, and then you can deny all knowledge with a clear conscience.'

'Thank you. Oh! I nearly forgot, Hodson's sister has been delayed until tomorrow; her mother has gone into hospital.'

'That's all we need. Okay, I'm off; I'll see you later.'

Zander met Oxbee being dropped off as he went out through the security gate.

'Morning, Fred. Sorry about not picking you up but I was in a bit of a hurry. Everything all right?'
'Yes, what happened here?'
'I'm on my way to the Prime Minister's Office. I'll explain on the way.'

They arrived at the old colonial building that was the Vanmalla Parliament House. It was situated about a hundred yards from the shoreline in down town Malla. The whole area was surrounded by a rough-built brick wall, which had metal rails on top. These rails extended to the height of about seven feet and they were in need of a coat of paint; the wall, however, had recently been whitewashed.

'As I was saying, I need to interview Sydney's brother but I have no authority and he just would not speak to me unless I force him I'm hoping this will do it.'

They went into Parliament House and asked to see the Prime Minister's secretary. They were directed to the Prime Minister's office.

'May I speak to the Prime Minister's secretary please?'
'Have you an appointment?'
'No, I'm afraid, not but if you tell him Mr Zander would like a word with him.'

The receptionist excused himself and went into an office directly behind his desk, emerging a few minutes later.

'I'm afraid the secretary is out of the country with the Prime Minister but his assistant is aware of you and would be happy to speak to you if that would be all right.'
'Yes, that would be fine.'

They were taken along the corridor, past a door that said Parliamentary Chamber, and another that said Prime Minister. The receptionist knocked and they were invited in.

'Good morning, Mr Zander. I'm Marcus Rees, the Prime Minister's Assistant Secretary. How can I be of help?'

Zander turned and looked at the receptionist. Rees got the message and asked him to leave.

'Sorry about that, Sir, but this is a bit of a delicate situation and I'm not sure who to discuss it with. The Prime Minister has indicated that he wants me to work for him. Are you aware of that?'

'Yes, but he has only told his personal staff of his intentions; it is not general knowledge.'

'Well, the thing is, I want to interview a particular individual whom I believe to be a corrupt policeman; he is a police superintendent and is very hostile towards me. What I need is the authority to insist that he answers my questions where and when I want them answered. Is it possible to arrange that?'

'I will have to speak to the PM directly because this is something he's not mentioned to parliament yet and he's not delegated the powers to investigate.'

'If he could perhaps brief the Police Commissioner to give me written authority, that would do it I should think.'

'All right, Mr Zander, I'm due to speak to the PM's personal secretary in about fifteen minutes and I will ask him to pass your message on. May I say, Mr Zander, that the PM is very impressed with the way you conduct yourself and I'm sure he will respond as soon as he's able.'

'Thank you very much, Sir,' said Zander who turned and left with Oxbee following open-mouthed.

'You've certainly made an impression with him, Adam.'

'Amazing, isn't it. I'm embarrassed by it I must admit but I'm pleasantly surprised by how cooperative the locals are.'

'If I was you I'd lap it up and hope he gives you a generous salary.'

'I don't think there is much chance of that; this is a Third World country.'

'The Prime Minister is obviously intent on stamping out corruption. Good luck to you both, I say.'

'Thanks. Now let's get back to the real world and find out who killed Mrs Platton.'

They drove to the police headquarters and went straight to Sir George's office.

'Have you any idea what time she was killed, Sir George?'

'Yes, old boy, about midnight and still in her night clothes which was very little.'

'Anything else?'

'Yes, here's a copy of the report; she was shot through the heart with a .38 round and it went right through, smashing her spine on exit. It looks as if she opened the door and the gun was pushed into her chest and fired. The weapon was several inches away when fired. She might have stepped or fallen back when poked in the chest with the barrel of the weapon.'

'Thanks. We'll go and have a word with Sydney.'

Zander scanned the report as they headed for the mezzanine floor and he then handed it to Oxbee as he arrived at the Chief Inspector's office. He knocked and went in.

'Hello, Sydney, do we have any leads?'

'No, nothing. Mr Platton was out on a dive cruise on the other side of the reef. The sea started to get rough so in the early hours of the morning they decided to come back, as they couldn't dive in bad weather. He came ashore at seven this morning, off-loaded, moored up and went home and he found his wife lying in the open doorway. We're doing house-to-house enquiries to see if there was any activity noticed in the area around midnight.'

The phone rang and Kaba answered it.

'It's for you - the Prime Minister's office.'

'Zander. Hello, Sir. Thank you very much I will arrange it this very minute.' Zander handed the phone to Kaba. 'I have an appointment with the Police Commissioner, Sydney. How do I get there?'

'He's in what we call the penthouse; his office is on the next floor up, top of the stairs, turn left. What's that about, Adam?'

'I need to interview your brother and he will hardly speak to me let alone answer questions.'

'Good luck. The commissioner is a good man but God help you when it comes to my brother, Bertram.'

'That's his other name. You're right, Sydney, it won't be pleasant, but it has to be done. You stay here, Fred, and I'll pick you up when I get back.'

Zander went upstairs to the top floor where the carpets were plush and the decor was sombre; it was mainly dark wood panelling and there were several framed pictures of previous Police Commissioners. The secretary ushered him into the aide's office.

'Good morning, Mr Zander, we've been expecting you.   The Commissioner has somebody with him at present but he should be free in a couple of minutes. Please take a seat.'

Zander sat down in a small waiting area and picked up a magazine with a story about the Manchester Police. He had just started to read it when the door to the commissioner's office flew open and a policeman in uniform was marched out accompanied by a sergeant hurling torrents of verbal abuse at him.

'Get out of my sight, you horrible little man,' screamed the Sergeant.

The sergeant saluted the inspector and marched out of the office.

'Sorry about that. It was a disciplinary interview; we have them once a week. I will tell him you're here.'   He opened the door and spoke and then said, 'Mr Zander, you may go in now.'

Zander went in feeling a little nervous and was surprised to see that the commissioner was white.

'Morning, Zander,' said the Commissioner with a Jamaican accent.

'Good morning, Sir Thank you for seeing me.'

'I bet you thought I was going to be black.'

'Yes I did. You're the first I've seen in the police force.'

'I knew it; I could see it in your eyes.'

'I'm sorry, Sir, I didn't mean to be rude.'

'Not at all, you're not the first. I was brought in last year to try and sort this lot out, hence the military-style disciplinary interview; the word soon gets around. It's an up-hill struggle but I'm getting there. Now, I'm told you wish to interview one of my officers but feel you need some qualified authority. What do you want?'

'You're obviously a forthright person so I'll come straight to the point. I would like your authority in writing to interview anybody of superintendent rank and below.'

'You've got it.'

'If I get any opposition, can I have your backing to have the interview conducted with one of your senior officers present?'

'Yes, my assistant will be present if there's a problem. Are you expecting any?'

'Yes, possibly. Superintendent Kaba can be a very difficult man.'

'If he's one of your targets, I suggest you read his file. My aide will let you have it. Kaba is under observation by Internal Affairs - I put it no stronger than that but you might need a word with them.'

'Thank you for your cooperation, Sir, it's appreciated.'

'Not at all. If the grapevine is right, we will be doing a lot of work together. My Aide will let you have the letter of authority when it's ready.'

'Thank you, Sir,'

Zander turned and went out closing the door behind him. He thanked the aide and asked for the Internal Affairs file on Kaba. It took him ten minutes to scan the file and then he headed back to the mezzanine floor.

'We've got a lead, Adam. A blue Toyota Land Cruiser was seen driving by just after midnight. There are not many Land Cruisers in Vanmalla, I do know that,' said Sydney.

'Arnold Day drives a blue Land Cruiser; I've seen him driving it.'

'I'll leave him to you then.'

'Can I declare a conflict of interests at this stage? I've spoken to him once, but my involvement has changed since then.'

'Okay, I'll have a word with him.'

'Good. I'll be interviewing your brother today if I get the chance.'

'I've been thinking about your activity and workload and I think it's about time you had an office here in the HQ, don't you?'

'I would appreciate that.'

'The office three down from mine is yours if you want it.'

Zander and Oxbee went and had a look. It was a glass-fronted office with two desks, phones, chairs, a filing cabinet and a typewriter. They walked to Kaba's office.

'I accept gratefully, thank you. Let's go to the office, Fred.'

Zander picked up the phone and called Heather.

'Is Arnie there?'

'No.'

'What time did he get back last night after I left?'

'About half past midnight.'

'Heather, there is going to be a lot of trouble. Have you got a sister or someone you could go and visit?'

'Yes, in the States. Is it going to be that bad?'

'Yes, very bad. If you think he might get angry if you tell him what you're doing, don't tell him - just go.'

'When will I see you?'

'Not for some time; not until this is over. If you could arrange with the people in the U.S. to ask for you to go there, that might make it easier.'

'Okay, I'll do it that way.'

He put the telephone down and looked at Oxbee.

Chapter 17 Twist in the Tail

'I had to warn her, Fred; besides, I wanted to find out what time he got home. Pop down to Sydney and tell him Arnie got in at half past midnight.'

Oxbee went out as the commissioner's aid came in.

'Your letter of authority, Mr Zander.' he said handing it to Zander.

'Thank you. I don't suppose you know where Superintendent Kaba is, do you?'

'Perhaps he's in his office; same office as this on a similar corridor on the other side of the building.'

'Thanks.'

'Let's go and see him, Fred. If he gets difficult, just back me up.'

Oxbee agreed and they headed off to the other side of the building where they found his office with his name on the door. Zander knocked and walked in.

'Ah! Superintendent Kaba, nice to see you. I've come to interview you to ascertain your whereabouts last evening.'

'Get out!'

'Don't react like that; I am quite within my rights to interview you. I am investigating the murder of Mrs Platton. I think you might know her.'

'I've never heard of her.'

'You're a liar. You went to speak to her recently and told her to stop spreading rumours.'

'Who said so?'

'Never mind who said so. I'm asking the questions and I would appreciate it if you would stop beating about the bush and start answering.'

'I don't have to speak to you. Now, get out,' he shouted and lurched up out of his chair.'

'Sit down and shut up, unless you are going to answer my questions.'

Kaba started to move around the desk.

'Fred, if he moves any further, shoot him.'

Oxbee drew his pistol and holding it in both hands he pointed it between Kaba eyes. Kaba was visibly shocked and staggered back and sat in his chair. Meanwhile Zander took the letter out of his pocket.

'This, Superintendent Kaba, is a letter from the Police Commissioner authorising me to interview anybody I wish. And I wish to interview you. Now, do I have to call the Assistant Commissioner and ask him to be present during this interview or are you prepared to continue here and now?'
   'Here and now,' Kaba whispered with his head hung in submission.

Zander looked at Oxbee and nodded and he put the pistol away.

'Did you speak to Arnold Day yesterday?'
   'No.'
   'I thought you were going to cooperate. You know the way we policemen work - we start by asking questions to which we know the answers. So, I'll ask that question again…Did you speak to Arnold Day yesterday?"
   'Yes, all right, I spoke to him.'
   'I know you did, because I was in the house next door and I heard him shouting at you. So what did you say to send him into a rage?'
   'I told him I'd received a complaint about him running drugs and I needed to take action.'
   'Were you going to charge him?'
   'No, just question him.'
   'No. You couldn't charge him because you're involved with the same thing, aren't you?'

'No, I just turn a blind eye.'

'I think it's a bit more than that. How do you get to drive around in a car that cost you more than a lifetime's income?'

'I saved.'

'I would like to see the invoice sometime. Well, enough of that for now - what happened last night?'

'I told him if he didn't shut that woman up, we were both in trouble. I also told him I'd been to see her and she wouldn't listen.'

'This was your telephone conversation.'

'No, I didn't tell him over the phone that it was Mrs Platton that had complained; that's why he was shouting. He came to my place and went wild. I didn't know he was going to kill her; I just thought he might rough her up a bit but not kill her.'

'Have you told anybody about this?'

'No.'

'Don't you think you should? You're a policeman, and you could have put him in jail for his own protection.'

'He threatened to say I was involved.'

'But you *are* involved up to your neck in drugs, *and* you're on Morris' payroll. That's where you got the car, isn't it?'

'He helped me with it, just a little.'

'I knew he was involved with you because all our investigations were pointing straight at him, but you're as much to blame as him in all these murders.'

'I had nothing to do with them. I just kept him informed.'

'Yes. You read the statements of the witnesses and all the other collated information and then told him. You also made up a story about Otis, which got him killed. Well, you won't be telling him any more because you're going to jail now.'

'You can't do that.'

'Oh! But I can, and I will. Get out of your chair and stand against that wall with your hands in the air – and do it slowly. Fred, watch him.'

Zander moved over behind Kaba's desk and opened the drawer from which he removed a pistol and a set of handcuffs, and then he handcuffed Kaba's hands behind his back.

'I'm arresting you on grounds of aiding and abetting murder. Anything you...'

Zander formally warned him and took him to reception and had him locked up. The Desk Sergeant would not do it until a chief superintendent was called and after Zander had explained the situation, Kaba was put in a cell.

'I'm going to brief the Police Commissioner - if you would like to come with me, Sir.' Zander said to the officer.

The officer accepted the invitation and all three of them went to see the commissioner. Zander briefed them fully giving the background to the case as well as his thoughts on Morris.

'If you will agree, Sir, I think Superintendent Kaba should be questioned by senior officers from Internal Affairs. I think this will take several days but once we have some hard facts, we must arrest Morris. Arnold Day will be arrested today, if it has not already been done. He most probably killed Mrs Platton, although, it could have been Superintendent Kaba who has been trying to shift the blame to Day. Whoever it was that killed her, it is going to take several days to sort out and I don't think we should arrest Morris until we have corroborated evidence; he's got too many slick lawyers on his side and if we get it wrong, they will get him off on a technicality.'
'Yes, Zander, I would agree with that. Raymond, you locked him up - would you like to take it on?'
'Yes, of course, Sir,'
'Good. Keep, Zander, informed - he's a good man.'
'Yes, Sir.'

They left the commissioner's office and were invited to the chief superintendent's office.

'Well, Mr Zander, you've certainly hit a big one with this case. I knew that Morris was a suspect because I go to the weekly briefings given by heads of departments. Of course, Bertram heard it there as well and then reported to Morris who promptly went and got someone killed. It's hard to take in, and I'm glad you went about it the way you did, otherwise it wouldn't have been permitted to get this far.'

'Chief Inspector Kaba was aware of what I was going to do. He wished me luck and I've had an abundance of that for which I am very grateful.'

'I would like you to give me a more detailed briefing on what's happened and which way you think the investigation should go. I have a lot of catching up to do.'

'Yes, of course, Sir. Every thing has been fully documented and I will arrange for the files to be sent up to you.'

Zander went through every thing in detail, calling on Oxbee to give explanations of certain parts, in particular the shooting at Joe's Joint. After some two hours of talking, Zander and Oxbee left and went in search of Sydney Kaba.

'Where have you two been?' I've been looking for you to tell you that Day is in jail and denies any involvement.'

'Your brother is in jail too and says that Day killed Mrs Platton. There is now a Chief Superintendent Raymond Manga in charge of the case and he is going to sort out the statements of your brother and Arnie Day.'

'Well, that's a load off my mind; I've had my suspicions about Bertram for some time. It all came to a head when he got that car. We were on reasonable terms then, and when I mentioned it, he went into a rage and accused me of all sorts, which was hurtful. His explanation was that he had been saving for years and had taken an advance on his pension and gratuity. I didn't believe him but I didn't pursue it further.'

'What did Day have to say for himself?'

'Nothing much. He admitted he had had an argument with Bertram because he had threatened to arrest him on drugs charges.   He says that Bertram was the person who arranged the smoke-screen of trips outside the reef to visiting ships, but that's all he will admit doing.'

'How does he explain being in the same road as Mrs Platton's house at about the time she was killed?

'He says he was returning from Bertram's house.'

'Is that possible?'

'Yes, my brother's house is nearby. It would not have been the most direct route, but if his Land Cruiser was pointing in that direction at Bertram's, he might as well go around the loop to get back on to the main route.'

'So, we have one word against another then. What about his pistol?'

'We found that in the glove box. It has been fired recently, but he denies that. We're getting tests done on that - the .38 - and on his hands. I questioned his wife about timings and she confirmed what you told me; she also gave me this note for you,' said Sydney handing over the envelope.

Zander quickly opened the note.

'Everything all right, Adam?'   Oxbee asked.

'Yes, she has gone to stay with relatives in Florida until this is over.'

'Yes. Day was a bit upset about that; she told him as he was arrested. She added that she would find it difficult to live with the embarrassment,' said Kaba.

'Yes, I can understand that. Look, I'm going to have a word with Sir George to see what the tests results are,' said Zander, and he walked through to reception and the morgue to the forensic department.

'Hello, Sir George. Any results yet?'

'They're doing the trace metal and paraffin test now - I'm just waiting the results. He says he hasn't handled a weapon in the last forty-eight hours - that's one of the questions we always ask - so we just need a positive result to prove him a liar. It looks as if the shot that killed her was from a .38; we have the bullet, which went through her and it's being tested now. Let's go through to the lab.'

The laboratory was small but reasonably well-equipped and exceptionally well-lit with white fluorescent strip lights. In the soundproof firing bunker, which could be seen from the laboratory through the window at the end of the room, a technician was in the process of taking a bullet out of the water tank used to catch them after a test-firing. The technician entered the laboratory and set the bullet that killed Mrs Platton, and the one he had just collected, into the dual microscope and adjusted the focus.

'It's a match, Sir George,' said the technician.

Sir George went over to the microscope and had a look.

'Yes, very distinctive. Anything on the trace metal test?'
'Yes Sir. Positive; he has handled a weapon recently.'
'To make life easy - I'm all for making life easy - all we need now is a confession.'
'Once Raymond Manga gets your report, there shouldn't be a problem except that I know Day can be a cantankerous old sod.'
'Yes, you are probably right, but that's a policeman's lot.'
'Thanks, Sir George,' said Zander as he headed out of the laboratory with Oxbee. 'What do you think possessed him to keep the revolver, Fred? He must have known we would come looking for him.'
'He didn't know his vehicle had been seen, and without that connection, we mightn't have got to him for a while, by which time he could have got rid of the revolver and established an alibi. The other thing I don't suppose he considered was that the superintendent was going to crack and give in. Mind you, I don't think he would have done if you hadn't ordered me to shoot him.'
'Surprising how that got his attention. It's nearly four o'clock and we didn't have any lunch today - do you fancy a pint and a bite to eat?'
'Good idea.'

They went to the upstairs bar in the Majestic and ordered club sandwiches and Slitz beer. While they were discussing the case and its eventual outcome, they were surprised to see Mr Platton stagger into the bar. He was very drunk and quite abusive to the barman even before the young chap had a chance to speak.   Zander went over to him at the bar.

'Don't you think you've had enough, Mr Platton? Maybe it's time to go home.'
'I am home,' he slurred as he lurched around to see Zander.
'I moved out; can't stay there.'
'Would you like me to take you to your room?'
'Yeah.'

Zander and Oxbee helped Platton to his room and put him to bed and by the time they left the room Platton was sobbing uncontrollably.

'Let's go to the HQ and see what the progress had been made.'

Sydney Kaba brought them up to date by explaining that Day had confessed after Manga had spent the afternoon shuffling between interview rooms. Attorney's had been called and statements made and signed. Arnold Day was charged with murder and Superintendent Kaba charged with corruption.

'All in all, a job well done, Sydney.'
'Yes, Adam, and with Hodson's sister coming tomorrow, we will have sufficient evidence then to bring in Morris. We could most probably do it now but I'm worried about getting it wrong.   When he is arrested I want him held until he's hanged.'
'I'm inclined to agree with you. I'm finished for now so I'll see you tomorrow when I've picked up Judy.'

Oxbee dropped Zander off at his sister's. As he went into the house, Zander decided that he was going to have a large whisky - or three - to see if that would take his mind off the case.   He also thought he would have another go at reading the book he started the evening before, but to no avail as he fell asleep in the armchair on the veranda. His sister woke him at eleven o'clock and said he should go to bed, which, he did. His hectic schedule had exhausted him and he slept well that night but woke with a start as Mary knocked on the door and told him that it was nine o'clock in the morning.

Oxbee collected Zander from his sister's and they arrived at the airport in time to see the flight arrive. Zander took a large sheet of paper out of the glove compartment and wrote "Judy" on it. 'Just in case I don't recognise her,' said Zander.

'Didn't you ask her name or what she would be wearing?'
'No, I didn't actually; I just assumed she would be a redhead, so if no redheads come down the steps, I'll hold up the sign.'

Only ten people got off the flight and the first out the door was a redhead.

'That's her, Fred. What a smart looking lady.'
'I would say stunning.'

They walked over to the customs area to collect her.

'Hello, Judy, I'm Adam Zander and this is Fred Oxbee. I'm sorry but I don't know your other name.'
'It's Stacus.'
'I'm sorry we have to meet under such circumstances. I've arranged for us all to go to police headquarters and meet the chief inspector in charge of the case and listen to the tape there. Have you listened to the tape?'
'No, Mr Zander. I must admit I was tempted but I couldn't face it.'
'Good. If you would prefer we can listen to it first and then advise you whether you should listen to it or not.'
'No. I've made up my mind - I'm going to listen to it with you.'

'Okay. Let's go into town; we'll go to the headquarters first and then drop you off at the hotel.

They parked outside the police headquarters and went in.

'Sydney, this is Judy Stacus. Judy, meet Chief Inspector Sydney Kaba.'

They exchanged pleasantries and went through to an interview room, which had been prepared for them. Kaba poured the coffee and as soon as they were all seated around the small interview table, Kaba put the tape in the machine and switched on.

'My name is Red Hodson. I am employed by Jon Morris as his farm manager. The first part of this tape is a summary of what I've heard but was unable to record at the time. The part that follows is a conversation that I recorded between Jessica Bray and Jon Morris. I was not blackmailing them - I just recorded it for my own protection.

'Jessica Bray shot Morris through the shoulder after giving him a pain killing injection. This was done to divert attention away from Morris, and to cover up the fact that they had planned, together, to dispose of Elly van Dam. Elly had been talking about her affair with Morris and Jessica got to hear about it. She thought the story was recent whereas in fact it was before Marty came on the scene. Elly kicked Morris out because she found out that he was running drugs and she wanted nothing to do with him. When Jessica confronted Morris with the story about the affair, he tried to explain that it was history but she would not accept that and insisted that something had to be done about it. The next part is their conversation.'

'What the hell can I do? There is no involvement between Elly and me. I've stopped foolin' around.'

'Except with Sal and your wife.'

'I keep my wife because of the kids, and I keep Sal for appearance and business purposes but there's nothing going on between us.'

247

'That's what you say, but I don't believe you.'

'But it's true, Jessica. You live with your husband who's a vicar; I don't ask you what goes on between you, do I? I don't want to know either.'

'Nothing "goes on", as you put it, Jon, nothing at all. Once I had slept with you, I wanted nobody else. Why don't you respond in the same way?'

'It's difficult for me; before we became lovers, I had many experiences and affairs, you know that.'

'I know you did, and you promised they would stop but they haven't.'

'I'm trying. I can't get rid of Sal.'

'No, I understand that right now, but she will have to go soon.'

'That is out of the question now she is responsible for the shipping of the special cargoes that Elly found out about.'

'All right. We will leave that for now. Reg is moving to the Ascension Islands to take up a new post but I won't be able to join him for several months. What I really want to happen is you to finish with all your women, including your wife, and then marry me.'

'You know I want that as well - I want it more than anything else, but it's just not possible yet.'

'Oh! But it is, at least it is possible to start the elimination process.'

'What do you mean by that?'

'Elly van Dam has to go.'

'What do you mean, has to go?'

'I want her killed.'

'You can't be serious, Jessica?'

'Oh but I am, and if you don't arrange it, I will.'

'Please Jessica; don't go over the top. That isn't the way to go.'

'It is for me and if you love me as you say you do, it can be arranged. There are enough people in this country that would kill for less than five hundred dollars.'

'Yes, you're right, but is that really what we want to get involved in?'

'Yes, it's the only way I will know for sure that you mean what you say when you tell me she means nothing to you.'

'But to kill her - that's asking a lot.'

'Are you telling me you are not capable of arranging for one of your workers to finish her off?'

'Let me think for a minute or two. She's due to get married shortly. Perhaps I could do something there, and she'll keep her mouth shut. If I don't give him another contract he won't get a work permit, and that could be it - they're gone.'

'Jon, you are missing my point. I want you to get her out of the way – permanently; not send her back to the States so you can go and visit her.'

'It's over. There is nothing between Elly and me.'

'Then prove it, Jon. Have her killed.'

'Don't push me, Jessica. What would you say if I said kill Reg?'

'There is no conflict; I have no other men friends. Reg is impotent and you know it.'

'All right, I'm sorry. I didn't mean anything by it.'

The tape hissed for a few seconds and then Hodson's voice was heard· 'Mom if anything should happen to me, please despatch this to Mr Zander - the address is on the covering letter and the package.'

Kaba stopped the tape.

'Well, Adam, more or less as you had thought.'

'Yes, but is this evidence acceptable in court?'

'Possibly not, but there is sufficient here to wrap it up, don't you think?'

'Yes, but we are going to have to work out some sort of strategy.'

'I don't think there is any need. I think we should meet at the police post near Two Snakes at six o'clock tomorrow morning and carry out a dawn raid there, and one at the manse at the same time. I'll get the sergeant you met out at Lilly's and a team to pick up Mrs Bray and we can go in and pick up Morris. So, I'll see you at the police post in the morning.'

'Yes, fine with me. Judy, I suggest that you stay away from Red's place until we have Morris and Mrs Bray locked up. I'll take you to your hotel.'

Zander dropped Judy off at the Majestic and Oxbee at the camp. His shoulder was still painful but because the Bronco was an automatic and had power steering, he was able to drive without too much difficulty. He headed off in the direction of his sister's but on the way he changed his mind and decided to go out to Two Snakes instead. During the journey he went over all the permutations of what might happen without considering his own safety or how foolhardy he was being. He arrived at the gate of Two Snakes only to have yet another confrontation with the difficult guard. He used the same excuse as before and pointed to the policeman guarding Hodson's house, and this got him in. Zander pulled up in front of the house and got out and spoke to the policeman. He went straight to Morris' house, opened the door and walked in. As he went into Morris' bedroom, he saw him standing in front of the mirror.

'What the hell are you doing here, Zander?'
'I've come to arrest you, Jon,' he said as he looked back towards the front door having heard a noise, but he saw nothing.
'Why did you do it, Jon?' Zander asked turning to find Morris slumped in the armchair pointing a pistol at him.
'Jealousy, I s'pose; I hate being a loser. When I was a kid I always got my own way, and later on that carried on because I selected people who were submissive or were prepared to work with me. I have little to do with those who resist my will. All was going well with Elly; I loved her more than anything. I know that sounds a bit of a cliché, but it's true. I'd had several affairs on the side but Elly meant so much. Then Martens turned up and the smooth-talking bastard ruined it all. Elly found out about my indiscretions and dumped me. I decided after much painful deliberation that I could live without her so I moved Sal down here.'

250

'The way I heard it, Elly threw you out because of the drug-running; she could put up with your fooling around but would not put up with the drugs.'

'That's not true. She didn't know about my special cargoes.'

'Oh, but she did. Elly had decided to kick you out before Marty arrived. Your mistake was getting Sal to interview Marty back in the U.S. If you had seen him, you wouldn't have given him the job; he's good-looking, young, and athletic and, I would suggest, a challenge to your virility. That's why you wouldn't have given him the job.'

'That's bullshit. Anyway I met Jessica; she came on a bit strong and put a lot of pressure on me to do something I was thinking of doing anyway.'

'So you were going to kill Elly anyway?'

'Yes, she was getting too big for her boots.'

'It seems to me that everybody has been well-disposed towards you actually, more than you deserve. Do you really think you will get away with killing me after so many other killings?'

'Possibly. After Elly, things started to go wrong. Each time I had a witness eliminated, you got closer. Killing Elly was all planned before you came on the scene. There is no one locally who could've nailed me, except perhaps Sydney, on a good day but I could most probably have bought him off using his brother. But, if you hadn't been here, I'd have killed Manuel when he didn't get the money and that would have been that. When I realised how good you really were at what you do, I tried to buy you off with the borrowed money story and I set you up the night of the party, hoping I wouldn't have to use it.

'The trouble was you were true to what your brother-in-law told us about you - in fact you're better. That shot from Valence was meant to kill you, you know so I was a bit surprised when you turned up. I'd decided to dispose of Valence using the snake because I knew that was the only thing that frightened him; I knew he had a phobia about them.'

'Why?'

'He screwed up and he had to go.'

'What about Hodson; why'd you kill him?'

'He was making some extra money shipping skins. I didn't want people checking on my shipping activities so I warned him off. He then told me he knew about Jessica and me plotting Elly's killing. He wanted me to leave him alone and said if I increased his salary he would keep his mouth shut. I couldn't take that chance so a couple of days later, when I thought I was fit enough, I took my .22 pistol out of the safe and we went up to the new grazing area and I shot him. I couldn't move his body back into the jungle as I wanted to because my shoulder hurt like hell, so I carried him as far as I could and then just dumped him.'

'I still think Martens was some sort of threat to you.'

'He was no threat; I don't care about him.'

'Maybe not, but you thought he was a threat as soon as you saw him. You knew then that there was no chance of ever getting Elly back so you decided to kill her.'

'No, Mr Zander, that was my idea.' Zander turned and saw Mrs Bray standing in the doorway pointing a .22 rifle at him. 'I knew Jon was hopeful of getting her back, but what we had going was so good I wasn't going to let that happen. You are the one person we didn't count on, Mr Zander. If you hadn't turned up here, Superintendent Kaba would have tied it all up, his brother wouldn't have been called back and it would all have ended with Manuel's death and Martens would have been hanged.'

'As a religious person and a vicar's wife, are you saying you could have continued to lead a normal life with the knowledge that an innocent man had hanged?'

'I don't class him as innocent. He was going to marry that whore and make her a legitimate family woman and perhaps give her children. People like her don't deserve that sort of luck.'

'You have an evil and vicious streak in you, Mrs Bray. How long would it have been before you turned that viciousness on Morris?'

'Mr Zander, I love him, and if I can't have him, nobody else will.' She quickly moved her arm and aimed a foot to the left of Zander and pulled the trigger. Morris was hit full in the face and died instantly. Zander dived at Mrs Bray and removed the rifle from her grasp. She collapsed to the floor, leaned back against the doorpost and sobbed. Zander went over to Morris and checked for signs of life but there were none. He then went to the phone and called police headquarters, and was told that the chief inspector was already on his way.

'Patch me through to his Land Rover please.'

The connection was not too good but good enough to explain the situation.

'How far away are you, Sydney?'
'About two miles. I'll be there in five minutes.'

The front door then suddenly burst open and the policeman and the gate guard flew into the hall.

'What happened?'
'There's been an accident; Chief Inspector Kaba is on his way.'
'Okay, Mr Zander,' replied the policeman and turned and left, taking the gate guard with him.

Jessica Bray was still sobbing.

'Did you know about the drug-running Mrs Bray?'
'Yes, but he promised me he was getting out of it and going to concentrate on ice cream and beef cattle.'
'And you believed him?'
'Yes, he showed me the plans. Sal was the coordinator and he had already agreed that she had to go.'
'You mean killed?'
'Yes, she knew too much and they fooled around, and I was going to have no more of that.'
'You're too possessive, Mrs Bray. What does your husband know of this?'
'Leave him out of it; he's done nothing.'
'But you wanted Morris for yourself?'
'Yes, and I would have had him if you hadn't interfered.'

The front door opened and Chief Inspector Kaba and his team entered.

'What made you come out here, Sydney?' asked Zander.

'I tried to contact you after you'd dropped Oxbee off, but when you hadn't arrived at your sister's, I put two and two together and guessed you were at Two Snakes. Did Bray do that?'

'Yes. I think she realised it was all over, and him killing me wasn't going to solve anything.'

'Sir George and his boys are on the way.'

'Jessica Bray can be taken away now, Sydney, and I think the next one to be arrested is Sal Klug; she's the one who organised the movement of the drugs.'

Chapter 18 Outcome of the Prosecution

'Come on, Fred; run me home I need some rest and a bite to eat. I expect you could do with something similar?'
'Yes I really could.'

They got in the truck and headed back to Riverside. Spark met him at the door and followed him into the dining room. Zander heard noises in the kitchen.

'Is that you, Sis?'
'Yeah, you all right?'
'Yes fine'
'Is there any chance of a snack?'
'Yes, beef sandwich be all right?'
'Yes thank you and a beer as well please.'

Mary took the beer in to Zander who was now on the balcony dozing. He had great difficulty keeping his eyes open. The beer perked him a bit and he was just about to sag again when Jenny gave him the sandwich.

'Jenny, could you come up with a list of food that would be suitable for the end of case party. I just want George to know the sort of food that would be preferable, say a curry and hot and cold finger buffet type items.'
'Yes of course, have you any sort of cash figure in mind?
'No, just stay away from oysters and caviar.'
'Okay, I understand.'

Zander had his beer and sandwich and then went for a lie down for an hour. He woke to the noise of what sounded like a speed boat going down the river. He got up, took a shower, dressed and went through to the dining room for another beer. His sister came out of the kitchen.

'Are you all right?

'Yes, today was a bit of an anticlimax now that the investigation is over and I just felt exhausted, not that I had done anything physical. I'm feeling fine now; is it all right if I phone Heather? She is back in the US now and she left me a note and a phone number.'

'Yes, of course.'

Zander got out the note and dialled the number.

'Hello this is, Adam Zander, could I speak to Heather Day please? Thank you.'

Zander tried to formulate what he was going to say, and was mulling it over when she came on the line.

'Hi, Heather, are you all right? Good, look I'm going to be here for several more weeks during the court proceedings. Once the cases are over I'm going to take a couple of weeks off and go back to the UK to sort out my business affairs then come back to Vanmalla and take up the post working for the Prime Minister. I'm also going to take a couple of weeks away as well before I actually sign the dotted line. Would you then be prepared to come back and live with me? You would, that's fantastic.'

They spoke for a further fifteen minutes during which time Heather agreed to go to Barbados with him for two weeks and he agreed to take up the post in Vanmalla after they had been to Barbados. Zander could not hide his excitement.

Jenny noticed he had changed from the half-asleep exhausted detective to the Adam Zander she knew and loved. Zander excitedly explained his plans. At that moment Stan Jones came in from work.

'Adam has decided to stay in Vanmalla and work for the PM., and Heather has agreed to move in with Adam once court proceedings are over for Arnie,' said Jenny.

'Will you be using the place we arranged or will you be moving next door?' Stan asked.

'I don't think Heather will want to stay next door somehow, I think she will put it on the market soon. I might be wrong but that's how I see it. In the long term I would like to get something more substantial than the place in town, but we will have to wait and see. I will go along with whatever Heather wants at this stage.'

Time seemed to pass quickly for Zander during the days preceding the court proceedings. He had arranged his flight back to the UK using the chief prosecutor's forecast for the length of the cases. The chief prosecutor actually overestimated the time and Zander had several days free before his flight back to the UK during which time he contacted those he wanted at the party.

On completion of his case Superintendent Kaba was sentenced to fifteen years' hard labour in the state prison.

Jessica Bray's case was quite short as Zander was the only witness. There was a short disruption as the Reverend Bray tried to make a protest in the court, but the judge was having none of it. He threatened Day with contempt of court and jail. She was sentenced to death by hanging as was Arnold Day a week later.

Zander went back to the UK to become a consultant and a silent partner in his investigation agency. He phoned Heather from England and arranged to meet her in Miami prior to their departure for Barbados.

He phoned his sister from Miami to be told that Jessica Bray was hanged the previous day at dawn and that Arnold Day was to be hanged on Monday of the following week.

'Jenny, would you have a word with George and arrange the party for the Saturday after we get back on the Thursday?'
'Yes of course, what about the guests?'

'I have mentioned it to them all; I just didn't have a date. Would you have a quick ring around and tell everybody?'

'We have two weeks; it might be better if I get Stan to send out invitation cards.'

'That would be brilliant.'

'Good luck and good fortune on your holiday in Barbados.

On his return from Barbados, Zander visited the Prime Minister on Friday to take up his new post. On Saturday they all went to the mess for the party.

To Zander's surprise there were well over a hundred people assembled in the mess.

'What's going on, Sis?

'I'm afraid when the invitations went out the American Ambassador took over. He sent me a note asking me not to mention it to you but they wanted to say thank you for all you have done in solving this case. So, I backed off and let them get on with it. '

The Ambassador approached Zander with an outstretched hand. They shook hands vigorously whilst the Ambassador reached into his inside coat pocket and brought out an envelope which he handed to Zander. Zander looked at him quizzically.

'What is this?

'Remuneration for services provided. You have been forthright and thorough and we are grateful; if we can be of any assistance to you in your new role, please just ask.'

'Thank you very much, Sir.'

'Now let's party,' said the Ambassador.

The End

Bob P-S is in the process of finishing the sequel, covering Zander's dangerous and exiting escapades in attempting to stamp out corruption within government, customs, police and the civil service in Vanmalla. The book is called "Mosquito Coast Corruption & Murder"

If you would like to pre-order a copy please send an e-mail to: bob.p-s@virgin.net

Websites for those who would like to work from home:

---

www.bpsWorkFromHome.com
This website is dedicated to researching Internet home business ideas and opportunities that can help you start a new Internet home business or grow the one you already have.

---

www.InternetIncome4U.co.uk
Earn income around the clock, the websites are set up for you and are free as is the training and support. You have nothing to pay and nothing to lose.

www.WorkFromHomebps.com
Top ten mistakes Free Report - The Top 10 Search Engine
Optimization Mistakes

www.WorkFromHomebps.com/realestate/
Real Estate Investing Basics

www.bobps.successuniversity.com
Listen in on a live opportunity seminar

www.WorkFromHomebps.com/party/
If you are planning a party soon, either for your boy or
girl, then we have some general party ideas to help make the
planning process as simple and hassle free as possible.